DARK PRINCESS

EMERGING

THE CHILDREN OF THE GODS
BOOK NINETY

I. T. LUCAS

Dark Princess Emerging is a work of fiction! Names, characters, places, and incidents are products of the author's imagination or are used fictitiously and are not to be construed as real. Any similarity to actual persons, organizations, and/or events is purely coincidental.

Copyright © 2024 by I. T. Lucas

All rights reserved.

No part of this book may be reproduced in any form or by any electronic or mechanical means, including information storage and retrieval systems, without written permission from the author, except for the use of brief quotations in a book review.

Published by Evening Star Press, LLC.

EveningStarPress.com

ISBN: 978-1-962067-60-7

1

SYSSI

The sounds of the cappuccino machine thumping and hissing were even more soothing to Syssi than her favorite Mozart piano concerto because they signaled the start of her evening with just her mate.

Given Kian's frown, though, they weren't having the same effect on him.

His expression as he looked at his phone indicated that clan business was once again intruding on their family time, and on a Sunday evening, that was worrisome.

It must be an urgent matter for anyone to bother him now.

When the cappuccinos were ready, she carried them to the couch. "Bad news?"

Kian set his phone aside as he took the cup she handed him. "It was just a text from Onegus about a matter I asked him to investigate." He took a sip and sighed. "Superb as always, my love. Thank you."

"You are welcome." She sat next to him, cradling her cup in her hands and hoping he would share with her what Onegus had reported so she would know whether she needed to worry about it or not.

Not knowing made her overactive imagination go places that were probably much worse than what Onegus had found out.

"It took a long time for Allegra to fall asleep tonight," Kian said as he wrapped his arm around her shoulders. "Was it because of my bath-time story?"

She cast him a reproachful look. "You need to tame your Captain Grouchy Face stories and make them more age appropriate. Allegra was overexcited and only relaxed after I read *Puss in Boots* to her again."

The illustrations in the book never failed to make Allegra smile.

"I'm sorry," Kian said, but judging by his sheepish smile, he wasn't sorry at all.

Her husband was on a mission to prepare their baby girl for a future as the clan leader, and he used his bath-time stories to convey complicated issues and teach her cause and effect. The problem was that Allegra was much too young to understand the cautionary messages in these tales, and her father was much too stubborn to accept that he needed to wait a few years before their daughter was ready for them.

"Bad guys snatching children is not age-appropriate for Allegra, even if Captain Grouchy Face saves the day, beats up the snatchers, and returns the children to their parents."

"Noted." Kian took another sip of his cappuccino. "How would you tell the story? Should the bad guys snatch a favorite pet instead?"

He was incorrigible. "Stick to Captain Grouchy Face saving cats stuck up trees and helping find lost pets."

"Boring."

Syssi laughed. "I like boring. Boring means that nothing bad is happening. Give me boring all day, any day." She glanced at his phone and decided that she wasn't going to wait for Kian to volunteer what was so troubling about the text. "So, what was so urgent that Onegus was messaging you on a Sunday evening?"

"I told you about what Roni's discovered. Onegus has been working on the organizational chart through the weekend. We've been brainstorming ideas for how to restructure our operations to deal with the pedophilia ring while maintaining our fight against trafficking without reducing the number of rescue missions. At least not significantly. We are also undecided about who should lead the new operations. Onegus suggested

Peter, but I'd rather it was led by a Head Guardian. I told him to speak to Bhathian."

"Bhathian is in charge of the training programs," Syssi pointed out. "He can't do both."

Kian nodded. "We can put Kri in charge of training and move Bhathian to lead the new effort. I'm also deliberating whether we should put another Head Guardian in charge of the trafficking operations. That will free Onegus from the day-to-day scheduling and organization and allow him to focus on the big picture for both divisions."

"You should do that." Syssi took another sip of her cappuccino and put the cup on the wood saucer, which was a permanent decor piece on the coffee table. "I also think that the two divisions need separate names, and they shouldn't be the trafficking division and the pedophilia division. That just sounds nasty."

"They deal with nasty stuff."

"I know." She leaned her head on his shoulder. "But the people who are doing the fighting are not nasty, and they need their divisions to have names that they are proud of and are motivated by."

Kian snorted. "These are not high school football teams. Our Guardians don't need any of that to do their jobs. Their motivation is their sense of purpose."

"Symbolism matters, my love." She lifted her head and turned to face him. "I would even go a step further and commission two different styles of uniforms. When soldiers go into battle, they rally under a banner and wear specific insignia. It builds unit cohesion and strengthens resolve. You might be right about our Guardians not needing it, but since you are including the new Kra-ell recruits, it might help them integrate better and reinforce their loyalty. They are proud people, and titles matter to them."

"You make a valid point, my wise mate." Kian kissed the top of her head. "So, what names would you suggest?"

"Frankly, I hadn't given it any thought before. It just occurred to me now that you started talking about organizational charts." Syssi thought of borrowing names from famous football teams, but nothing really resonated with her. "We can keep it simple. How about Saviors for the teams saving victims of trafficking, and Avengers for the teams taking out pedophiles?"

"I like it." Kian finished the last drops of his cappuccino and set the empty cup down. "As for the uniforms, right now everyone is wearing the same black fatigues, and I wouldn't change that for the new division because we need to maintain anonymity, but maybe we can issue pins or patches to denote the two branches."

"That's probably good enough." Syssi lifted her legs onto the couch and tucked them under her. "If you're thinking of putting Bhathian in charge of the Avengers, who do you have in mind for the Saviors?"

"Arwel, if he's up to it. If he's not, I might have to put Peter in charge of the Avengers and Bhathian in charge of the Saviors. Onegus will have to promote Peter to Head Guardian, though, which I don't think he will have a problem with, but some of the other Guardians might. Several have been waiting for a promotion."

"That reminds me." Syssi leaned away slightly. "Do you know when Arwel is going to induce Rob?"

Kian's lips lifted in a knowing smile. "I don't think they have decided on the date yet, but I have another piece of information that you might find even more exciting. Rob and Gertrude have a thing going on."

"What?" Syssi sat up straighter. "How come I didn't know about this, or better yet, how come your mother and Amanda didn't find out? Is the village rumor mill broken?"

Kian chuckled. "I think they are just in the initial stages of their relationship. I saw them together at the clinic when I went to check on Jasmine and Ell-rom, and the looks and smiles Rob and the nurse were exchanging over their shared lunch were telling."

"That's wonderful news. It makes me happy

that Rob has already found someone. Gertrude is so perfect for him that it's surprising Amanda hasn't thought of matching them. I guess she thought it was too early." She frowned. "Now that I've said it, I realize that it might be indeed too soon after Rob's horrible breakup with his fiancée just days before their wedding. I hope it's not just a rebound romance for him. Gertrude deserves better."

Kian shrugged. "Looked like they were into each other, but I'm not an authority on the subject of romance."

"Oh, but you are." Syssi leaned in and planted a kiss on his lips. "You are the best at it because you are real, and you are all in."

"I am." He wrapped both arms around her and pulled her onto his lap. "And so are you."

"True." She kissed his cheek. "As impossible as it seems, our love grows stronger over time." She leaned her head on Kian's chest.

For some reason, her thoughts wandered to Ell-rom and Jasmine and their nascent relationship. They probably couldn't imagine loving each other more, but they would. "I hope Jasmine wakes up soon. I'm glad that at least Morelle is awake. It would have been much more difficult for Ell-rom if she was also still in a coma. Nevertheless, he is freaking out over Jasmine, and that's understandable. It is taking her a very long time to transition."

"Yes and no." Kian rubbed his hand over her arm. "Some have taken even longer, so I'm not worried, but my mother is impatient for Jasmine to wake up. Morelle encouraged her to investigate what happened to Jasmine's mother after Ell-rom suggested that your vision might have been about finding her and not Khiann, but we can't send Guardians to peek into her father's mind to find out what happened to her because Jasmine wants to do it herself and we need to ask her permission first."

"Why would my vision show Jasmine's mother? I mean, it's possible that she has the same eyes as her daughter, but I didn't ask to be shown where she is. I asked to be shown where Khiann was."

"It's just a loose hypothesis, and Ell-rom suggested it as a reach. His reasoning was that when you asked whether Khiann was dead or in stasis, the vision might have revealed something about Jasmine's mother, who might somehow be important to finding Khiann. Jasmine's father never talked about her mother and never took her to see her mother's grave. She doesn't even know where her mother is buried or how she died."

It was a far-fetched idea, but maybe Ell-rom's hunch had been inspired. They still didn't know the extent of his talents, and Amanda was eager to test him as well as Morelle, but since he was glued to Jasmine's side, he couldn't accompany his sister to the university tomorrow.

Amanda was well aware of Ell-rom's death-ray talent, so she wasn't going to examine that or anything that might trigger it, but she wanted to find out whether he had any precognition or telepathic ability in addition to that.

Initially, Morelle used her recuperating as an excuse not to go, but Amanda figured out that she was simply afraid and convinced her to come by explaining what was involved and that it wasn't a big deal. What had finally convinced Morelle, though, was a promise to show her the nursery she had created for Evie and Allegra that now cared for twelve more little ones, with four full-time nannies and a large group of part-time students. It was such a lovely initiative, and Syssi was proud to have played a big part in making it happen.

"Perhaps you should ask for another vision about Khiann or directly about Jasmine's mother," Kian said, surprising her. Usually, he tried to talk her out of seeking visions.

"I can do it right now." She pulled out of his arms and sat beside him.

His eyebrows rose. "Here? Won't I affect your concentration?"

"You might," she admitted. "But I want to try. I've become too dependent on using Allegra to enhance my power. I need to go back to basics and do this on my own." She touched his hand. "If it doesn't work, I can always try again another time with Allegra next to me."

Again, he surprised her by nodding his approval. "Should I move to give you more space?"

"No." She put her hand on his thigh. "You can stay right where you are. Just try not to distract me with your handsomeness."

He laughed. "I'll do my best to tame my magnetism."

Syssi closed her eyes, letting her awareness of the room fade away.

She could feel Kian's solid presence beside her, but instead of distracting her, his warmth was a steadying anchor as she reached for that ethereal space where visions dwelled.

When the familiar sensation of floating began to overtake her, Syssi asked to be shown who the woman in the desert was and how she would help them find Khiann.

Having learned a long time ago not to force visions or direct them too specifically, she opened herself to whatever images might come, trusting that what she needed to see would be revealed in its own time and way.

As the familiar scene from her previous vision materialized, the woman appeared as before, wrapped in traditional male desert clothing, the fabric billowing in the hot wind, with only her striking eyes visible—brown with swirling flecks of gold that seemed to catch the sunlight.

This time, however, new details emerged. Behind the woman, mountains rose against the horizon, but not the barren peaks Syssi had seen when she'd followed the woman's gaze. Green slopes were dotted with oak trees, and in the valley below, she saw stone houses with flat roofs. Some of them were half-ruined, but others were livable, and people were milling around, men and women in ragtag fatigues. As their voices carried on the wind, she tried to discern the language they were speaking. She'd heard it somewhere before, but she couldn't remember where and what it was.

Listening intently, Syssi tried to catch familiar words, and the vision obliged, isolating a conversation between two women who were standing next to a jeep and bringing it closer to her as if she was standing right next to them. When she heard one of the women mention Azerbaijan, things clicked into place, and when, a moment later, the other woman mentioned Kermanshah, Syssi's suspicion was confirmed.

She had read about those places recently enough to remember the names.

The two places the women were talking about were in Kurdistan, specifically the part controlled by Iran, and Jasmine's mother was Iranian.

As the vision began to fade, it zoomed back to the golden-eyed woman, and Syssi caught one final detail—a distinctive pendant that was partially hidden by her scarf. It looked like it was carved from amber or some similar golden stone.

Opening her eyes, Syssi let out a breath. "I saw

the same woman, the same place, but this time I got more clues. I'm pretty sure it was Kurdistan, but I'm not sure whether the woman was Jasmine's mother, and I was being shown the past, or it was Jasmine in the future, looking for her mother in the area of Azerbaijan and Kermanshah, which were both mentioned quite clearly. There was another clue—a pendant that the woman wore, which I didn't see in the previous image, but it was partially hidden under her scarf, and I couldn't see the design. I think it was made from amber, and it looked old."

Kian nodded. "Kurdistan spans parts of Iran, Iraq, Syria, and Turkey, so Jasmine's mother, Kyra, might have been originally from the area controlled by Iran. We have to talk to Jasmine's father, but Ell-rom was very clear that Jasmine wanted to handle that herself. Perhaps we can start investigating the Kurdish angle without directly involving her father just yet. I would love to get Roni digging deeper into Kyra's past and maybe focusing on that region, but he is too busy to tackle it right now. I will have to ask Shai to sift through what he can find online and prepare a summary for me."

"That's a good idea." Syssi winced as her head started to throb. "The vision felt different without Allegra's boost. It was just as clear as the ones I had with her help, maybe even clearer because I felt more in charge and found it easier to steer it where I wanted it to go, but it's taken more out of me. It was draining." She gave Kian a smile. "Next vision, I'm definitely summoning with Allegra in the room. It doesn't affect her, but it boosts my energy."

2

MORELLE

As Morelle walked beside Brandon toward the vehicle parking area, her anxiety grew with each step. The morning sun felt warm on her scalp, reminding her of her compromised appearance, although why she was bothered by that was unclear.

As someone who had spent her entire life on Anumati covered from head to toe, she could have been bald under the hood and the veil, and no one would have known or cared.

She had been a statement—a thing—a princess—a priestess in training, but not a female with desires and mundane concerns like being fond of her beautiful hair.

Resisting the urge to run her hand over the soft fuzz of new growth, she clutched the purse that was more for appearances than to hold anything of importance. She didn't have anything to put in it other than her earpieces or the teardrop, but she was wearing both, so the thing was empty.

Brandon put his hand on the small of her back. "Are you nervous or excited?"

"A little bit of both," she admitted. "I'm excited to see the world beyond the village. As for the testing, I'm nervous about Amanda having the same results as the head priestess. I might have no special talents."

The priestess had put her through countless tests and pushed her to her limits by any means available to her, whether it was starvation, isolation, exhaustion, or even beatings, but despite feeling the power prickling under her skin and the desperation to use it, nothing had ever happened. In time, Morelle had accepted that the feeling of energy circling just under the surface was nothing more than her frustration and restlessness.

"Having special abilities is not as important as you might think." Brandon led her into a big hall made of glass. "I don't have any special talents either, and I'm a council member, which is an important position in the clan that is based on merit. It's not just about the talents you are born with. It's the abilities you develop and your drive to succeed." He pressed a button that was located on a panel next to a set of metal doors.

"What is this?" she asked, pointing at them.

"It's an elevator or a lift that takes passengers up or down. I'm sure you had them on Anumati."

"We did, but the first and only time I used one of those was in the spaceport. The temple and the palace were only two stories high, and we used the stairs."

The spaceport elevators had been crafted mostly from glass, which had made the experience of traveling in them terrifying.

The speed had been dizzying, and the passing levels rushed by in a blur.

Thankfully, this elevator had no windows at all, only a mirror, and Morelle couldn't tell how fast it was going, only that it was going down.

Still, the small space wasn't free of traps. Her own reflection still startled her despite having seen it multiple times over the past several days, and it wasn't just because of the lack of hair. Morelle was still getting used to being outside without her robes and veil, her face and body exposed for all to see that her eyes were blue, not black and huge, and that she had actual breasts that were clearly outlined by her blouse.

When the doors opened, it was to a large hall with many rows of vehicles and many thick columns that held up the ceiling.

The vehicle Kian stood next to was larger than the others, and it was black. She recognized his two bodyguards, the friendly redhead and the stoic blond.

"Good morning," Kian greeted her and Brandon.

"Good morning." She smiled and offered him her hand like she had seen Brandon doing.

The sooner she learned Earth customs, the better.

He shook it lightly and then exchanged greetings with Brandon.

The redhead opened the back door for her. "My lady?" He offered her a hand as if she needed help getting inside the vehicle.

Striving to be polite and abide by Earth customs, she accepted his hand.

When they were all seated in the vehicle, she glanced at the Odu who was sitting behind the wheel and offered him a smile through the small mirror mounted above him.

Morelle was no longer anxious around the Odus after spending four days at Annani's and being served by them. She'd also met Kian's, Amanda's, and Alena's Odus at the family dinner on Saturday, and they had all been perfectly pleasant and accommodating.

The entire family had been just wonderful, welcoming her and Ell-rom with open arms. It was enough to melt even her cynical heart and make her experience profound gratitude toward her mother, who had sent her and Ell-rom to Earth to find their father.

But, even though she would have loved to know Ahn, Morelle was grateful to Ani, the queen of the gods, for sabotaging the settler ship and having it arrive on Earth seven thousand years later. If they had arrived on time, they would have most likely perished with all the other gods, and even if they had arrived after the bombing, they wouldn't have been welcomed by such a loving family.

Kian, who was sitting across from her in the roomy interior of the vehicle, regarded her as if trying to guess what she was thinking about. "If you are wondering why Amanda and Syssi are not here, they have gone ahead to prepare the lab. They are also going to stay and finish the rest of their workday after we leave."

"I wasn't wondering that at all. But what do they need to prepare for me? Amanda said that the tests are very simple, and the lab is set up for them."

"They're clearing the space," he explained. "The lab usually has quite a few people working there—researchers and research assistants, as well as volunteers and paid participants. We thought it best to have your testing done privately."

The unspoken implication hung in the air. They didn't want witnesses to whatever might happen in case she exhibited a deadly talent like her brother's.

Morelle's stomach tightened.

On the one hand, she yearned to have an incredible gift like his, something that would indicate that she was also remarkable, but on the other hand, she was terrified of what it could be.

"Are you concerned about what Amanda might discover?" She leveled her gaze at Kian.

"There is that," he admitted easily, "but we are also a large group, and none of us look like the average human."

"In what way?" she asked.

The redhead leaned forward. "We are better looking by a lot."

"Oh." She smoothed her hand over her head. "I guess that's the gods' heritage that's apparent in your visage and my bald head standing out."

Kian crossed his legs. "Even without hair, you are a very striking female, Morelle. You will draw attention because you are beautiful, not because of what is or is not on your head. Be prepared for curious looks as we walk from the parking area to where the laboratory is located."

It was nice of him to say that she was beautiful, and it was also good that he warned her about the looks she would get. Morelle would have thought that they were directed at her because of her baldness.

"Thank you for telling me. I would have felt very awkward otherwise." She shifted in her seat. "I'm excited about seeing the place of learning where Amanda works and also about visiting the nursery, but I'm afraid that the visit will be a waste of time. I don't have any talents. After all the tests that the head priestess put me through, I will be very surprised if Amanda finds that I do."

The head priestess had always been disappointed when nothing she'd tried caused Morelle to manifest a talent. But what if she'd been looking for the wrong things or used the wrong approach to reveal them?

As the vehicle began moving, the windows turned opaque, and Brandon took her hand. "The vehicle drives autonomously until we reach a certain distance from the mountain entrance. It's one of our security measures, so the entrance to our village remains a secret."

"Is it because of me?" Morelle narrowed her eyes at him. "So I won't know where it is?"

"It's standard protocol for everyone living in the village," Kian said. "If one of our people gets captured, the information cannot be tortured out of them."

"By whom?" she asked. "The Doomers or the humans?"

"The Doomers," the redhead said, "but also the humans to a lesser extent."

Morelle still didn't know much about those terrible enemies who had been mentioned on several occasions, and every time she asked Brandon about them, he found a clever way to change the subject, which was starting to annoy her.

Although she had to admit that when the method was kissing, she didn't mind as much.

They had done a lot of that after the first time, and she was eager to explore more, but Brandon insisted on taking things slow because she was still recuperating.

That was a good incentive to push herself on that weird machine Gertrude had guided her to use.

"What happens if the vehicles all break down?" Morelle asked. "Amanda mentioned something about a pulse of energy that can disable all electronic devices on Earth. How would people find their way back home?"

A pulse like that wouldn't have interrupted life on Morelle's home planet because the Kra-ell were not as dependent on electrical energy, and gods lived underground, so their tech was protected, but the impact on Earth would be catastrophic.

"Council members and Head Guardians know the way," Brandon said.

That made sense, and she hoped that one day she would be entrusted with that knowledge, too. Morelle didn't want to be the outsider with the secrets anymore. She wanted to be a valued member of her community.

At some point, the windows turned clear again, and the Odu took over the driving. At first, the world outside the windows didn't seem much different than the one she'd seen in the village, but then they reached a populated area with tall buildings that were covered in glass and gleamed in the morning sun.

"The facility where the lab is located is called a university," Brandon said. "Does that translate well to Kra-ell?"

She nodded. "The gods have them. The Kra-ell don't, or at least they didn't when I was there."

"According to the gods who arrived not too long ago, the Kra-ell have institutions of high learning now," Kian said. "But nothing that compares to the elite universities of the gods. Those are reserved for their upper class, and even commoner gods can't get in."

She shook her head. "Thousands of years later, things are still pretty much the same over there."

"It seems to me that time on Anumati moves at a different rate." Kian crossed his arms over his chest. "They are such an ancient civilization, and they live forever. They don't want things to change. They are comfortable with how things are."

3

BRANDON

Brandon held on to Morelle's hand as their group made its way through the campus, which was buzzing with activity, but as more people turned to stare at their unusual-looking procession and then their gazes landed on her, he switched and placed it on her lower back.

Her muscles were so tense that he wrapped his arm around her and tugged her closer against his side.

"Is there a movie shoot going on, and no one told us?" someone murmured, but it was loud enough for his immortal hearing to catch.

"Has to be. Look at that stunning woman. She must be an actress with that perfect face and starved look. I bet it's a sci-fi movie, given that shaved-off hair."

"I'm going to Google it. She looks familiar."

Morelle must have heard everything as clearly as he had, but judging by how stiff her posture remained, she didn't understand that the comments were complimentary.

He leaned closer to her ear. "They are saying that you are beautiful, and they think we are actors on our way to film a scene in a movie."

"The woman said that I looked starved," Morelle whispered. "I didn't understand what she said about my shaved-off hair. The translation must have been inaccurate."

It made sense that the term science fiction did not translate well to Kra-ell. "They think that you are an actress in a futuristic movie, and having a shaved head is the style of the future. They might also think that you are playing the part of a soldier in an elite unit. They usually shave off most of their hair for practical reasons."

"Is that why they assume I am a performer of fictional stories?"

"Performers are usually the most attractive people. They are chosen for their looks." He smiled as her shoulders relaxed slightly. "They think you are gorgeous, which, of course, you are."

"Thank you," she whispered back. "I don't know why this is important to me, but for some reason, it is."

Looks were important to everyone because people wanted to be deemed attractive and desirable, and although Morelle had grown up in a warrior culture that worshipped strength above all, some things were universal.

She lifted her chin and actually smiled at a group of passing students, causing several of them to stumble.

When they reached the lab, Amanda sauntered toward them with a big smile on her lips and her arms open wide to embrace Morelle. "Welcome to my domain."

Syssi followed with her own embrace and then hugged her husband as if she hadn't seen him in weeks instead of mere hours.

That was what Brandon wanted.

He wanted to be loved like that.

"Can I see the nursery?" Morelle asked. "I've been thinking about it and imagining it since you told me about it at dinner."

Brandon's heart squeezed at her enthusiasm.

Her natural affinity for children had taken him by surprise. He'd watched her with Allegra on Saturday, and the way she'd instantly connected with the child had been heartwarming.

"It will have to wait until after the testing," Amanda said. "I only cleared the lab for two hours, so we don't have time to visit the kiddos now, but we can visit them after we are done."

Morelle looked disappointed, but she nodded. "I understand."

As Amanda and Syssi led Morelle deeper into the lab, Brandon and Kian stayed in the seating area that was located by the entrance and was comprised of a row of six chairs and two small side tables on each end. Stacks of old magazines that had seen better days had been left on the tables.

Anandur and Brundar had remained outside, guarding the entrance to the lab.

"Any progress with InstaTock?" Kian asked as he sat down.

Brandon shook his head. "Not much since I'm dedicating most of my time to Morelle. I had a few ideas sketched out and ran them by Kalugal. He suggested that I show them to a sample of our target audience—Lisa, Parker, and Cheryl. He also told me that Cheryl is an expert on the platform."

Kian nodded. "So I've heard. But there is no rush with InstaTock. Morelle's well-being takes precedence, and she needs you." He smiled. "It would seem that the most unwavering of bachelors is off the market."

Brandon lifted his hands. "What can I say? I was enthralled by Morelle from the first moment I saw her."

The past four days had been extraordinary. Morelle was unlike any female Brandon had ever been with or known, and he'd known many over his long life.

She was fierce and guileless at the same time, and she had a darker edge that fascinated him. It was just a hint of the Kra-ell ruthlessness and tenacity that emerged at certain moments.

She was exciting.

The many kisses they had shared had been a trial of his self-control, and so far, he had proudly managed not to take it any further despite Morelle's encouragement.

She might have believed herself to be ready for more, but he knew better. She was still recuperating, getting stronger each day, and learning more about the new world she found herself in. They had unlimited time to explore each other's desires, and rushing things would only diminish the experience.

Each night, after Morelle fell asleep, he'd slip away to his own house, returning before she awoke. Annani had offered to let him stay, but he'd declined the invitation even though he'd originally planned on sneaking in at night.

He had realized that he needed to slow down for his own sake as much as for Morelle's. This was new territory to him as well, and he needed time to adjust to thinking about himself as a committed male and not the free agent he had been throughout his life.

Different skills were required for seducing a female than for maintaining a relationship.

"She needs time," he'd told the Clan Mother. "Even if she doesn't realize it yet."

Morelle had spent millennia in stasis and,

before that, her entire life in enforced isolation. Everything was new to her, including feelings, experiences, and choices. He wouldn't risk overwhelming her with physical intimacy before she'd had time to process the emotional connections she was forming for the first time in her life.

4

MORELLE

Morelle sat across from Amanda, trying her best to focus on the series of cards being shown to her.

"Just tell me what you think the next card will be," Amanda instructed patiently. "Don't overthink it."

Morelle stared at the back of the card deck. "Circle?" she ventured.

Amanda turned over the top card. It was a random shape. Another miss.

After an hour of various tests that included cards, dice, and random images, Morelle's results were consistently poor. Worse than poor, actually. She scored lower than the random chance would predict.

"Are you deliberately choosing wrong answers?" Amanda asked finally.

Her smile suggested that she was saying that

jokingly, but Morelle was sure she meant it seriously.

She straightened in her chair. "I'm truly trying. My head hurts from the effort. Maybe I'm trying too hard?"

Amanda exchanged glances with Syssi. "Even someone with no precognitive ability should be able to guess correctly around fifty percent of the time with simple coin tosses, and knowing that, you should feel no pressure. It's a simple exercise." She pulled out a coin from her drawer and showed it to Morelle. "This side is called heads because it has a face on it. The other side is called tails, and it has this design. So far, is that clear?"

Morelle nodded.

"Now let me demonstrate how this is done."

She tossed the coin in the air and called out her predictions. After twenty tosses, she'd guessed correctly nine times.

"That's normal for someone without a precognition gift." Amanda handed the coin to Syssi. "Now watch what happens when a talented seer does it. Syssi can go on and on and guess correctly each time."

Syssi smiled. "That's not true. I get tired after a while. I call it mental fatigue, and then I do worse than average."

She started tossing the coin and calling her predictions, but she kept missing repeatedly.

Her forehead creased in concentration as she

tried again and again, but her success rate remained remarkably low. "I don't get it. I'm not mentally fatigued, and this shouldn't be happening." She stared at the coin in her hand. "It's like my ability is muted somehow." Her eyes widened suddenly. "Or nullified."

"What do you mean?" Amanda asked.

A chill ran down Morelle's spine as the implications of what Syssi had said dawned on her. But then she remembered what Ell-rom had done while she was with him in the room, and her shoulders relaxed. She hadn't nullified his ability.

"Morelle might have a talent that is the opposite of Mia's," Syssi explained. "Mia enhances others' abilities." She turned to Morelle. "You might be suppressing them."

"That's impossible." She leaned over the desk and whispered, "I didn't nullify Ell-rom's ability." She glanced in the direction of where Brandon and Kian were sitting, but they were too far away to hear her when she lowered her voice.

Syssi, Amanda, and Kian knew about it, but Brandon didn't, and even with how much she cared for him, she wouldn't tell him before Kian said it was okay. They were going to test Ell-rom's ability as well, and only once they had all the information would they inform the council.

"Maybe you need to be aware of someone using their power to nullify it?" Syssi suggested. "You were sleeping in your bed at the time, and you weren't aware of what your brother was thinking or doing."

Morelle nodded. "That's true."

"Were you trying to block me just now?" Syssi asked. "Perhaps wishing I would fail?"

Morelle shook her head vigorously. "Of course not. I wasn't trying to block you or even thinking that you might fail. I was sure you would do as well as Amanda had predicted, and I was curious to see your ability in action. If anything, I wanted you to succeed."

Amanda tapped her chin thoughtfully. "We should test this further in the village. We have more people with various abilities there. I don't have any special talents myself, so you can't test your nullifying ability on me. Kian might have supernatural business acumen, but we're not about to risk the clan's finances by testing if you can nullify that."

A horrible thought suddenly struck Morelle. "What if it was me after all, and I've damaged Syssi's ability permanently?"

"There's an easy way to check," Syssi said, not looking alarmed in the slightest. "If you could wait outside for a few minutes, I can try again without you present. That will also test the effect of proximity on your nullifying ability."

"Okay." She rose to her feet and walked toward the door.

"I need to stay outside for a few minutes to see

what's happening," she said to the men as she approached them.

"I know." Brandon stood up. "We heard. I'll wait outside with you."

She hoped he hadn't heard their hushed discussion about her brother's gift. A glance at Kian revealed that he didn't look happy, but it might have been because she'd damaged his mate's talent.

"I'll stay," he said. "I want to make sure that Syssi's ability returns to normal."

She swallowed hard. "I really hope Syssi's talent is not harmed."

When Brandon took her hand, she was grateful for his support, and as they stepped outside the lab and he closed the door behind him, the tall redhead regarded them with a raised eyebrow.

"What's happening?"

"Amanda and Syssi are testing a theory," Brandon said. "They need Morelle out of the room to conduct the experiment."

"I see." The redhead smoothed a hand over his short beard. "I might as well entertain you with some stories as we wait. This very spot where we are standing now is where we fought off a group of vicious Doomers. My brother and I bought time for Kian, Amanda, and Syssi to escape."

Morelle frowned. "If this location was compromised, why does Amanda still work here?"

A smile curled the redhead's lips. "You think like a warrior. I like it. And to answer your question, the location is no longer compromised because we eliminated those Doomers. And their leader?" He paused for effect. "He became Amanda's mate."

"What?" Morelle stared at him in disbelief. She opened her mouth to ask more questions when the laboratory door opened.

"All clear," Amanda announced cheerfully. "Syssi's abilities are working normally now."

"That's a relief." Morelle put a hand over her chest.

Syssi joined them in the hallway. "Since we can't conduct any more tests here, how about we go see the nursery now?"

"I would love to." Morelle cast a quick glance at Kian. "If you have time, that is. I know you are eager to return to your office."

He chuckled. "And miss the opportunity to see my princess? No way."

For a moment, she got confused but then realized that Kian had meant his daughter. For some reason, Earth males used princess as a term of endearment.

As they headed toward the ground floor, Morelle's mind raced with implications. If she truly was a nullifier, what did that mean for her place in the clan? Would they see it as an asset or a threat?

Brandon squeezed her hand as if he could read her thoughts. Perhaps he could. He seemed to have an uncanny ability to sense her moods. Then again, if she was a null, she would have nullified his ability, right?

This discovery was very confusing and kind of disappointing. She'd hoped for something much grander than the ability to nullify the talents of others.

5

KIAN

As the limousine glided along the winding road back to the village, Kian considered the implications of what they'd discovered earlier.

The tactical advantages of a null, someone who could potentially neutralize the abilities of others, were immediately apparent. Morelle could be effective against any enemy who possessed supernatural abilities, but most Doomers didn't have any beyond thralling, and even that was limited to humans and could affect a minimal number of them. She might be useful against Navuh's compulsion power, without which he would lose his hold over his followers, and that could be tremendously helpful in taking over the island. But the question was how strong her nullification was and from how far it could be implemented.

Given that Ell-rom had used his power next to Morelle and her nullifying hadn't affected him, it probably meant that her power wasn't all that strong.

Then again, she had been a kid at the time, and her power might not have fully manifested yet. Morelle and Ell-rom were twins, but they were fraternal, not identical, and the discovery that they had different powers really wasn't surprising.

If her nullifying ability was strong, though, she could pose a threat to the clan if she turned against them for some reason.

The tenuous peace and cooperation in the village was in part reliant on the compulsion placed on all members not to harm each other. Morelle could potentially nullify the compulsion, releasing everyone to act as they pleased.

It wasn't a likely scenario, but the issue needed to be addressed.

First, though, they needed to find out the extent of her power, and he didn't want to wait a moment longer than necessary to do that.

Kian pulled out his phone and typed a message to Amanda: *Can you wrap up things early and return to the village? We need to continue testing Morelle's ability ASAP.*

Her response came quickly: *I need to finish a few things first, but Syssi and I will try to get back as soon as we can. Need to coordinate test subjects. Cassandra would be ideal because her explosions are easy to verify. Can you check with Onegus if she's working from home today?*

Cassandra's power was indeed perfect for testing Morelle. There was no ambiguity when she made things explode, especially not now after all the training she had put into gaining better control over her talent. He forwarded the request to Onegus, asking him to check with his mate about her availability.

When the chief answered a few moments later that Cassandra was available, Kian texted Amanda. *Done. Cassandra is ready when we are. I suggest we test Morelle's nullifying power on Arwel. Poor guy would love a break from everyone's emotions. We could try Toven's compulsion, too, though that's trickier to test.*

Amanda: *Good choices. Can you arrange for them to be available? We can do the testing at Mother's house.*

Kian: *Will do. I'm inviting them for a late lunch at two o'clock to be sure that you and Syssi make it back on time.*

As Morelle shifted in her seat and looked at him instead of Brandon, Kian realized that she must have noticed the rapid exchange of texts and was wondering about it.

"Amanda and I are organizing more testing," he said. "We are exchanging ideas about the kinds of abilities we should test to see how your nullification works."

"When?" she asked.

Kian liked how direct Morelle was. Her speech patterns were similar to Jade's in that she didn't mince words, but somehow the effect was different. More refined.

"I'm inviting a few people to my mother's house for a late lunch, which reminds me that I should let her know so she can put her Odus to work." He typed a lengthy message to his mother, explaining Morelle's possible talent and the people he wanted to invite to her house for lunch.

When she replied immediately with an emoji of a thumbs up, he smiled. His mother had only recently started to use emojis in her texts, and she was having a blast with them.

"What kinds of powers will I have to nullify?" Morelle asked.

Should he tell her? Did it matter if she knew ahead of time?

Maybe. It was better if she didn't know.

"I'd rather not tell you to see if you can nullify their powers without knowing what they are."

Morelle nodded. "I knew that Syssi was a seer, and Amanda reminded me of the fact before handing the coin to Syssi. It will be interesting to see if not knowing makes a difference."

"I also want to test at what distance your power works and if you can aim it at a particular person or if it is blanket nullifying."

Brandon put his hand on Morelle's thigh. "You

don't have to do this all at once. We can test some things today and continue with others tomorrow."

Determination settled over Morelle's features. The princess didn't back down from challenges. "I'd rather get answers sooner than later. Not knowing is stressful. Knowing my limits will help me control this so-called talent."

She was obviously not happy with what the Fates had given her, and Kian could understand that. But the truth was that most immortals who had powers above the standard thralling and shrouding were not too happy about them. Arwel would give away his gift if he could, and so would Cassandra. Toven, Kian wasn't sure about. Being able to compel others was too useful an ability to pass up, and as long as the one wielding the power used it conscientiously, Kian was glad to have the option to use it for the clan's benefit.

Drova, on the other hand, was too young to use it in any capacity, and if Morelle could nullify her power not just temporarily but for a while, that would definitely be beneficial for the clan.

His phone buzzed with another message from Amanda: *Syssi suggests testing distance limitations, too. Does Morelle need a line of sight? Physical proximity? Can she nullify through walls?*

All were excellent questions.

He typed back: *We also need to check if she can selectively nullify and for how long.*

"More test candidates?" Morelle asked.

"No, more parameters. Distance, selectivity, and duration of the effect. The more we understand about how your power works, the better we can utilize it."

"Or guard against it?" she asked.

Kian met her gaze. "The more control you have, the less chance of accidents."

6

ANNANI

After sending Kian the thumbs up, Annani instructed her Odus on what to prepare for lunch and took a moment to think about Morelle's talent.

She had never heard of such a power. None of the gods she had known could nullify another's power, but then they could not use their other talents on fellow gods either. They could only use them on immortals and humans.

It suddenly occurred to her that since not all gods were equal, it was possible that royals might be able to use their powers over commoners.

Things were different on Anumati, though. The Eternal King could compel the entire planet, other gods could read the minds of their fellow gods, and the rare duos like Aru and Aria could communicate telepathically.

Still, her grandmother had never mentioned that in any of their nightly talks, so perhaps that was not the case, or maybe it was such an obvious thing to her that she had not thought it was worth mentioning.

Could Annani compel Aru, Negal, and Dagor because they were commoners?

Should she even suggest testing her hypothesis?

It seemed offensive, and she would rather not do that, but she was curious, and knowing herself, it would gnaw at her until she got an answer. It would be much simpler to ask her grandmother tonight.

For now, though, she should put it aside and call Ell-rom. He needed to join them for lunch and be there for Morelle while she was being tested.

"Good morning," he answered immediately. "Did you hear anything from Morelle?"

"Not from Morelle herself, but from Kian. He texted me a few minutes ago that they are on their way back and that it seems Morelle's talent is the nullification of other paranormal talents. Kian has invited several people with different abilities to join us for a late lunch so Morelle's ability can be tested under various conditions. I thought you would want to be here to witness it and also to enjoy a meal with the family."

There was a moment of silence on the other end. "Morelle can nullify other talents?" He sounded both surprised and excited. "If she can nullify my ability, that would be a huge relief for me."

"I do not know how her talent works. Kian's text did not elaborate. But if you join us for lunch, you will find out together with Morelle and the rest of us."

He hesitated. "I really want to be there for Morelle, but I don't want to leave Jasmine. For some reason, I have a feeling she's going to wake up today, and I don't want her to open her eyes and find herself alone in this room."

"Oh?" Annani sat up straighter. "What makes you think today is the day?"

"I'm not sure," he admitted. "I just woke up this morning expecting to see her eyes open. I actually jumped up from my cot to look at her, but it hasn't happened yet."

"How long have you had this feeling?" Annani knew better than to dismiss premonitions.

"Just since this morning." His voice held a mixture of hope and uncertainty. "Perhaps I'm just impatient. It has been so long, and Bridget keeps saying that Jasmine is doing great and still growing taller, and it just makes sense that she should wake up any moment now."

"Never doubt your instincts," Annani said. "I have learned to listen to my gut over the millennia, and it has never steered me wrong. If you believe that today is the day, Jasmine will wake up soon. Stay with her."

"I feel terrible." He sighed. "I should be there for Morelle while she's discovering her ability."

"You are exactly where you need to be." Annani pushed to her feet and started pacing. "You and Morelle are no longer alone, and you are not each other's only support. You have a sister and an entire clan caring for you. I will be here for Morelle while you take care of Jasmine."

"Thank you." He sighed in relief. "I'm so grateful for everything you've done for us."

"And I am grateful for having you and Morelle in my life. Your arrival was one of the greatest gifts the Fates have bestowed on me. Now focus on your mate, and I will keep you updated about Morelle's testing."

"Thank you. I will call you if anything changes over here."

"Please do. I am keeping my proverbial fingers crossed."

Only after ending the call did Annani wonder if Ell-rom knew what crossing her fingers meant. He had learned so much since waking up, but there was still so much he did not know, and many phrases did not translate well into Kra-ell.

When she spotted the golf cart approaching, Annani did not wait for her Odus to open the door and announce her family's arrival. Instead, she went to the door herself, opening it just as Morelle was climbing out.

Her sister's face showed signs of fatigue, but the moment her eyes landed on Annani, a smile spread over her face, and she walked straight into her arms, hugging her with careful gentleness. "Did you hear?" she asked.

"Yes." Annani smiled, holding her close. "This is a remarkable gift."

Morelle pulled back slightly, searching Annani's face. "Really? I was thinking about what it could mean on the way home, and I realized that it wasn't much. Most immortals don't have unique paranormal talents for me to nullify."

Annani took her sister's hand and led her to the living room. "Every power has its purpose and a place in the balance of things. Your talent will prove valuable. I have no doubt."

Kian and Brandon, who had walked in behind them, murmured their agreement.

"It depends on many factors, but we will know more once the second round of testing is done," Kian added as he looked at his watch. "I'll let you rest until lunch, and I'll come back at two o'clock."

Annani put a hand on his arm. "Are you sure you want to leave only to come back in an hour?"

If her home office were available, she would have offered it to him, but it had been converted to guest quarters, and she knew that Kian would not want to work from her bedroom, sitting on her pink swivel chair and putting his papers on her tiny white desk.

"My house is right next door, and I have a fully equipped office there." He leaned and kissed her cheek. "Take care of Morelle," he whispered. "I think she's disappointed with her talent."

"Do not worry." Annani patted his arm. "I will take good care of her."

7

DROVA

Drova glared at the massive history book in her lap, muttering curses under her breath. Of all the punishments Parker could have devised, he'd chosen the absolute worst. Public humiliation would have been better.

Even a good old-fashioned whipping would have been preferable to this torture.

"The rise and fall of human civilizations," she read aloud mockingly. "As if I care about what humans did thousands of years ago."

She'd started on the first chapter, but even though her English was pretty good by now, the book had many words that she didn't understand, and sometimes she was reading them wrong in her head. She had to use the translating software that William's crew had designed, and it was making the already boring reading even worse.

The chime of the doorbell startled her so badly

that she nearly dropped the heavy tome, but for once she welcomed the interruption, not even caring if it was someone looking for her mother. Though with Jade working from her office at Ingrid's design center, few people came to the house. That was where Drova had been spending most of her time lately, but between the hours of twelve and four, she was supposed to be studying, or as she preferred to call it, serving her sentence.

When she opened the door and found Pavel standing there, her heart made a silly little flutter that she immediately tried to quash, but it wasn't easy. He looked so handsome in the black fatigues of the Guardian force, the fabric fitting his tall, lithe frame perfectly.

"You are officially a Guardian? When did this happen?"

"Official as of this morning," he said with a grin. "Though we're not called Guardians because Onegus does not want to offend the old timers who've spent many decades to achieve what we did in mere months. The new Kra-ell recruits are called either Saviors or Avengers, depending on which division we are assigned to, and we've not been assigned to either yet."

"Come in and tell me all about it." She stepped aside, trying not to stare at how the black fabric stretched across his shoulders.

She headed toward the couch but changed direction at the last moment, leading him to the dining table instead. If he sat next to her on that couch, she would have trouble breathing. It was safer at the table where the huge stack of books could serve as a barrier.

He pulled out a chair and sat down while glancing at the books. "What's all that?"

"My punishment." She waved a dismissive hand over them. "Tell me about those divisions. It's the first time I'm hearing about them."

"That's because they are new. The Saviors will continue the work of rescuing victims of trafficking. The Avengers is a new division, but no one's saying exactly what it will be doing yet." He straightened in his chair and waved a hand over his fatigues. "When we get our posts, we will receive a special insignia to designate us as one or the other."

"I wonder what the other division is for," Drova said. "Maybe they are finally going after the Doomers? I never understood why the clan just hides from them. They should do a preemptive attack and eliminate the threat. They keep saying that there are many more of them than there are of us, but that's precisely why they need to attack first and catch the filthy Doomers by surprise. They know where they are, so I really don't get why they hesitate."

Pavel regarded her with an amused smirk that was too sexy to be allowed. "There are a lot of innocent people on that island. The clan doesn't want to harm them."

Drova crossed her arms over her chest. "I get that, but life is not fair. They should think of their people first and then about the harm the Doomers are doing to the entire world. I think the collateral damage of a few dozen innocents is acceptable."

"What if it's a few hundred?"

She narrowed her eyes at him. "Even a few thousand. As I said, life is not fair, and you need to choose. It's either us or them. There is no middle ground."

He lifted his hands and clapped. "Spoken like a true Kra-ell."

"I take that as a compliment."

He nodded. "It was meant as such. I happen to agree with you, but the Clan Mother decides for the clan, not us, and she is too soft and merciful."

Drova let out a breath. "Yeah, she is, which is a damn shame since she has so much power that she does nothing with. Still, I can't complain since she invited us to live with them. But frankly? If it were me, I wouldn't have done that. It was a mistake."

"Why not?" Pavel waved a hand over his uniform again. "We strengthen them. Thanks to us, they can launch this new division and do whatever they plan to do with it. They didn't have enough warriors before."

That was true, and if that was the reason the goddess had invited them, then her decision had merit, but Drova wasn't sure that the Clan Mother had thought that far in advance. She'd just wanted to be the Good Samaritan who offered a hand to a bunch of displaced Kra-ell.

The goddess was lucky that the Kra-ell were generally honorable people. Others, who were less concerned with honoring their pledges and expressing their gratitude, might have bitten off her offered hand.

"I want in," she said without having given it much thought. "Maybe that could get me out of this stupid punishment." She gestured at the history book she'd left open on the table. "I'd rather fight any day of the week and twice on Sunday than read another page of that boring book."

Hopefully, Pavel had learned that human phrase and didn't ask her to clarify.

It seemed that he had because he reached over and picked up the book. "What is it about?"

"Human history. That's Parker's idea of justice," she grumbled. "He's making me read all these boring books, and then he will test me on them. As if I need to know any of this."

Pavel began flipping through the pages. "My English reading skills could use improvement. Perhaps we could read these books together to help me get better at it? In the Guardian training, we are assigned reading about technical stuff. You know, guns, rifles, grenades, ammunition, and many other things, and it takes me forever to get through it because I read so slowly."

Drova kept staring at him. "Reading about guns and ammunition is exciting. This is the most boring stuff you can imagine. Why would you want to read about human history? It had nothing to do with us."

"I value education." He ran a hand over his sleek, long ponytail. "It's the greatest equalizer. It doesn't matter who you are born as, if you educate yourself, you can best the most highborn prince or princess. By rejecting it, we Kra-ell doom ourselves to be as ignorant as the Doomers."

A laugh burst from her throat. "Ignorance will doom us to be dumb as the Doomers? That's one hell of a tongue twister but so apt."

Pavel grinned, and Drova's heart did that annoying flutter again. "Exactly. I don't want to be as dumb as a Doomer."

She leaned back to get some more distance between them. "Jade says that the Doomers are breeding for brains instead of brawn now, so they won't stay dumb forever."

It was obvious that the clan had spies in the Doomer camp, but Jade either didn't know who they were or didn't want to share it with her untrustworthy daughter.

"I guess so. But I'm sure they are not teaching their warriors history. They might teach them physics and chemistry so they can make better weapons, but I bet they won't teach them any of this." He tapped the book. "I think that by learning about the mistakes of others, you can avoid making the same mistakes yourself. Also, reading manuals about strategy written by successful generals has a lot of merit."

"I suppose," she conceded.

"Think about it," he said. "The clan has been influencing human development for thousands of years. Don't you want to know how they did it? What worked and what didn't?" He tapped the book again. "This isn't just about what humans did. It's about how gods and immortals shaped their progress."

Drova hadn't considered that angle. "We are not immortals or gods, and we can't do what they have done, but I get what you are saying."

Having won the argument, Pavel looked smug. "It doesn't matter that we are neither. We're living among gods and immortals, and we should understand their past. Know what shaped them."

"Yes, you are right," she conceded, not because she agreed with him but because it had occurred to her that if she appeared to do so, Pavel might come over more often to study with her. "We will need to find a way to work our study sessions into your training regimen and my shadowing sessions with my mother. She thinks I will learn about governing the Kra-ell by trailing her and watching what she does."

"There is no better way to learn." He grinned. "We will figure out something."

8

ARU

The stark room in the office building across from the keep felt almost too ordinary for such unusual circumstances.

As it turned out, the clan had several such spaces reserved in the various office buildings they owned that were intended just for meetings like this one.

Aru sat behind the desk with Negal and Dagor flanking him, facing the three men Turner had selected and vetted. All were recently retired Special Forces veterans with excellent service records and a thirst for carefree travel after years of service.

Their military bearing was still evident even in their civilian clothing. Time would soften their postures, though, and would make them a little less rigid.

Aru and his teammates had gone through a similar metamorphosis.

"I understand Turner has explained the basics?" he asked.

The oldest of the three, who'd introduced himself as Marcus, nodded. "Minimum of a three-year commitment, extended travel assignments, all expenses paid, and specific locations to visit. He was light on the details."

"That's because some aspects of this assignment are unconventional." Aru chose his words carefully. "We'll need to implant tracking devices to monitor your progress and the locations you visit. You will be provided with an itinerary, but you don't have to follow it strictly. As long as you visit the general vicinity, that's fine with us."

He watched their reactions closely, but none showed alarm. If anything, they seemed curious and somewhat amused.

"Is this some kind of a reality show?" asked the youngest, Jake, his eyes moving between Aru, Negal, and Dagor. "You guys look like actors."

Aru allowed a small smile. It was actually a good idea to let them think that they were taking part in a reality show. "I can't reveal the nature of the project or even hint at it. What I can tell you is that you'll be well compensated for your time and discretion."

"Of course," Marcus said. "That's why we are being paid the big bucks, right?"

Aru nodded. "The procedure of implanting the trackers will be done in a secret facility, and we will use hypnosis to make you forget where it is and that you underwent any procedure at all. I'm telling you this ahead of time to give you an opportunity to change your minds. Nothing will be done to you without your consent."

Marcus exchanged glances with the other two. "We trust you because Turner vouched for you. I wouldn't have agreed to the hypnosis otherwise, even though the three of us have been subjected to it during our service. That and other methods were used to make us forget certain details of our assignments. Naturally, I can't tell you what those other methods were."

"And I wouldn't ask you to reveal them," Aru assured him, even though his curiosity was piqued. "Not now and not under hypnosis. You have my word. We respect your professional discretion as we expect you to respect ours."

The third man, who'd been quiet until now, spoke up. "You mentioned compensation, and Turner said it was going to be generous. I would like to know more."

"Of course." Aru pulled out three folders and slid them across the desk. "Monthly deposits to accounts of your choosing, plus all travel expenses covered. The amount is listed on page three."

The men examined the documents, eyebrows rising at the figures. Aru had expected haggling, but the amounts seemed to meet their expectations.

Diamond prices had been falling over the last two years, so the stash they had brought with them was worth much less than it was when they had first arrived on Earth, but Kian had promised to find the three of them work in the clan so they could afford to finance the fake search. Well, it wasn't entirely fake. They were sending these humans to the places they would have gone to themselves, so these men might get lucky and uncover some of the missing pods.

"That's more than enough," Marcus said. "If you need us beyond the three years, we will happily renew the contracts."

"Don't you want to settle down?" Negal asked. "Start a family?"

The humor bled out of Marcus's expression. "I've seen too much shit to want to bring kids into this world." He looked at his companions. "Right?"

The two nodded but without much enthusiasm.

Aru had a feeling they didn't share Marcus's sentiment. "We will talk again in three years and many times before that, so you don't need to decide anything now."

Jake nodded. "Sounds good."

"Let's talk about passports," Negal said. "Do you want to use your own, or would you prefer alternate identities?"

"Our own," Marcus answered without hesitation. "Keeps things simpler."

"Are you sure?" Aru asked. "As former Special Ops, you are probably restricted as far as where you are allowed to travel. Tibet is part of China, and we might, at some point, send you into China proper. Russia and its former republics are also on the itineraries."

"That's fine. We were not that kind of Special Ops. Strictly military, commando missions."

Aru regarded them for a long moment just to give Negal more time to peek into their heads and check if they were hiding anything that could undermine their mission.

Finally, he nodded. "Very well. We will need your passport information to book flights for you."

"How much contact will we have with you?" Jake asked.

"Minimal," Dagor said. "Emergency protocols will be established, but otherwise, you're on your own."

"That's good," Jake said. "We are all tired of taking orders."

"When do we start?" Marcus asked.

"If you sign the documents today, we will meet here tomorrow and take you to where the medical procedure will be done. After that, you will be given money to purchase what you need to trek through Tibet. We will book flights for you for

Thursday. We can also arrange transport to the airport, or you can handle that yourself."

"I'll leave it up to you," Marcus said. "Either way is good."

They spent the next hour going through paperwork, answering questions about emergency protocols, communication methods, and travel arrangements.

The men were thorough but not suspicious, accepting the unusual nature of the assignment with professional detachment.

After the final handshakes, Aru watched them leave, waiting for the door to close before turning to Negal. "Well?"

"Clean," Negal confirmed. "No deception, no hidden agendas. They think it must be a reality show or some kind of government experiment, but they're not particularly concerned either way. They are happy with the pay and the all-expenses-paid travel."

"Dagor?" Aru asked.

"Drones attached and tracking," he reported. "I'll watch what they are saying from now until they return here tomorrow."

"I should thank Turner," Aru said. "These men are perfect. They are experienced enough to handle themselves in any situation, disciplined enough to follow instructions without asking too many questions, and motivated by both money and the promise of traveling the world."

"You should call Kian as well." Dagor opened his laptop. "Tell him that we found hosts for our trackers and are ready to move into his village."

9

BRANDON

Morelle hadn't said much in the hour or so since they had returned from the university, but her nervous energy was palpable, and with every passing minute, she was growing even more agitated.

"There is no reason for you to be so stressed. You know almost everyone who's joining us for lunch. You've already met Toven, so it's just Cassandra and Arwel who are new. Their mates are not even coming because they couldn't drop what they were doing on such short notice."

Truthfully, he was thankful that Jin wasn't coming. Cassandra and Jin were both headstrong and somewhat intimidating females, and they might have overwhelmed his princess. Meeting them one at a time was preferable.

Or maybe he was underestimating Morelle and was letting his overprotective instincts cloud his judgment. She might be anxious now, but she was a fighter.

"I'm not nervous about meeting new people." She put down the fashion magazine she'd been pretending to browse for the past hour. "I'm nervous about testing my so-called talent. I don't even know if I want it to work. In fact, I think it would be better if I had no special talent at all. You said that most immortals can't do more than thrall and shroud. I'd rather be like everyone else."

"Oh, but my dear Morelle, you are not an immortal. You are a goddess."

"Half goddess." She crossed her legs. "Half Kra-ell. So, I'm more like the immortals than the gods, right?"

"Not quite." He leaned forward, bracing his elbows on his knees. "The Kra-ell have paranormal abilities and are long-lived. Most humans have no special abilities at all, and their lives are short in comparison."

"I feel pity for them." Morelle picked up the magazine again and started flipping through the pages. "These women are nearly as beautiful as the goddesses, though."

"Not all women look like that, and even these models don't look as good in real life. These photos have been heavily manipulated."

"Oh." She closed the magazine. "That's trickery."

He laughed. "That is just the tip of the iceberg."

Seeing her confused expression, he realized

that he shouldn't have used idioms she had no reference for, but before he could explain, Morelle took a deep breath, rose to her feet, and walked over to the full-length mirror positioned next to their bedroom door.

She looked beautiful in the high-waisted dark blue trousers and white short-sleeved shirt. The outfit was deceptively simple, but the quality of the fabrics elevated it to quiet elegance. He made a mental note to thank Melinda for her exceptional work in putting together Morelle's wardrobe.

"You are stunning, sweetheart." He moved to stand behind her, placing his hands on her shoulders.

Funny how that casual endearment felt natural even though he'd never been one to use such terms before.

Morelle was tall for a female, the top of her head reaching his nose when she was wearing flats. In heels, they were nearly eye to eye, though he'd noticed she hadn't touched any of the higher shoes in her closet.

"I have a question," he said.

She turned to face him. "What do you want to know?"

"You're tall for a goddess or an immortal but not for a Kra-ell." He studied her face. "Did you wear elevated shoes under your robes to appear taller?"

She shook her head. "Not all Kra-ell are tall. Some tribes are a little shorter than others."

"Really?" This was new information. "I didn't know that. All the Kra-ell in the village are quite tall."

"Shorter stature is not common, but it's not unusual either." A shadow passed over her face. "It was just one more way I was made to feel inferior. But even if I had wanted heeled shoes, there weren't any available. I wore what other acolytes wore, but unlike them, I never took off the robes and veils when others could see me."

"I'm so sorry." He rubbed her arms. "That must have been difficult."

Morelle's shoulder lifted in a slight shrug. "When you know nothing else, it becomes your routine, a way of life. You don't think about it."

"Like a bird that has been caged since it hatched that doesn't know what to do when the cage door is left open."

As the doorbell rang, Morelle closed her eyes briefly. "Not me. I would have flown away the moment that door was unlocked." When she opened them again, there was new determination in her gaze. "We should join the guests."

"Yes, we should." He stepped aside and opened the door for her.

In the living room, they found that Syssi and Amanda had already arrived, along with Cassandra and Arwel, but Toven and Kian were still not there.

"Hi." Cassandra approached Morelle and offered her hand. "Welcome to the village, Princess Morelle. I'm Cassandra, Onegus's mate, and I—"

"Don't!" Amanda cut in sharply, raising her hand. "We don't want Morelle to know what your talent is before she tries to nullify it."

"Got it." Cassandra's smile never faltered. "I'll show you later." She winked.

Arwel stepped forward next, and Brandon studied the Guardian closely. The empath couldn't turn off his ability. It was constantly active. If Morelle's nullification worked passively by proximity, Arwel should already be feeling its effects.

Standing behind Morelle, Brandon raised an eyebrow in question.

Arwel's slight head shake could have meant either that the null wasn't working or that he couldn't feel the emotions of others anymore.

"Let's sit down," Annani said. "Kian and Toven will be here any moment, and we can start lunch then."

Brandon guided Morelle to the dining table, noting how she chose a chair that would allow her to keep everyone in view. It was a warrior's instinct, he realized, and his chest filled with pride, even though he had nothing to do with that.

"So, Morelle." Cassandra sat across from her. "How do you like life in the village so far?"

10

MORELLE

Throughout lunch, Morelle studied Cassandra with fascination. The immortal was strikingly beautiful, her features enhanced by the same kind of facial paint that Amanda wore. On Anumati only warriors painted their faces, and that was in order to appear more fearsome in battle, not to enhance their beauty. Yet the effect was undeniable.

When Cassandra caught her staring, she smiled. "Is there anything you want to ask me?"

"I'm curious about the Earth custom of females painting their faces to enhance their appearance," she admitted. "My sister doesn't do that, and neither does Alena. Is there a reason some females do it and others don't?"

Casandra chuckled. "I work for a cosmetics company, and my job is to convince every woman that she must use these paints, as you call them, to enhance her natural beauty, but the truth is that it is completely up to the individual. Some females don't leave the house without applying the paint first, others do it only for special occasions, and many never do."

Morelle frowned. "How do you convince females to use your company's products?"

"Advertising. We put pictures of gorgeous women in magazines next to a photo of our products, and the message is that if you use them, you will look just as beautiful as the model."

Morelle remembered seeing that in the magazine that Annani had given her. "Brandon says that the photos have been manipulated and that the women don't really look as lovely in reality as they look in the pictures."

"That's true," Cassandra admitted.

Morelle hesitated for a moment, but she couldn't help what needed to be said. "That's cheating, isn't it?"

"Not really," Cassandra said. "Everyone knows that the pictures are altered. We are selling dreams and fantasies, and we don't even charge much for it. A woman can spend a little money on a new eyeliner and feel fantastic for at least a little while thinking that it will make her look beautiful."

That was such an interesting concept. The cosmetic company was cheating in how it presented its products, but the customers knew about the cheat and bought the product anyway because they were actually buying hope.

Then, a thought occurred to her. "Do you use your special ability in your work?" She still didn't know what Cassandra's talent was, but surely there must be some connection.

Cassandra laughed. "My talent isn't really suited for advertising. Though it might make for some interesting commercials." Her eyes sparkled with mischief. "Would you like to see what I can do? But we should probably step outside for this."

As lunch was mostly over, everyone got up and followed them to Annani's backyard, and Cassandra carried an empty drinking glass with her for some reason.

She walked up to a garden chair, put the glass on top, and they returned to the covered patio where everyone was assembled.

"Try to nullify my power," she said.

Morelle frowned. "I don't know what power I'm trying to stop." She still wasn't entirely sure how her nullification worked. "I will just think about stopping whatever it might be."

She concentrated, and the familiar energy humming under her skin sizzled pleasantly as if it had just woken up from slumber.

Morelle shook her head. *You're imagining it. It's not happening.*

She disregarded the feeling, letting it fizzle, and

leaned against Brandon, who was standing behind her.

Cassandra turned to look at the glass she'd left on the green garden chair. "Here it goes."

For a moment nothing happened, but then, with a sharp crack, the glass exploded into countless glittering shards.

Startled, Morelle jumped, throwing her arms out to shield Brandon.

"Relax," Cassandra said. "My explosions are contained. The toughest part of learning to control my talent was aiming at a specific object so I wouldn't accidentally blow things up when I got angry or excited, and to moderate the power of the explosion so the pieces wouldn't fly too far away."

Morelle was still trying to convince her heart to stop racing, but she'd calmed down enough to realize that Cassandra's power was somewhat similar to Ell-rom's. It was also destructive, but the female had learned to control it. If Cassandra could be trusted, perhaps she could help Ell-rom master his death-ray ability.

"Let's try again," Amanda suggested. "Now that you know what to expect, see if you can block it."

One of Annani's Odus appeared with a broom and a new glass. He swept the broken shards into a bin and put a fresh glass on the green chair.

When he returned to the house, Cassandra looked at Morelle. "Ready?"

"Yes."

This time Morelle focused on the glass, imagining Cassandra blowing it up, just as she had done with Syssi's coin tossing.

Cassandra concentrated, but the glass remained intact.

"It worked!" Amanda clapped excitedly. "Let's test the range. Morelle, go inside while Cassandra tries again. Stay by the window and watch her. After that, we will try it without a line of sight."

"I'll go inside with you," Brandon offered.

Morelle nodded.

She could see Cassandra clearly through the glass door and maintained her focus, picturing that glass exploding.

When Cassandra attempted to use her power, nothing happened.

"Remarkable," Amanda said as she joined Morelle and Brandon inside. "Now, let's move away from the glass doors, and I'll tell you about how I met Dalhu. It's quite a story. He actually kidnapped me, and I fell in love with him anyway."

"He did what?"

Morelle suddenly remembered what Anandur had told her about Amanda mating the leader of the Doomer team, who had come to harm the clan. She'd been so preoccupied thinking about her newfound ability on the way home that she'd forgotten to ask how it had happened.

"Oh yes," Amanda launched into the tale,

gesturing animatedly. "My Dalhu used to be a Doomer—"

A sharp crack from outside made Morelle jump.

While she'd been distracted by Amanda's story, Cassandra had successfully shattered another glass.

"Perfect!" Amanda beamed. "So, the nullification requires conscious attention. When you're distracted, it doesn't work."

Morelle frowned. "I don't understand how it works. I wasn't trying to stop Cassandra. I was just watching the glass and expecting it to shatter. Maybe my effect is on the object and not on the power affecting it?"

Amanda tapped a finger on her red-colored lips. "That's an interesting theory. I wonder how we can test it."

"Easy," Brandon said. "Arwel's talent does not work with objects. If Morelle can nullify it, then her power works on the talent, not the object."

"True, true." Amanda walked out the glass doors and called everyone inside. "Okay, everyone. You know what to do to activate Arwel's talent." She turned to Morelle. "Do your thing. Try to stop Arwel from doing what he's doing."

The Guardian looked pained, and she wondered what was causing it. Maybe she could stop his pain?

Morelle concentrated, clearing her mind of

Amanda's fascinating story of how she had fallen in love with the enemy of her clan, and she imagined Arwel smiling.

Then it happened, and he smiled. "Unbelievable. It went quiet up here." He tapped his temple.

"What's your talent?" Morelle asked.

"I'm an empath, and I can't block people's feelings. It's not as bad with immortals because they project much less than humans, but they bombarded me just now, and then it suddenly stopped. How did you know what to do?"

"You looked in pain, and I wanted you to feel better."

"Fascinating," Amanda said. "I need to do some thinking. This nullifying talent is not what I expected."

"Should we try mine?" Toven asked.

Morelle was exhausted after blocking Arwel's pain, and she really didn't want to try again with Toven.

Amanda looked at her. "You look tired, but since we've dragged Toven over here, can you summon a little more energy and try again?"

"Of course. But can we do that sitting down?"

"Naturally." Amanda led the procession to the living room, where everyone found a place to sit.

"I'll make it simple," Toven said. "Look at me and try to stop whatever I'm about to do."

Morelle nodded.

Toven turned to Brandon. "Tell Morelle that she is ugly and that you hate her."

"No," Brandon said with a smile.

Morelle was confused. "Why did you tell Brandon to say such hurtful things, and why are you two smiling about it?"

"My talent is compulsion," Toven said. "You just blocked me from forcing Brandon to say those nasty things to you."

"Ha." She looked at Brandon. "How did I do it without knowing what he was doing?"

"Good question," Amanda said. "Your nullifying ability behaves differently with each talent. I will need to study it some more. But not today."

Morelle let out a breath. "Thank you. I feel like I need to lie down and sleep for a few hours."

11

ELL-ROM

Ell-rom closed his laptop and put it down on the bedside table. He'd been practicing English with the help of the AI teacher every day for long hours, but today, he couldn't concentrate. The feeling that Jasmine would finally wake up was so strong that he kept lifting his head from the screen and looking at her, hoping to see her eyes open.

It wasn't very conducive to learning.

Jasmine had been unconscious for ten days, which was a long time, but not as long as some of the other transitioning Dormants, who had taken weeks. Everyone was telling him that he had nothing to worry about, and maybe they were right, but Ell-rom was all out of patience.

He needed his Jasmine back.

He had memorized every detail of her face during his long vigil—the arch of her eyebrows, the curve of her cheeks, the slight parting of her lips as she breathed.

So, when there was the tiniest change in her breathing pattern, he noticed it immediately, and his heart rate accelerated rapidly.

He jumped out of his chair and stood at her side in a split second. "Jasmine?" he whispered, taking her hand.

Her fingers twitched in his grasp, and her eyelids fluttered while the steadily beeping monitors beside her bed picked up their pace.

"My love?" He leaned closer, hardly daring to breathe. "Can you hear me?"

A small furrow formed between her brows, and she turned her head slightly toward his voice. Her lips moved, though no sound emerged, and her eyes remained closed.

"Bridget!" he called out, not taking his eyes off his mate's face. "Jasmine is awake!"

The door opened a moment later, and Bridget walked into the room. She stood next to him and smiled. "Welcome back, Jasmine. Ell-rom missed you like crazy."

Was that a ghost of a smile he was seeing?

It vanished as quickly as it had appeared.

"I'm here, my love," he said softly. "Can you open your eyes and look at me? I've missed you so much. You're transitioning, and you've grown taller by more than two inches. I don't know if you'll be happy or upset about that. Bridget says that if you don't like the extra inches, she will gladly take them. She is right here beside me, so she can confirm that she said that."

He was throwing everything he could think of at Jasmine to cause her to want to wake up, and it seemed to be working.

Her eyelids fluttered and opened briefly before closing again.

"I'll dim the light," Bridget offered. "It might be too harsh for her."

She pulled out her phone and adjusted the lighting using an application that controlled everything in the patient room. He didn't know how it worked and didn't care.

"Try again, my love. The lights are dimmer now."

When Jasmine's eyes opened this time, they stayed open, though unfocused at first. She blinked several times, her gaze gradually sharpening until it found his face.

"Ell-rom?" Her voice was barely a whisper, rough from disuse.

"Yes." He had to fight back tears of relief. "Welcome back."

She tried to lift her hand to his face, but her coordination was off. He caught her hand and pressed it to his cheek. "I've missed you so much."

"How long?" she managed to ask.

"Ten days," he told her. "You've been transitioning and taking your time because your body was growing."

Her eyes widened slightly at that, and he wondered whether she'd heard him before when he had told her that she had grown in height.

"How much taller?" Jasmine asked.

"Two inches," Bridget said. "Now you are the standard height for a supermodel. Congratulations."

To his relief, Jasmine gave a weak laugh. "Yay. Did my ass shrink?"

He frowned. "I hope not. I like your ass just the way it is."

Chuckling, Bridget motioned for him to step aside. "I need to check a few things."

When Jasmine's eyes widened in fear, he brought her hand to his lips and kissed it. "I'm not going anywhere. I will just give Bridget room to work."

Jasmine nodded.

As soon as Ell-rom made room for her, Bridget stepped forward. "How's your vision? Any blurriness or light sensitivity?"

"A little blurry," Jasmine admitted and licked her lips. "Can I have a sip of water?"

"Of course." Bridget moved over to the sink, filled a paper cup with water, added a straw, and brought it over to Jasmine's lips. "Not too much. Just a little sip."

As Bridget continued her examination, Ell-rom

kept eye contact with Jasmine, unwilling to take his eyes off her even for a moment.

He'd known she would wake today and had felt it in his bones, but the reality of having her conscious and alert again was overwhelming.

Bridget adjusted the bed so Jasmine was slightly more upright, allowed her another sip, and then handed Ell-rom the cup.

"Morelle?" Jasmine asked.

"Awake and doing well," he assured her quickly. "And she's even discovered her special paranormal talent. She can nullify others' abilities."

Interest sparked in Jasmine's eyes. "That's unusual."

"So I've been told." He smiled, amazed at how quickly her mind was working despite just waking.

"You should be with her," Jasmine said as her eyelids slid shut. "Stay?" she murmured despite her previous statement.

"Of course." He leaned over her and pressed a gentle kiss to her forehead. "I'm not going anywhere. Annani is taking care of Morelle, and so is Brandon."

Jasmine probably hadn't heard that because she was already asleep, and the only reason Ell-rom wasn't panicking was that Bridget didn't seem concerned.

Unbothered by her patient dozing off, the physician finished noting her vital signs. "Everything looks good," she said quietly. "She'll probably sleep for a few more hours but don't worry. This sleep will be natural, not transitional unconsciousness."

Ell-rom nodded, not taking his eyes off Jasmine's peaceful face. He should probably text Annani and tell her that his prediction had been correct, but for now he just wanted to savor this moment, watching his mate sleep and knowing that when she woke again, she would be stronger and stay awake longer.

12

MORELLE

The Odus were just clearing away the dinner dishes when Annani's phone rang. Her sister's face lit up as she checked the screen. "Ell-rom," she said, tapping the speaker button and placing the phone on the table. "I have Morelle and Brandon with me, and I activated the speaker function so they can hear you clearly. How are things over in the clinic?"

"Jasmine is awake!" Ell-rom's voice carried both joy and exhaustion. "Well, she was, and she is asleep once again, but Bridget says that it's a normal sleep, not a transitional unconsciousness. Jasmine was conscious and perfectly coherent, just very weak."

Morelle's heart leaped. Annani had told her about Ell-rom's choice to remain by Jasmine's side because he'd had a feeling she would wake up today. "Congratulations, Ell-rom," she said with as much cheer as her tone could carry. "That is wonderful news. I'm starting to think that you have a precognition talent. You had a feeling it would happen today, and it did."

Annani smiled smugly. "It runs in the family. I also get gut feelings, and they are never wrong."

Morelle cast her sister a smile. "I can't claim to have experienced the same, so it must be just you and Ell-rom."

She wondered what talent their other half-sister had. Annani had revealed during dinner that their father had sired another daughter with a goddess before he had met Annani's mother. The revelation was startling enough but not as shocking as the fact that Areana was mated to the clan's archenemy. Contact with her was limited to clandestine phone calls that her mate didn't know about, and that put her at great risk.

Ell-rom didn't know about that yet, and Morelle couldn't wait to tell him.

"Can I come over and see Jasmine?" Morelle asked. "I'll gladly sit with you until the next time she wakes up."

"Of course," Ell-rom said. "She asked about you, and I told her about your nullification ability. I can't wait to hear how the testing went."

"I'll tell you all about it when I get there."

"I'll arrange for a golf cart." Brandon turned to Annani. "Would you like to join us?"

She shook her head. "I don't want to distract

anyone from Morelle and Jasmine's first meeting. I'll wait for the ceremony tomorrow."

"Ceremony?" Morelle asked. "What kind of ceremony?"

"When a Dormant completes the first stage of transition, the doctors perform a simple test to verify that they are indeed immortal. They make a small cut on the Dormant's palm and time how quickly it heals."

Morelle frowned. "That seems kind of crude. I'm sure that there must be better ways to test it."

Annani shrugged. "It is quick, practical, and decisive. Even those with the most diluted immortal blood heal significantly faster than humans. Over time, it has become more than just a test, though. It was made into a ceremony, and a celebration with family and friends present to witness and welcome new immortals into their everlasting lives."

"Jasmine will love it," Ell-rom said. "She heard about the ceremony from Margo, Frankie, and Gabi, and I know that she will want to have the same experience."

Ell-rom had told her about his and Jasmine's time in the clan's keep, and the three gods and their mates who had helped find their pods and had also become good friends. He was excited by the possibility of them moving into the village, but there was something that the gods needed to take care of first. Something about trackers that had to come out of them and get implanted in human volunteers.

"The cart is here," Brandon announced. "Are you ready to go?"

Morelle stood quickly, smoothing the fabric of her trousers. "Yes." She turned to Annani. "Thank you for dinner and lunch and everything else."

"Stop thanking me, Morelle." Annani waved a hand in dismissal. "It is my pleasure. Give my love to Jasmine and tell her that I will come to see her tomorrow."

Brandon said his thanks as well and got the same answer from Annani. They headed outside, where a Guardian was waiting with a cart.

"Good news." He beamed at them. "It's always a good day when a Dormant transitions."

"Thank you, I think." She looked at Brandon. "Is that what I'm supposed to say?"

"You could also say something like 'good news indeed' as an affirmation." Brandon helped her into the cart even though she was steady enough on her feet now and didn't need assistance.

She'd noticed that he loved to find excuses to touch her, and she was more than happy to oblige him. The contact sent pleasant shivers through her body.

"Your customs are confusing," she said as he climbed in behind her.

"The clan believes in marking important moments," he said. "As Kian says, every reason for celebration should be taken advantage of. Life is full of hardships, so when there is an opportunity to rejoice and celebrate, it should be taken."

"Indeed," she said, following his advice from before.

Her comment had referred to speech conventions, but she liked his answer about celebrations.

"Can I tell Ell-rom everything about the tests today?" she asked. "Or are some things supposed to remain confidential?"

"You can tell him everything."

"Good." Morelle let out a breath. "I don't like keeping secrets from Ell-rom."

She also didn't like keeping secrets from Brandon, but she had no choice. Kian and Annani wanted Ell-rom's ability to remain a secret for now, and she couldn't go against their wishes.

13

ELL-ROM

"I'll wait out here." Brandon sat down on one of the chairs in the waiting area of the clinic. "You go ahead and sit with your brother in Jasmine's room."

Morelle looked conflicted for a moment but then nodded. "We will leave the door open."

"That's okay." Brandon pulled out his phone. "I need to make a few calls, so you can close the door if you want to."

Morelle shook her head. "I'd rather leave it open so I can see you."

"I promise not to run away." He winked at her.

"Not funny." Morelle cast Brandon a mock glare and then followed Ell-rom into Jasmine's room.

Ell-rom didn't have a problem with leaving the door open. He still remembered how desperately he had clung to Jasmine those first days after he had woken up from stasis and how anxious he'd been every time she had left his side, even for a little while.

"You are really connecting with him," he said as they sat down on the two chairs in Jasmine's room. "It's like it was for me with Jasmine." He smiled. "I'm a true believer in the Fates now."

Morelle chuckled softly. "You were always quick to believe in higher powers, and I was always the skeptic who didn't believe in anything."

He tilted his head. "How about now? Are you still a skeptic?"

She let out a breath. "Less than I was before. After Mother came to me in my dreams and told me things I didn't know before, I had no choice but to believe that the soul goes on." She shrugged. "And if that's true, then maybe all the rest is true as well."

"You don't sound convinced."

"I'm not. I'm not a fan of the Mother of All Life."

He nodded. "I get it. She's not easy to love, but that's what makes her real. The universe is not purposely cruel, and neither is she, but it is also not benevolent, and neither is she. They are both largely indifferent."

She narrowed her eyes at him. "Then why bother praying to her or even caring if she exists at all?"

"Because we need a compass. That's all religion is. Its purpose is not to aggrandize a deity who is above our material concerns and our opinions. It is to guide us on our journey."

Morelle shook her head. "We used to have these kinds of discussions, and neither of us succeeded in convincing the other, so we shouldn't get into that again. I'd rather tell you what Annani told me today over dinner. We have another half-sister."

"I know that."

She frowned. "And you never mentioned her to me?"

"Frankly, I'd forgotten about her. Annani mentioned Areana once and promised to tell me her story, but we both forgot about it somehow."

Morelle perked up. "Then I have a lot to tell you. Areana is Ahn's daughter from a goddess he was involved with before he met Annani's mother, so she's a half-sister to both Annani and us." She leaned forward. "But here's the shocking part. She's mated to the leader of the Doomers."

"What?" Ell-rom managed to keep his voice low. "How did that happen?"

"It's quite a story." Morelle crossed her legs. "Areana sacrificed herself to give Annani a chance at love. Annani was engaged to this evil god named Mortdh, but she fell in love with Khiann. When she broke the engagement, Mortdh was enraged, and our father feared that he would start a war. He asked Areana, his older daughter, if she was willing to mate Mortdh in Annani's stead, and she agreed."

"That was noble of her."

"It was. Ahn offered her to Mortdh, but he was offended by the offer, claiming that Areana was used goods because she was a widow. However, it was mostly because she wasn't Ahn's successor, and it was actually the throne that Mortdh was after, not Annani. He left in a huff and tasked his immortal son Navuh to escort Areana to his stronghold in the north. During the journey, Areana and Navuh fell in love."

"But she was promised to Mortdh."

"This is where it gets complicated," Morelle continued. "Mortdh, who was enraged at being deprived of his chance to mate the next ruler of the gods and become ruler himself, murdered Khiann, and the gods' council that was led by Ahn sentenced him to entombment. Only they had to catch Mortdh first, and he wasn't about to let them do that. He flew over and dropped a bomb over the gods' assembly, killing them all and getting caught in his own attack. At least, that's the theory." She paused. "There is another theory that Mortdh wasn't the one who bombed the gods and that it was the work of assassins sent by our grandfather, the Eternal King, but no one knows for sure what happened. Anyway, Areana thought that her whole family was gone, and she mated Navuh, who later founded the Doomers—the clan's archenemies. Annani only recently discovered that her sister had survived and managed to establish secret contact with her."

Ell-rom's eyes drifted to Jasmine again, checking for any sign of waking. "I've heard the part about Mortdh, Annani, and the bomb, but not about Areana's part in all of that. Does she help the clan against the Doomers?"

"I don't think so," Morelle said. "The contact is very clandestine, and Annani didn't share many details. It must be a very difficult situation for Areana. She loves her evil mate, and she loves her sister. Her loyalties are split."

"I don't envy her that position." Ell-rom glanced at Jasmine again. "I'm glad that all my loyalties are aligned." He turned back to his sister. "Tell me about the testing. How did it go?"

"The results were interesting." Morelle grimaced. "Sometimes I needed to know what ability I was trying to block in order to nullify it, and sometimes I didn't. Cassandra, the chief's mate, can blow up things with a thought, which is similar to what you can do. I didn't know what her talent was the first time I tried to block it, so my nullifying effect didn't work. Once I knew, just my thinking about her not blowing up the glass was enough to stop her. Then Amanda told me to go inside the house and try again, and it worked, but when Amanda distracted me, it didn't."

Ell-rom chuckled. "I'm getting confused."

"Wait, that's not the end of it. Arwel, who is an empath, didn't tell me his talent either, but I could see that he was suffering, and I wanted to give him relief even though I didn't know what he was suffering from. I blocked the influx of emotions easily. So far, though, it seems that I need to be actively thinking about a talent for the nullification to work."

"That's good news," Ell-rom said. "It means you can't do it accidentally."

"Exactly. It also explains why I didn't nullify your ability when you killed that guard. I didn't know what you could do. Besides, I was asleep."

The sound of a bedsheet rustling had Ell-rom on his feet instantly.

"Jasmine?" He took her hand. "Morelle is here, my love. Would you like to meet her?"

Jasmine's fingers twitched in his grasp, her head turned slightly, and then her eyelids fluttered.

This time, when they opened, her gaze was clearer than before. She looked first at Ell-rom, a small smile forming on her lips. Then she shifted her gaze to look at Morelle.

"Hi," she managed, her voice still rough.

"Hello, Jasmine." Morelle rose to her feet and smiled at his mate. "It's a pleasure to finally meet you in person."

As Ell-rom watched his sister and his mate meeting for the first time, his heart was so full that it felt like it might burst. His two worlds, past and present, old family and new, were finally coming together.

14

ANNANI

Annani lay sprawled across her bed, staring at the ceiling as her mind raced with questions about Morelle's newfound ability to nullify powers. She needed to talk to her grandmother about it, and she would do so as soon as Aru called.

Ogidu sat at her desk, waiting for the conversation to begin so he could write down notes. Tomorrow, Syssi would go over them and add them to the growing stack of transcribed conversations between Annani and the queen of Anumati.

Getting Ogidu to do that was a good solution that freed Syssi from coming over each night to take the notes herself. It had become too much of a burden, and when Annani suggested that Ogidu take over, Syssi was relieved. The Odu transcribed everything faithfully and accurately.

When her phone rang, Annani answered using

the speaker function so her Odu could hear Aru clearly. "Hello, Aru. I am ready."

"Hello, Clan Mother. Aria and I are ready, too."

"Grandmother," she greeted formally through the twins' link. "I hope I find you well."

"My dear one," Aru said, somehow conveying the regal tone of Queen Ani's mental message communicated to him through his sister. "I am well. And you?"

"I am well, thank you. I have updates about Morelle. Today, we tested her abilities, and we discovered that she is a null. She can disable the paranormal abilities of others. So far, she was able to stop the mate of my son from guessing coin tosses, another member of my clan from using her power to blow up a glass container, block an empath from feeling the emotions of others, and prevent a god from compelling an immortal. Are you aware of any such abilities among the gods on Anumati?"

"Ah, yes," Queen Ani said after a pause. "The Nulls. They were rare, and they were eliminated during the early purges. Your grandfather saw them as a threat. A null could theoretically neutralize even his powers. He made up some reason for hunting them down. I do not remember what it was. El can be very inventive and very convincing."

Annani absorbed the information and thought of Morelle. "Were they considered dangerous?"

"Naturally, but the truth is that I do not know much about that ability. I have never encountered one of them, and as you know, our written records cannot be trusted. El has them altered according to his whims."

That was a shame, but perhaps some of what had been written about them could be of use.

"I wish to understand how their power worked so I can help Morelle. According to those written records, did they need to be aware of the ability they were nullifying?"

"Please remember not to put too much trust in what I will tell you because the information is not reliable. If I cannot verify it myself or get a firsthand report from a trustworthy source, I treat our records as fiction. The way the story goes, the ability varied from god to god, and it was believed that they could create general dampening fields that affected everyone around them, rendering them helpless."

"I can see how that could have been perceived as dangerous." Annani filed away this information for Amanda's research. "Were they born with this ability, or did it develop over time?"

"They were born with it, of course, but it usually manifested in response to a trigger, either stress or necessity or both. I wonder what triggered it for Morelle. Was she harassed in the temple she grew up in?"

"Yes, but I do not think it was overly traumatic. She has a very strong personality."

"Obviously. She is my granddaughter."

Annani stifled a chuckle. "Ell-rom has a much mellower personality."

On the other hand, he could kill with a thought, so that evened out the playing field between the twins, but her grandmother did not know that.

"Yes, so you have told me. I hope he finds his strength. Has he manifested any talents yet?"

"No, not yet," Annani lied.

They did not know the extent of Ell-rom's power and how it worked, so there was not much she could actually tell her grandmother. When she knew more, she would tell her.

"That is a shame. After all the predictions and the prophecy, I expected more from those two."

Annani's gut clenched. "A prophecy about the twins?"

"Yes, and El took it very seriously, which was one of the main reasons he was so obsessed with eliminating them. The prophecy said that his downfall would come from his own blood and that there would be two of them, a brother and sister who shared a womb."

Chills ran down Annani's spine.

If Ell-rom's death ray could work across the universe, he could be the downfall the Oracle talked about, but what part would Morelle play in toppling the Eternal King?

"The prophecy must be about Ell-rom and Morelle," Annani said. "But how can it be when they have no way of ever reaching Anumati?"

"I do not know. We are immortal, and what is not possible now might become possible in the future."

"True." Annani sighed.

She just hoped that it would not be made possible by the Eternal King suddenly allowing communications and transportation between Earth and Anumati. Nothing good would come of that.

"Keep an eye on them, my dear," Aru said for the queen. "A null could be a powerful asset in the right circumstances."

"I will. There is one more question I would like to ask before we continue to our nightly lesson, or what time we have left for it. Can all royals exert power over commoners? And by that, I mean a mental power like compelling them to do things? Or is it done just by a select group of very powerful gods?"

"Of course, royals are more powerful. Did you think that they could rule over commoners just because of their pretty glow? Naturally, not all royals are gifted with special powers, but those who are gifted always come from royal stock."

15

MORELLE

Bright morning sunlight spilled across the polished stone floor of Annani's entryway as Morelle adjusted the ankle straps on her sandals. Brandon stood nearby, keys to one of the village's electric carts dangling from his fingers.

"Are you sure you don't want to ride?" he asked. "It's quite a distance to the clinic."

"I want to walk." Morelle straightened, smoothing the fabric of her dress—a flowing blue sundress that Brandon claimed matched her eyes perfectly. "I need the exercise." She smiled. "Walking is much easier than the torture sessions Gertrude puts me through on the Pilates Reformer."

"Perhaps, but you can take a break any time you want." He glanced at his watch. "If we want to make it in time for the ceremony, we can't even stop on the way for a quick rest. I will have to carry you on my back." The grin that spread over his face indicated that he found the prospect enticing rather than bothersome.

Not that she would ever allow him to carry her. Not unless she collapsed and couldn't take another step.

She gave him a look that made him chuckle and raise his hands in surrender. "Alright, I won't push it. But remember that the offer stands in case you need it. Don't try to be a hero and impede your progress."

Morelle nodded. "I will push myself, but not to the point of collapse. I've been driven back and forth between here and the clinic enough times to have a good estimate of the distance. I should be able to make it without issues."

"Indeed," Brandon said in an encouraging tone that was just a little insincere. "Let's go. A celebration awaits."

Morelle was excited for Jasmine and the confirmation of her immortality that was about to occur, but she was also a little apprehensive about living with her brother's mate under the same roof.

Ell-rom reported that Jasmine had woken up a few times during the previous evening and the night, and Bridget was going to release her after the ceremony, which meant that she was coming home today.

Their interaction the previous evening had

been brief, and Jasmine had been friendly and seemed deeply in love with Ell-rom, but Morelle hadn't been able to assess her personality in the few minutes of wakefulness.

Hopefully, they would get along just fine.

As they stepped outside into the warm morning air, Morelle took a deep breath, savoring the fresh scents of the greenery filling every corner of the village. Everything about this place seemed designed to delight the senses—the colors were vivid, the air was fresh, and the sounds gentle, unlike the harsh winds of Anumati she had grown to detest even though she hadn't known anything else.

Morelle had often thought about the gods living in their grand underground cities and secretly commended them on their good sense. Anumati's climate wasn't hospitable.

In comparison, Earth was how the priestesses described the Fields of the Brave.

As Morelle lifted her face to the sun and closed her eyes, Brandon's hand found hers, his fingers intertwining with her own. "You really like the outdoors."

She opened her eyes and smiled. "Here I do. Back where I came from it was rare that the conditions were hospitable enough for a stroll in the gardens, and I was also covered from head to toe."

A female jogging past smiled and waved. "Good morning!"

"Good morning," Morelle called back after recovering from the surprise.

She was still getting used to showing her face so freely and getting friendly responses from strangers.

They passed the training grounds where several Kra-ell were running in formation, the sound of their synchronized footfalls bringing back memories of watching warriors train from the temple's windows.

"You're doing it again," Brandon said.

"Doing what?"

"Getting lost in memories." He squeezed her hand.

She smiled. "I can't stop comparing everything. Even these warriors seem different than those I saw training back home. The expressions on their faces are more relaxed. I don't know if it's the wonderful weather or the freedom."

"It's the freedom," he said. "That was what motivated me for long decades to produce films and television series celebrating the human spirit and pushing the idea of freedom. But it's a never-ending struggle, and I'm tired of the constant setbacks. One generation of humans fights against oppression, sheds blood, sweat, and tears to earn and safeguard freedom, and the next takes it for granted and gives it up, sacrificing the hard-won rights their parents fought for on this or that altar of propaganda pushed by those who want to take it away. The cycle of naivety and stupidity is disheartening."

Morelle had only a vague idea of what he was talking about because she knew so little of Earth's history. There was only so much Brandon could cram into the days since her awakening, especially since she preferred to spend their private time kissing rather than talking about history and politics.

As they passed by the village café, a woman with blue hair waved at them. "Are you heading to the ceremony?"

"We are," Brandon replied. "I hope we are not late."

"The place is already packed, but I don't think they are going to start without Annani." The woman walked up to them and offered her hand to Morelle. "I'm Marina, by the way. Peter's mate." She smiled warmly.

Was Morelle supposed to know who Peter was?

She glanced at Brandon, but he didn't offer an explanation.

"It's nice to meet you," she said before realizing that the female didn't have earpieces.

To her great surprise, Marina answered in Kra-ell. "The pleasure is all mine, Princess Morelle."

"How do you know Kra-ell?"

The female looked at Brandon with a raised brow. "I guess you didn't tell her about the compound."

"There was no time." His hand tightened on Morelle's hand. "And speaking of no time, we'd better head in."

"Of course." Marina smiled at Morelle. "I work in the café, so when you need a break and want to talk to someone, you can find me here most of the time."

"Thank you. I will do that."

It would be nice to have a friend who did not belong to her immediate family.

Morelle had never had friends, and she wasn't sure what to do with one, but she could start by asking Marina about the compound that Brandon hadn't had time to tell her about.

As they entered the clinic, the space was already crowded with people, and to Morelle's great disappointment, all the chairs were taken. She'd pushed herself on the walk, and even though she'd made it without having to ask Brandon to carry her, she would have loved to get some rest.

Amanda's mate noticed her looking and pushed to his feet, motioning for her to take his place, but before she could take him up on his offer, she was ambushed by a woman with long blond hair.

"I'm so happy to see you up and about, Morelle! I'm Margo." Without warning, she threw her arms around Morelle in an enthusiastic hug.

Startled, Morelle stiffened for a moment before forcing herself to relax. This was normal here, she reminded herself. That was how clan people showed their affection.

"And I'm Frankie," said a short woman with dark hair, stepping forward for her own hug as soon as Margo released her. "And that's Gabi and Ella." She gestured to two other women who were approaching more sedately but with equally warm smiles.

"We are good friends of your brother," the one named Gabi said. "He and Jasmine stayed with us and our mates in the clan's keep, and before that, we journeyed with Jasmine to Tibet and helped her search for your pod."

As emotion tightened Morelle's throat, she turned to Brandon. "Can you please convey a message to them that I owe each one of them a life vow?"

She'd already given it to Jasmine for saving them, but these females were part of the rescue mission and deserved it as well.

"We don't need a translator." Frankie pushed her hair aside to show the earpieces she was wearing. "We all have them. And there is no need for you to vow anything. We're just so happy that you're both okay."

"More than okay," Margo added with a knowing look at Brandon. "The Fates seem to be working as quickly on your behalf as they did for Ell-rom. You've already found your special guy."

16

JASMINE

Jasmine smoothed the fabric of her new nightgown—one of several that Ell-rom had brought for her to choose from—and tried not to fidget as she waited for the ceremony to begin. The decision hadn't been easy. She had very nice nightgowns that were meant to entice but were not appropriate for the occasion, and she had simple ones that were just oversized T-shirts, and those were not appropriate either.

Not only was this the start of her new life as an immortal, but the ceremony would also be recorded, and she wanted to be able to show it to her children one day and not be embarrassed by how she looked and what she wore on this most important occasion.

In the end, she chose one of the silk nightgowns. It was a bit much, but it worked with the matching robe over it.

Margo had arrived earlier armed with a curling iron and a cosmetics bag and had done a great job with her hair and makeup. She did not go overboard but made sure that Jasmine would look great in the video.

It was quite silly to put so much thought and effort into her appearance, given that she didn't even need the test to prove that she had turned immortal.

Jasmine had grown taller by over two inches during the ten days she'd been unconscious, so there was no doubt that she had transitioned into immortality. The ceremony was purely for show, but then she thrived on those. After all, she was a professional actress, and she loved the attention.

Ell-rom, on the other hand, looked stressed. "Are you comfortable?" he asked. "Do you need another pillow?"

"I'm perfect," she assured him, reaching for his hand. "More than fine. I feel amazing." It was true. Despite having been unconscious for many days, she felt stronger and more vital than she ever had before. Colors seemed brighter, sounds clearer, and even her sense of touch was enhanced. The texture of the sheets against her skin, the warmth of Ell-rom's hand in hers—everything felt more vivid.

Through the open door, she could hear the excited chatter of her friends in the waiting room, and the thought of them all gathering to witness this moment filled her with warmth.

"The camera feed is working perfectly," Julian announced, making one final adjustment. "I should have done this a long time ago." He stepped down from the ladder and folded it. "The camera is trained on you, and everyone outside will be able to watch the ceremony on the screen in the waiting room."

"Thank you," Jasmine said. "I wish they could all be in here with me."

"The room would burst," Julian chuckled. "You can have up to four people in here. Ell-rom is one, the Clan Mother is two, and you can have two more."

"Morelle," Ell-rom said. "I want her to be here."

Jasmine nodded. "And Margo. We started this journey together."

They had been abducted together by Alberto the scumbag and then rescued together by the clan.

"No problem." Julian lifted the step ladder. "I'll watch it on the screen." He did a little head tilt and strode out of the room.

Was he really offended at not being invited to be in the room? Or was he goofing around?

A moment later, Margo burst into the room, the excitement practically radiating off her. "I'm so glad you picked me. Thank you. By the way, the Clan Mother has just arrived, so we can start as soon as you are ready."

"I'm ready. I just wish that the rest of the girls could be here with me."

"Don't worry about it. We will celebrate tomorrow at Ella's." She leaned over and pretended to whisper. "Are you allowed to drink? Because we are planning on lots of margaritas."

Jasmine chuckled. "I don't know. I'm on a clear liquids diet for now, so I can play dumb and say that I thought margaritas qualify."

Margo laughed, and Ell-rom looked horrified, but when Jasmine was about to tell him that she'd been joking, Annani entered with Morelle.

"What a joyous occasion," Annani said as she approached the bed and kissed Jasmine's cheek. "I know that I am supposed to wait for after the test, but since it is just ceremonial, I will say it now. Congratulations, and welcome to the clan."

"Thank you, Clan Mother."

"It is Annani to you, my dear. We are family." The goddess floated over to the one chair that remained in the room but then stopped and looked at Morelle. "I should stand, or I won't be able to see anything. You should sit down."

Morelle looked aghast. "It is not proper for me to sit while you are standing."

"Oh, such nonsense." Annani waved her sister over. "We are sisters, and you are still recovering. I can see how difficult it is for you to stand. Do not try to deny it."

Morelle hesitated for a moment, looking

unsure about how to deal with her stubborn and forceful sibling.

"I'll sit for a few moments until the ceremony starts." She smiled at Jasmine. "But first, how are you feeling this morning?"

Jasmine studied Morelle, still struck by how different the siblings looked despite sharing the same striking blue eyes. Where Ell-rom's expressions were soft and gentle, Morelle looked like a beautiful and deadly blade.

Not that it made any sense. Ell-rom was the one with the deadly power, while Morelle's special ability was stopping others from using their gifts.

Jasmine put on her friendliest smile. "Excited. A little nervous. But mostly just ready to get out of here."

"I understand perfectly." Morelle returned her smile, which was a little more reserved but appeared genuine.

"No need to be nervous," Annani said. "We know what the test results will be."

Well, she was not the one who was going to have her palm cut with a knife, but Jasmine had a feeling that the fierce Clan Mother wouldn't have batted an eyelid.

When Bridget entered with her ceremonial tray, Jasmine gulped as she saw the small surgical blade gleaming under the fluorescent lights. She was not a fan of knives, or needles for that matter.

"Alright, everyone, quiet down," Bridget

commanded the crowd outside the door. "Who will be filming the ceremony?"

Kian filled the doorway, holding up his phone. "I will."

That was an unexpected honor. "Thank you," Jasmine said. "That's very gracious of you."

He smiled. "It's not every day that we welcome a new immortal into the family."

Family. The word echoed in her mind. She was not just any member of the clan. As Ell-rom's mate, she was part of the clan's royal family, so to speak.

"Okay," Bridget said. "I also need someone to time it."

"I will." Margo held up her phone, the stopwatch app open.

"Kian?"

He raised his phone in response, the camera already recording.

Bridget turned to Jasmine. "Your left hand, please."

Ell-rom's grip on her right hand tightened almost imperceptibly as Jasmine extended her other hand to Bridget. The doctor's fingers were cool and steady as she positioned Jasmine's palm upward.

"This will sting," Bridget warned, though Jasmine already knew that from Margo and her other friends who had all transitioned recently.

"Now," Bridget said as she struck.

The knife's edge was sharp enough that the

initial cut barely hurt, but then the pain bloomed bright and sharp.

Jasmine stifled the urge to wince and forced herself to watch.

The blood welled in the shallow cut, and as Bridget wiped it off, the edges of the wound started knitting together. The healing was so rapid that they could all see it happening before their eyes.

"Thirty-three seconds," Margo announced when the incision closed, and Jasmine's palm looked unmarked save for a faint pink line that was already fading. "That's incredibly fast, right?" She looked at Bridget.

The doctor frowned as she examined Jasmine's palm. "Very fast, especially given how long the transition took. Usually, the closer to the source the Dormant is, the easier the transition and the faster the healing time. But you have two contradicting indicators."

"What do you mean by close to the source?" Jasmine asked although she had guessed what the doctor had implied.

"The closer you are to pure god blood, the faster you heal. It means that there aren't many generations separating you from your godly ancestor."

A heavy silence fell over the room as the implications of this settled in.

Jasmine felt Ell-rom's fingers tighten around hers.

Annani put her hand on her shoulder. "Your mother must have been more than she appeared, my dear girl."

"This is definitely something we need to investigate," Kian said, lowering his phone. "But perhaps we should save that discussion for another time? This is a celebration. Welcome to immortality, Jasmine."

As if on cue, a cheer erupted from the waiting room where the others had been watching the ceremony either through the open door or on screen, and people repeated Kian's welcoming.

Tears stung the back of Jasmine's eyes, and then some spilled out the corners.

She quickly wiped them off. "Thank you, everyone. I can't express how grateful I am for this incredibly warm welcome into your wonderful community."

17

ARU

Aru leaned against the desk in the underground clinic, listening to Merlin explaining the procedure in clinical detail to the three humans.

Marcus, the oldest of them, paid little attention to the explanations and seemed much more interested in exchanging smiles with Hildegard than concerning himself with the upcoming surgery.

"Any questions?" Merlin asked.

Jake shook his head. "It's all pretty straightforward. Let's get it done. Who's going first?"

"I will." Marcus pushed to his feet. "I can't wait to get in bed and have this beauty take care of me."

Hildegard giggled. "You are such a flirt," she said. "Come on. I'll get you ready."

Aru followed them to the operating room, while Merlin went into one of the rooms where the trafficker had been placed, the patient sedated and waiting for the tracker to be removed.

Jake and Wade had remained in the waiting room with Dagor and Negal.

After Marcus changed into a surgical gown behind the screen, he walked to the bed and laid down, with Hildegard admiring his physique unabashedly.

The guy was still young and in great shape, and he exuded confidence. No wonder the nurse was taken with him.

"Do your worst, Hildy," Marcus said. "Is it okay if I call you Hildy?"

She chuckled. "Since you already did, go ahead." She prepared his arm with a local anesthetic.

"Do you always work in secret underground facilities?" he asked.

She smiled while inserting the needle with practiced precision. "No, not always. I work wherever I'm needed."

"And where might you be needed tonight?"

"Tonight?" Hildegard's smile turned playful. "I'll be monitoring your recovery in the fancy hotel suite we booked for the three of you. Depending on how well you handle this procedure, we will figure out what to do with the rest of the time."

Marcus grinned. "Trust me, I heal fast."

"We'll see about that," she said, checking that the area was properly numbed, and then doing the same thing on his other arm.

It made sense not to put the two trackers next to each other in case that created interference.

Merlin walked in with his surgical tools. "Ready to begin?"

"Born ready, doc." Marcus winked at Hildegard. "Though I wouldn't mind if the lovely nurse held my hand."

"Sorry, big guy. I need both hands free to assist," she said. "But I'll be right here monitoring your vitals."

As Merlin made the first incision, Marcus didn't even flinch and kept up a steady stream of flirtatious banter with Hildegard. "So, about tonight—"

"Less talking, more lying still," she chided playfully.

"Almost done," Merlin announced. "First tracker is in place. Hildegard, would you close?"

The first one was the tracker that had been removed from Dagor, implanted in the trafficker, and now found a new home in Marcus. The second tracker was built by William and his crew, and it was for the benefit of Aru's team so they could monitor the humans and make sure they were following instructions.

As Hildegard began suturing the small incision, Marcus continued undeterred. "You never answered about tonight."

She tied off the last stitch with expert efficiency. "Tell you what—if you're feeling up to it after the procedure, we can discuss it over takeout in the hotel."

"I'm already feeling up to it."

"We are not done," Merlin said as he implanted the second tracker in Marcus's other arm.

Negal, who had been watching from near the door, stepped forward. "My turn next?"

Merlin shook his head. "Hildegard needs to stitch up Marcus on his other side, and then we will get him out to the recovery room and you on the operating table."

The procedure for removing the tracker was much more complicated than implanting it and took more time.

As Hildegard helped Marcus walk out of the operating room and into one of the patient rooms in the clinic, Negal took his place on the operating table, and unlike Marcus's casual demeanor, his jaw was tight.

"You okay?" Aru asked.

"Fine," Negal replied. "I'm ready for this thing to be out of me so I can join Margo in the village."

The ladies were there to attend Jasmine's transition ceremony, and Aru would have loved to accompany them, but this needed to be done first.

Soon, they would be free to live with their mates in the village and stop pretending to search for pods that would probably never be found. The question was what they would do while there.

Margo had a bunch of ideas about all of them

working for Perfect Match, but that wasn't what Aru wanted to do. Dagor would probably want to join William's crew and work on building new things and learning all he could from the clan's tech genius. Negal was a soldier through and through, and he would most likely want to join the Guardian force in some capacity.

Aru wanted to work on advancing the resistance against the Eternal King, but he wasn't sure how to go about it. Perhaps Queen Ani would have some ideas for him.

When it was his turn, Aru lay back on the table and closed his eyes.

"Last one," Merlin said cheerfully as he began administering the local anesthetic.

The procedure itself seemed to pass in a blur. Before Aru knew it, Merlin was announcing that he was finished and Hildegard was applying the final bandage.

"Time to take care of our guests' memories," Merlin said.

"I'll handle it." Aru pushed to a sitting position. The local anesthetic was making his thigh feel strange, but he ignored it.

He approached the waiting room where the three men sat, already dressed and ready to go. Marcus started flirting with Hildegard as soon as she walked in, and the other two seemed content to watch.

"Gentlemen," Aru said. "Please look at me for a

moment. You've had a routine medical examination in preparation for your upcoming assignment, and everything went well. You'll remember coming to a private clinic, but not the exact location."

The men's eyes glazed slightly as the thrall took effect. Even Marcus fell silent.

"Hildegard will accompany you back to your hotel to monitor your recovery," Aru finished.

Given that the procedure had been simple on their end, it wasn't really necessary for the nurse to accompany them, but Merlin thought it was prudent in case they experienced discomfort or their bodies rejected the implants for some reason. No one wanted them to seek treatment in a human hospital or clinic.

"I'll make sure they rest properly," Hildegard assured him with a wink.

Dagor appeared in the doorway. "The car's ready whenever you are."

As Hildegard helped the men to their feet and guided them toward the exit, Marcus seemed to shake off some of the thrall's effect. "So, what did you say about dinner?"

"Let's see how you're feeling in a few hours," she said.

After they'd gone, Dagor turned to Aru with an expectant grin. "Let's celebrate with a bottle of whiskey or two upstairs and then start packing."

"Not yet," Aru said. "I don't want to jinx it, as the humans say. I want to wait until they're actually on the plane on their way to Tibet before I start celebrating."

"Can we at least do the drinking part?" Dagor asked. "The packing can wait."

"We can do that." Aru clapped him on the back. "And once they are in the air, we can drink some more."

18

ROB

Rob peeked over the rim of his laptop screen, watching as another group of well-wishers left the clinic, their animated chatter carrying across the village square. The celebration for Jasmine's transition had drawn a small crowd, but things were settling back to normal, and it was time for his daily lunch date with Gertrude.

Well, it was more like a lunch delivery than a date, but it was just as sweet.

As usual, he'd ordered two cappuccinos and two turkey club sandwiches with pickles and mayo but no mustard, which was exactly how she liked them.

It was such a simple thing, bringing lunch to someone you cared about, but it meant so much to Gertrude. The way her face lit up when she saw him walk in every day at noon made his heart swell anew with emotion each time.

The thought triggered an unwelcome comparison to Lynda, and he tried to push it away, but memories had a way of intruding when least wanted, and suddenly he was back in their house, watching Lynda sprawled on the couch, phone pressed to her ear, jabbering with one of her countless vacuous friends and ignoring him.

And that was when she had been at home.

Most of the time, he'd returned to an empty house, and if he cared to be honest with himself, he had been relieved because he hadn't needed to deal with her and had a few moments of peace and quiet for himself.

Even though she didn't work, dinner had never been ready for him, not even takeout or delivery. Lynda only ordered food when she was in the mood for something, and since she was constantly dieting, that hadn't happened often either.

He'd rationalized it then, made excuses for her. She was busy with an active social life, and he had no right to make demands. Now, with distance and perspective, he could see how stupid he had been. How he'd settled for scraps of affection because Lynda was hot, and she'd convinced him that he was so damn lucky to score a woman like her.

The fault was his for having believed her, for thinking he wouldn't find anyone better, for buying into the notion she was the best he could ever hope for.

Stupid.

How could a smart guy like him be so stupid?

Gertrude was nothing like Lynda. She looked at him like he mattered, listened when he talked about his work and shared with him her own stories and dreams. She made him feel valued just for being himself.

He was falling in love with her.

The realization wasn't new, but it still scared him. The words sat heavily on his tongue sometimes when they were together, wanting to spill out, but fear held them back. Fear of being wrong again and misreading signals.

After all, he'd thought that Lynda loved him in her own way.

He gathered up the tray and the bag of sandwiches and carefully arranged his features into an easygoing smile. He crossed the few feet that separated the café from the clinic.

Gertrude deserved his best self, not the brooding version that appeared when he felt weighed down by past hurts.

Using his hip to push open the clinic's glass door, he entered the space that had become one of his favorite places in the village.

"Rob!" Gertrude's face lit up with that smile he'd come to live for. "Can you give me a minute? I need to finish something for Jasmine."

"Sure." He set down the tray and bag on the side table, settling into one of the waiting room chairs. "Don't take too long. The coffee is getting cold."

"I won't." She blew him an air kiss before disappearing into Jasmine's room, her blue scrubs making a soft swishing sound as she walked.

Rob watched her go, marveling at how something as simple as an air kiss could make him feel more cared for than all of Lynda's grand gestures ever had. Because Lynda's gestures had always come with strings attached, with expectations and subtle manipulations he'd been too blind to see at the time.

Shaking off those thoughts again, he focused instead on his plans for the near future. He'd finished his final project for his old company, tying up all loose ends neatly. He could start his work in William's tech heaven, but he wasn't sure whether it was prudent to start a new job before his transition.

Maybe he and Gertrude could spend a few days together and go on some real dates or even a mini vacation.

The thought made him smile.

Between her work at the clinic and his need to finish his old project, they hadn't had as much time together as he would have liked.

"Okay, I'm back." Gertrude sat down beside him, pressing a quick kiss to his cheek. "Jasmine is getting discharged today, but since she was in a coma for so long, Bridget wants her to come in for a few Pilates sessions to strengthen her muscles."

Rob couldn't quite hide his disappointment. "I was hoping you could take some time off now that the clinic is empty of patients. I'm done with the project I needed to finish for my previous job, and I thought I would take a mini vacation before starting my induction process, transition, and work for William."

Her answering grin was mischievous. "How about a vacation right here in the village? Hildy is spending the night with the humans who were implanted with the gods' trackers, making sure that they are okay, so she's only coming back tomorrow."

Rob loved the sound of that.

He'd spent a couple of nights with Gertrude, and they had been the best sex he'd ever had, but the idea that Hildegard was sleeping in the next room over had bothered him even though the houses in the village were built with the best soundproofing money could buy.

"So, we have the house to ourselves?"

"Yup." Gertrude's eyes sparkled. "And I'm cooking dinner."

"Oh, sweetheart, you say the nicest things." He leaned in, capturing her lips in a kiss that held all the words he couldn't quite say yet.

When they parted, they were both slightly breathless. "The coffee's getting cold."

"Don't care," he murmured but reached for the cups anyway.

As he handed her one, their fingers brushed, sending little sparks of electricity through him. Everything with Gertrude felt like this—natural and exciting at the same time, comfortable yet thrilling.

"So," she said, taking a sip of her coffee. "About a vacation. What did you have in mind?"

"Honestly? I just want to spend time with you. No interruptions, no work obligations, just us. But I'm open to suggestions. We can do anything you like."

She smiled sheepishly. "Do you like gardening?"

"Never tried it. Why?"

"My herb garden has been neglected while I was in the keep, and it needs work. I was planning to take care of it now that I have more time, but perhaps we could do it together. I can teach you."

Of all the things she could have suggested, that was probably the one he liked the least, but did it really matter what they did as long as they did it together?

All he wanted was more time with her.

"I'd love to work in your herb garden."

"Awesome. We could also go on hikes. There are several beautiful hiking trails in these mountains."

That was also not one of his favorite things to do, but then Rob didn't really have favorites. He liked his work, and he liked reading. He didn't even play video games like most of his coworkers.

"It all sounds great, but right now, I'm most interested in tonight's dinner plans."

19

PETER

Peter stared at the thick folder Roni had just placed on Onegus's desk, its contents threatening to spill out, and when Onegus opened it and started leafing through it, the images he glimpsed made his stomach turn. After years as a Guardian, he thought he'd seen the worst humanity had to offer.

Clearly, he'd been wrong.

"These are just the preliminary findings," Roni said, his face grim. "There are several large networks and many smaller ones. They're using social media apps, gaming platforms, and even educational websites as covers."

Onegus leaned forward in his chair, his expression, usually professional and impassive, showing his disgust. "That's why we're creating the new Avengers division. This requires an entirely different approach than our usual tactics. More precise targeting and elimination. We are not giving these monsters second chances."

The implication was clear. While the Saviors would continue their rescue missions, the Avengers would focus on eliminating the distribution networks and the end users. It was a much darker mission, but it needed to be done. If they could deliver an effective blow to the buyers and cut off the money supply, it would affect the traffickers as well.

"I need someone to head this new division," Onegus continued. "I'm offering you the job if you are interested, but I will understand if you want to pass. It's a dirty job."

"But someone has to do it," Peter completed the sentence. "I'll be honored to lead this effort, Chief."

"It also comes with a big promotion. You will become a Head Guardian and sit on the council during sessions dealing with security. Now that there are more civilian members on the council, Kian has agreed to more military members as well."

Peter was stunned. He hadn't expected that. There were several excellent Guardians more deserving of the promotion than he was, and he had no idea why Onegus had chosen him.

"I'm speechless, Chief. Thank you."

"Congratulations." Onegus smiled. "I understand that the timing might not be right given that you're getting married this Sunday. Your bride is probably expecting a honeymoon."

Marina wouldn't want him to pass this up, and not just because of the big-ass promotion. She would want him to fight evil and save children by eliminating the demonic monsters who preyed on them.

"We weren't planning anything special, and Marina will not only understand but also encourage me to get to work on this as soon as possible."

A ghost of a smile crossed Onegus's face. "You sound very sure of that."

"I know my mate."

Roni clapped him on the back. "You picked a good one, Peter. Sylvia and I are not married yet, but I know she would have also given up our honeymoon to do this, and if you ever need a techno-nullifier, she will be happy to help."

Onegus tilted his head. "That's an interesting way to describe Sylvia's ability. Did you hear about Morelle's talent?"

Roni nodded. "Of course. Cassandra told my mother and grandmother, and I found out about it five minutes later. You know how things work here."

"What can she do?" Peter asked.

"Morelle is a nullifier. She was able to stop Cassandra from blowing up a glass cup, but only after learning what Cassandra's talent was. There is still a lot to be learned about her ability and how it can be utilized. What we know now is that she needs to be close for her nullifying to work, and she can't do it when she's distracted."

Peter nodded. "Now I get the new name for Sylvia's talent. It definitely sounds better than the electronics disrupter." His eyes fell on the folder again, and his expression hardened. "So, what's our first target?"

Onegus nodded to Roni, who began spreading photographs and documents across the desk. "We should start with collecting intel. What Roni could find on the internet is of little use to us. We need boots on the ground." Onegus leaned forward. "I don't suggest infiltrating the networks. It's enough that we have Guardians hovering close enough to collect the information we need. Thralling, shrouding, and compelling are, of course, authorized. "

Peter studied the materials. "I would like to start with a small covert operation to get a feel for what we are about to face."

Roni leaned against Onegus's desk and folded his arms over his chest. "These aren't the regular thugs we are used to dealing with. Some of these bastards have serious security—private armies with military-grade weapons. They're selling 'protection services' to others in their sick little network."

"I know that you're thinking of an undercover

approach," Onegus said. "That's good to start with, but you need a solid team to back you up if you get in over your head. I want you to give it some thought, and then we will brainstorm this together. It's new territory for all of us."

"What about Turner?" Peter asked. "Perhaps he can give us some insight."

Onegus shook his head. "This is not what he's used to dealing with. He deals with hostages in the hands of militias and drug cartels, and he can handle military operations. He has no experience with this type of criminal activity." Onegus rubbed his hand over the back of his neck. "I've been around for a long time, and I've never encountered depravity on such an industrial scale."

It seemed that even the chief had trouble dealing with this filth, which meant that the Guardians he needed to recruit would have a hard time as well. Perhaps they needed a little help from the clan's therapist.

"I wonder," Peter said, "if the Kra-ell will have the same emotional response as we do. To be effective, we need to lock our feelings behind a steel door, or we could get ourselves killed even by well-armed humans."

"They do," Onegus said. "I spoke with Jade, and she reacted like any decent person would. She was shocked and disgusted."

"Then we need Vanessa to help prepare us for this."

Onegus nodded. "Good suggestion. It wouldn't have occurred to me to ask her. Although I'm not sure she will be able to help. This is even beyond the scope of what she's dealing with at the sanctuary."

"If she can't, she will know someone who can," Peter said. "Show me what you've found so far," he said to Roni.

The hacker began laying out the network he'd uncovered, pointing to various photographs and documents. "This guy here seems to be one of the main coordinators, but he's not at the top of the food chain, which makes him an easier target. He operates behind a dozen shell companies, but they all lead back to this estate in Beverly Hills."

Peter studied the aerial photograph of a sprawling estate. "Security?"

"We need to find out," Onegus said. "We can hire a human team to do the snooping, or you can do that after you assemble your team."

"I'll do that." Peter was already calculating how many people he would need for an operation like this.

"But here's the kicker," Roni said. "You need to be careful because they might have kids on the property."

Peter felt his jaw tighten. "That's not a problem during the recon mission. But later, when we go in, we might need a blanket thrall. Did you speak with Yamanu?"

Onegus nodded. "As usual, he's available on a case-by-case basis."

"I'll need at least eight people," Peter said after a moment's calculation. "Not for the recon, which can be done by just two Guardians with experience in that sort of operation, but for the extraction. Two for perimeter control, four for entry, and two for extraction. I will also need surveillance drones."

Onegus lifted a hand. "Slow down. We are not there yet. You're getting married on Sunday. Take the rest of the week to put your team together and review the intel. We can plan the first operation for the week after."

"I'll take Monday off, but I can go out on Tuesday." Peter's mind was already racing with possibilities, considering which Guardians would be best suited for this type of work. "I'll have a preliminary team roster for you by Thursday."

He was pushing it, but the sooner they began, the sooner they would get this ball rolling and the sooner the monsters would be six feet under.

"One more thing," Roni added, pulling out another document. "We've identified several smaller operations that might make better initial targets. Places to test the team's capabilities before we tackle something like that estate."

"Smart," Peter reluctantly agreed. In his mind, he and his team were already storming the mansion. "We'll need to work out our dynamics before attempting anything too ambitious."

Roni put everything back into the folder and handed it to Peter. "Homework. I'll probably have another stack just as big by Thursday."

"Thanks." Peter grimaced.

"See ya in a couple of days." Roni clapped him on the back. "If you need me sooner, you know where to find me."

When the hacker left, Onegus leaned forward. "There is one more thing I need to discuss with you that I couldn't bring up with Roni here."

Peter arched a brow. "What could you possibly be hiding from Roni? The kid knows everything."

"He doesn't know this, and I need you to keep it to yourself. Don't say anything to your teammates until you get the green light from me."

Peter's curiosity was piqued. "You have my word."

"Our mellow and charming Prince Ell-rom can kill with a thought, and I need you to bring back disposable targets for him to practice on."

20

BRANDON

Brandon held Morelle's hand as the golf cart wound its way through the village paths toward Annani's house.

Thankfully, she hadn't argued when he'd suggested that they hitch a ride with Annani, which meant that she was exhausted.

"Jasmine's mother might be an immortal." Annani kept up a steady stream of conversation, speculating about Jasmine's godly ancestor. "Maybe she is one more of Toven's children. He traveled all over the globe and had countless paramours. Orion and Geraldine are probably not his only progeny." She continued with the story, telling Morelle about Cassandra meeting Onegus at a gala, the connection between Cassandra and Roni, and then how that led to Geraldine and Orion joining the clan.

Morelle tried to keep up, but Brandon could

tell that she was tired and confused by the way her responses were growing shorter and the way she was leaning against him.

When they reached the house, she also leaned on him as they walked inside.

"You should rest," Annani told her. "I'm planning a small family dinner, so maybe a little nap before?" She patted Morelle's arm.

Morelle smiled. "I might take your advice. I'm very tired."

In her room, she sat on the couch, toed off her flats, and sighed as she settled onto the soft cushions. "Stay with me?" She patted the space beside her.

"Always." He sat down, and she immediately leaned against him, her head resting on his shoulder. "Perhaps you should lie down?"

"Not yet. I don't want you to leave."

His heart soared at her admission. "I won't go anywhere. I'll stay right here and watch you sleep." He wrapped his arm around her shoulders. "After all, I have a lot of experience doing just that."

"I'm worried about sharing the house with Jasmine," she said quietly.

"Why?" He stroked her arm.

"What if we don't get along? What if she finds me too intense? Too direct?" She let out a small laugh. "The head priestess used to say I was exhausting to be around."

Brandon's chest tightened at the hint of old

hurt in her voice. "The head priestess was an idiot." That earned him another laugh, less strained this time. "From what I've heard, Jasmine is easygoing and friendly. I'm sure you two will get along fine."

Morelle shifted slightly, looking up at him. "It feels odd to me to share Ell-rom with someone else. He was always mine, and now he is also hers, and I'm trying to adjust to that, but I know there will be tense moments with Jasmine and me competing for his attention."

"I guess that's natural." He kept rubbing her arm. "I'm sure it was difficult for Annani to share Kian with Syssi, but she grew to love Syssi like her own daughter. Maybe that's the answer. Instead of feeling like you are losing a part of Ell-rom to Jasmine, think of it as gaining another sister."

Morelle chuckled. "What if she doesn't want to be my sister? Annani was fortunate with Syssi being so sweet and accommodating. Very few people are like her."

He was starting to understand what Morelle was really concerned about. She feared that Jasmine wouldn't like her and might try to keep Ell-rom away from her.

It wasn't a baseless concern because things like that happened in families, but Brandon didn't think it would in this case. He didn't know Jasmine well, but from what he'd heard about her, she was too smart to try to come between the twins even if she didn't like Morelle. Not that it was remotely possible.

Morelle was magnificent, and she had a good soul. So what if she was a little rough around the edges? She'd been raised as a Kra-ell priestess.

It was remarkable that she was as accommodating as she was.

"You are going to get along just great, but if you are so concerned about it, you could always stay with me. I have a whole big house all to myself, and you can have your own room, so don't think that I'm suggesting that to pressure you into anything. It's just—"

Her laugh interrupted him. "What if I don't want my own bedroom?" Her eyes held a mischievous glint. "What if I want to share yours?"

Brandon's throat felt suddenly dry. "That would make me the happiest male alive. No expectations. Holding you in my arms through the night would be enough."

"And what if that's not enough for me?"

Her words sent heat coursing through his veins. "Princess, you're killing me," he groaned, reaching for her.

When their lips met, it was fire and need and barely restrained passion. Morelle's hands found his shoulders, pulling him closer, and he lost himself in the taste of her, the feel of her body pressing against his.

A knock at the door jerked them apart, and

Brandon had to take several deep breaths before he could trust himself to stand and answer it.

Morelle's throaty giggle did not help matters.

Adjusting himself, Brandon cracked the door open, finding Ogidu standing in the hallway.

The Odu bowed. "Apologies for disturbing you, Master Brandon. The Clan Mother wanted me to inform you that dinner will be served shortly after Master Ell-rom and Mistress Jasmine arrive from the clinic. Master Kian, Mistress Syssi, and young Mistress Allegra will be joining us as well. The Clan Mother asked me to convey that dinner would be served at six o'clock in the evening."

"Thank you, Ogidu."

"You are most welcome, Master." The Odu bowed again and turned on his heel.

When Brandon closed the door, Morelle clapped her hands. "I'm so happy that Allegra is coming. I adore that little girl."

Brandon's heart squeezed at her obvious delight.

The image of Morelle with a child of her own—their own—flashed through his mind, but he quickly pushed it away. It was far too soon for such thoughts, no matter how appealing they might be.

When he returned to the couch, Morelle was sprawled over it, but she scooted aside, pressing herself against the pillows and making room for him to sit beside her.

He sat down, took her hand, and kissed the back of it. "You should follow Annani's advice and take a nap before dinner."

Morelle's eyelids drooped, but she fought to keep her eyes open. "I'm tired, but I'm also overexcited. I don't think I can sleep."

"Do you want me to tell you a bedtime story?"

A smile curved her kiss-swollen lips. "Yes, please. Something happy. Something about love winning against all odds."

Brandon smiled, thinking for a moment. "Let me tell you about ancient Rome, where a Vestal Virgin named Tuccia fell in love with a soldier..."

As he wove the tale, he felt Morelle's breathing become slower, and he continued the story even after he was sure she'd fallen asleep, his voice dropping to a gentle murmur.

She was so beautiful like this, all her usual sharp edges softened by sleep. The thought of her in his house, in his bed, was so tempting, but he meant what he'd said—he would be content just to hold her, to wake up beside her, and to share with her quiet moments like this one.

Still, her words echoed in his mind: "What if that's not enough for me?"

The memory of their interrupted kiss sent another wave of heat through him. He'd been trying to take things slow, to give her time to adjust to the new world she found herself in and all the difficulties she still had to face. But perhaps he'd been overthinking it. Morelle knew her own mind, and she wasn't shy about stating what she wanted.

She wanted him.

The realization both thrilled and humbled him. She wanted him, a former Hollywood producer who'd spent decades crafting stories about love without ever truly experiencing it himself.

Perhaps that was the reason he'd excelled at adventure stories and had only done so-so with romantic themes.

Was it love, though?

How could he be in love with a female he had known for all of a week?

But then, he had never felt like this before; his heart had never raced just because of a smile or ached when she wasn't near, and he'd never wanted to give someone everything he had and more.

Morelle stirred slightly in her sleep, murmuring something he couldn't quite catch. He pressed a gentle kiss to her temple, breathing in the clean scent of the soap she had used and her own unique fragrance underneath it.

"Sleep well, my princess," he whispered.

21

KIAN

Kian balanced Allegra on his hip as he and Syssi walked out their front door and headed to his mother's. Her small arms were wrapped around his neck, and her face perched on his collar.

"Are you cold, sweetie?" He rubbed her back.

"No."

"So, why are you sticking your nose into my shirt?"

"Dada smell good."

"Oh, I do?" He grinned at Syssi. "That's good to know."

Their daughter had recently started stringing words together and creating sentences, which, of course, was very advanced for her age.

"Amanda and I are planning a big BD party for you know who," Syssi said. "I still don't know what to buy her. She has everything."

"Are you talking in code because it's supposed to be a surprise?"

"I don't know." Syssi sighed. "I tried to find something about whether it was a good idea online, but there was nothing. It's also your BD."

"Mine should not be celebrated again on a grand scale. I had my big party last year." He stopped before turning into his mother's walkway. "But hers is a big deal milestone, and we should start talking about it and preparing her for it."

Syssi smiled. "We'll have a small celebration for you with just the family." She patted his arm. "I know that you don't like surprises, so I'm letting you know ahead of time. Amanda, on the other hand, loves them, and she is convinced that our little one would love a surprise party."

"Speaking of Amanda." Kian cast a glance at his mother's house. "I feel bad about her and Alena not getting invited to dinner." He adjusted Allegra's weight as she squirmed and pointed to show that she was eager to get to Nana's house.

Syssi chuckled. "The only reason we're invited is that your mother wants you to convince Jasmine to let us question her father instead of waiting for her to learn to thrall."

"Which might never happen," he agreed, settling Allegra on his other hip. "Most transitioned Dormants never develop the ability." He sighed. "But I'll need to find a way to explain to my sisters somehow that this isn't a slight against them without making it sound like I'm apologizing for Mother's machinations."

"You don't need to explain anything." Syssi stretched up to kiss his cheek. "Your mother will handle it perfectly well on her own like she always does."

"You're probably right. She's had a long time to perfect the art of managing family dynamics."

"Dada!" Allegra patted his face, demanding attention. "Go, Nana!"

"Yes, Princess, we're going in." He pressed a kiss to her soft cheek, marveling as always at how much love his heart could hold for this little girl.

He'd lived a very long time, and yet being a father was the best experience of his life. Well, it competed with being a husband. Both his ladies owned his heart.

As Ogidu opened the door with his usual bows and greetings, the three of them headed to the living room, where Jasmine and Ell-rom were already settled on the couch.

"Welcome to immortality," Syssi said. "How are you feeling?"

"Better every minute," Jasmine smiled. "Though Bridget says I need to take it easy for a few days."

"I'm sorry I couldn't be there for your ceremony. Amanda and I couldn't take time off."

"That's okay. You wouldn't have been able to see anything anyway. Bridget only allowed four people in the room. Ell-rom, the Clan Mother,

Morelle, and Margo. Kian had to film from the doorway."

As if summoned by the mention of her name, Morelle rushed into the living room with Brandon practically chasing after her, and her eyes immediately found Allegra.

The joy on her face was pure and unguarded, so different from the sharp-edged fighter she usually presented to the world.

Allegra stretched her arms toward Morelle, squirming in Kian's grip. "Illy!"

Morelle made a move to take his daughter, but Kian didn't trust her to hold his precious child while still weak and recovering.

Allegra might look like a bundle of fluff with her frilly dress, pink stockings, and black lacquered Mary Janes but she was solid muscle and baby fat, weighing over thirty pounds now.

He was absurdly proud of how healthy and strong she was.

"Why don't you sit down?" he suggested. "You can sit next to Jasmine, and Allegra can sit between you."

Understanding flickered in Morelle's eyes, but she didn't protest, and as she settled onto the couch beside Jasmine, Kian placed Allegra between them.

"Jadga!" Allegra reached for Jasmine with one hand while keeping hold of Morelle's fingers with the other. "Illy!"

"She gives everyone she likes nicknames," Syssi observed with a laugh. "Consider it an honor."

"I do," Morelle said. "We didn't have any little ones in the temple. Unlike Ell-rom and me, most acolytes joined at the age of ten."

It struck Kian again how much the twins had missed, growing up in isolation. It was a miracle that they had somehow turned out to be decent people. The head priestess, who had been the only one they'd had constant contact with, must not have been as bad as they remembered her. She must have done some good as well.

"Dinner is served," Ogidu announced from the dining room doorway.

"Perfect timing." Annani swept into the room.

As they migrated to the dining room, Kian noticed the careful attention paid to everyone's dietary preferences. Vegan options for Ell-rom and himself, Allegra's favorite foods cut into manageable pieces, and lighter fare for Jasmine and Morelle, who were still recuperating.

"Everything looks and smells wonderful," Kian said as he settled Allegra into her highchair between Syssi and himself.

"Our new family members deserve a proper welcome-home dinner," Annani replied, her smile warm as she gazed at Jasmine and Morelle. "Even if we must keep it small for now."

As they started on the first course, Kian watched the interactions around the table. Morelle and Jasmine were already falling into easy conversation, their initial awkwardness with each other melting away as they talked about Jasmine's acting experience. The Kra-ell were not into the performing arts, or any arts for that matter, and Morelle was fascinated by tales of actors bringing stories to life.

"Mama, look!" Allegra announced proudly as she managed to stab a piece of steamed carrot with her fork.

"Well done, sweetheart," Syssi praised. "Now try to put it in your mouth."

Morelle turned to look at Allegra and smiled, her eyes full of emotion, and Kian wondered what that was about.

Was she just enjoying the company of a small child because she'd never gotten to experience it before? Or was it the feeling of finally having a family?

22

MORELLE

Morelle couldn't take her eyes off Allegra as the little girl carefully maneuvered another piece of carrot into her mouth. There was something magical about watching a child discover the world, even in such simple acts. She'd met the other children in the family during the large dinner Annani had hosted on Saturday, but none of them was as special as Allegra.

Amanda's little Evie, who was nine months old and already walking and saying a few words, peeked at strangers from behind her mother's legs and only smiled when playing with her older cousin. Alena's newborn son was still too young to show much personality. Kalugal's son, Darius, who was six months old and had serious eyes and inner calm, seemed to evaluate everything around him, marking him as a future warrior or leader.

Allegra, though, was special. There was a spark in her, a brightness that drew people in. Morelle could easily imagine this child growing into a formidable female, leading the clan with the same grace and authority as her grandmother.

The thought made her smile.

She would be there to see it, to watch this remarkable child grow into the person she was meant to be.

"You're completely enchanted by her, aren't you?" Brandon murmured from beside her.

"She is adorable," she whispered back, watching as Allegra demonstrated her mastery of spork-holding to her attentive grandmother.

When the conversation shifted to Jasmine's mother, it finally drew Morelle's attention away from Allegra's antics.

"I don't remember much about her," Jasmine was saying, her voice soft and still a little weak. "All I have left from her is a jewelry box, the two rings and a gold chain that were inside, and a deck of tarot cards that was tucked in a hidden compartment." She smiled apologetically. "But as much as I searched the cards for clues, I didn't find any. Eventually, I just accepted that she wanted me to use them as a way to express myself, but now I question that once more. Maybe there was a message hidden in them somewhere after all."

"Was it a standard deck?" Syssi set down her fork. "I don't know much about tarot, but Amanda has delved a little into Wicca, so I know that there are several standard decks, and then there are decks made by various artists. She owns one that had a very limited print edition, and it's worth a lot of money. Maybe that's why your mother left it for you. Maybe it's valuable."

"It's not one of those." Jasmine sighed, absently playing with the stem of her water glass. "It's a nice deck that is no longer in print, but it was quite popular in the nineties when my mother got it."

Annani's eyes held that particular gleam that Morelle knew meant she was pursuing a theory. "Maybe the clue is in the jewelry box," she suggested. "Do you still have it?"

Jasmine nodded. "I do, but I don't want to take it apart. The box and the few items that were in it are all I have left of my mother."

Morelle understood that feeling all too well—the desperate need to hold on to any connection to a lost parent. She had nothing tangible from her own mother, just memories and that one dream visit that had pulled her back to consciousness.

"We can have the box X-rayed," Kian said. "There is no need to take it apart to see if there is anything hidden in the lining or maybe the wood itself. Will you allow us to examine it?"

Jasmine nodded, but she didn't look too happy about it. "I don't know why the sudden interest in my mother. I know that my quick healing indicates that I'm close to the source, but on the other hand, my long transition indicates the opposite."

"You grew two inches," Ell-rom said. "That's why you were unconscious for so long. Your body did that in ten days, and it required shutting down all nonessential functions to preserve energy for the growth."

Morelle smiled. Her twin was a deeply spiritual person, but that didn't mean that he wasn't pragmatic and logical as well. He always analyzed things, breaking them down into their base components and coming up with the most likely explanation. He only invoked the Mother of All Life when there was no other way for him to explain certain phenomena.

Jasmine shook her head. "That doesn't prove anything. Other Dormants have grown in height without being out for so long. Don't get me wrong, I would love to believe that my mother was an immortal or a goddess and that she's still alive somewhere, but that's not likely. My father was devastated after her death. He couldn't even look at me without getting sad or angry because I reminded him of her."

Syssi and Annani exchanged a look that spoke volumes, some silent communication passing between them, and at Annani's nod, Syssi turned to Jasmine.

"I had another vision about you or someone with eyes very similar to yours. We are starting to think that the visions did not show me you but your mother. Do you remember her ever mentioning Kurdistan or the Kurdish people? Did your father say anything about her being from that region?"

Jasmine frowned. "I remember her singing to me in what I assumed was Persian, but maybe it was Kurdish? I don't know the difference between them."

"Do you remember her wearing any special jewelry?" Syssi asked. "Some distinctive piece that has stuck in your memory?"

Jasmine shook her head. "No, why? And why are you asking questions about Kurdistan?"

"In my vision..." Syssi said, "the second one, I saw the same woman in traditional male desert clothing, with your eyes and a curvy body that gave her away as a female. She wore a pendant that caught the sunlight and looked like it might have been amber or something similar. It was partially hidden by her scarf, so I couldn't see the design, but there was something carved on it."

"I don't remember anything like that." Jasmine fiddled with her napkin. "Did she speak Kurdish?"

"She didn't, but some women a short distance from her mentioned two Kurdish towns. I remembered the names because I've read recently about the Kurdish women warriors and their rebellion against Iranian oppression. They are very brave, and they actually led the rebellion. Kurdish women have a long history of fighting for their freedom. They've been doing it for generations."

"Women. Life. Freedom," Annani said. "*Jin, Jiyan, Azadi.*"

"Something about this sounds familiar," Jasmine said.

"You might have read it or heard about it on the news," Brandon said. "Their cause is finally seeing some light in the Western media. You'd think that brave female fighters who wage war against the worst oppressors of women would be mentioned by every feminist organization in every country, but it seems like these organizations have lost their soul or rather sold it to the highest bidder."

Morelle frowned. "How can a soul be sold?"

"Easily." Brandon wrapped his arm around her shoulders and kissed her cheek. "And not even for a good price."

Allegra chose that moment to offer Morelle a slightly squished piece of zucchini. "Illy! Eat!"

That broke the somber mood and tension that had built around the table, and Morelle accepted the offering with exaggerated delight, making the child giggle.

"Good. Eat," Allegra declared, immediately turning to find her next victim.

23

JASMINE

Jasmine absently stroked the stem of her water glass as she tried to make sense of Syssi's vision. Why would the Fates show Syssi her mother instead of her? Was she meant to go to Kurdistan?

Maybe finding Khiann wasn't what she was supposed to do at all.

The thought made her stomach clench. She hadn't been certain about the role she was meant to play in reuniting Annani with her mate, but she wanted to help, and now everything had gotten muddled, and she didn't know what she was supposed to do.

"I want to bring up questioning your father," Kian said. "I know that you want to do it yourself, but if you hope to be able to thrall, I'm afraid that's not likely. Dormants who transition as adults rarely develop the ability. You are probably never going to be able to do that."

"Ell-rom is learning to thrall," she pointed out.

Kian kept his intense gaze on her, and it was intimidating, but she wasn't going to crumble under it.

"Ell-rom knew how to thrall and shroud before he went into stasis. He only needed to be reminded of the technique."

Under the table, Ell-rom took her hand and gave it a light squeeze. "There isn't really much use for thralling. It's forbidden under most circumstances."

"I know, but I only need it to get into my father's head and see what he knows about my mother. If he had something to do with her death, I want to be the first one to know."

There. She'd said it. That was her biggest fear.

"I understand." Kian's expression softened. "And I would feel the same if I were you, but would it really be so bad if you were the second person to learn it? The Guardian who will perform the questioning is not going to do anything to your father that you don't approve of. If he's indeed guilty of murdering your mother, you will decide his fate."

Jasmine hadn't expected that, and now she wasn't even sure that she wanted to take the responsibility. She just needed to know what had happened.

"I don't think he killed her. But I think he knows something."

"Would you like to know what Roni has discovered about your mother?" Syssi asked, her eyes soft and understanding.

Jasmine knew that the clan had conducted a background check on her, so she wasn't surprised that they had information to report. "Yes, please."

"Her name was Kyra Fazel," Kian said. "She came from Iran on a student visa in 1988 and a year later married your father and dropped out of the university. She changed her name to Kira Orlova, taking on his last name and just slightly changing the spelling of her given name, but that could have been enough to cover her trail if anyone from her homeland was looking for her."

Jasmine frowned. "Why would she need to hide?"

"She might have married your father without her parents' permission, and if they were traditionalists, that might have been a great offense." Syssi's eyes were sad and full of compassion. "She could have been in mortal danger."

Jasmine swallowed. "That never occurred to me. They were legally married, so it wasn't like she was dishonoring her family or something ridiculous like that."

Ridiculous was not the right word, not when young women were murdered by their own family members for their supposed dishonor, but right now, there was a child present, and even though Allegra was probably too young to understand, Jasmine didn't want to use that kind of language around her.

"Your father was a Christian, right?" Syssi asked gently.

"Yeah, Russian Orthodox, but he wasn't very religious. We went to church only a couple times a year."

"It doesn't matter how religious he was," Kian said. "By marrying him, she dishonored the family."

"I see," Jasmine whispered. "Do you think they got to her?"

"Not if my vision is right," Syssi said, a little too cheerfully, probably trying to defuse the dark mood that had descended upon the gathering and was starting to affect Allegra.

Jasmine let out a breath. "Thank goodness for your vision. It gives me hope." She turned to Kian. "Did Roni find anything else?"

"He tried to trace her family in Iran but didn't find any data he could even hack into. What reinforces my belief that your mother is alive is that he also found no records of her death, and she wasn't buried by any traditional means. She simply vanished from all records around the time of her supposed death."

"Good." Jasmine allowed herself a smile. "That's good."

"Do you know if your father legally married

your stepmother?" Syssi asked. "Because to do that, he would have needed to either prove that he was a widower or divorce your mother in her absence."

"They got married. I was there in the city hall when they did, along with my stepbrothers. But I don't know how he proved that he wasn't married anymore."

Syssi turned to Kian. "Wasn't Roni supposed to look into that?"

"Roni is swamped with a big project I assigned to him. It will be some time before he will be free to pursue this. It would be easier to find out all of this information by getting into your father's head."

Syssi cleared her throat. "I don't want to be a spoilsport, but isn't it forbidden?"

"Not when the life of Jasmine's mother is on the line," Annani said.

Jasmine didn't think her father could do anything about her mother at the present time, but if it was convenient for Annani to excuse the thralling this way, she wasn't going to say anything.

Syssi nodded. "Now that we've cleared up that issue, I think we should hurry with the investigation. I don't know why I was shown this vision when I asked about Khiann. Maybe it's like when I saw the pod, there's an urgency to find your mother, and that's why the Fates showed her to me." She paused. "Or perhaps your mother has a talent that could help us find Khiann. After all, if she left you a deck of tarot cards, she clearly had an interest in the esoteric. She might have been aware of having a special paranormal talent."

The logic was sound, Jasmine had to admit. And if there was truly urgency involved, they shouldn't wait. "I agree that waiting for me to develop a thralling ability does not make sense, but I want to be there when he's questioned."

"That's not a problem," Kian replied.

"I go where Jasmine goes," Ell-rom said, his tone leaving no room for argument.

Kian's expression tightened. "That complicates things. We'll need to assign at least two Guardians for your protection, probably more. And with the new division being formed, we're already stretched thin."

"What new division?" Brandon leaned forward.

"It's too early to discuss it," Kian said curtly. "The council will be informed once we have a solid plan of action."

The sudden tension between the two men was palpable, though both were clearly trying to hide it. Jasmine glanced at Morelle, and her slight nod indicated that she'd noticed it, too.

Somehow, the brief moment of shared understanding gave Jasmine hope for the future of their relationship. Morelle seemed like someone who could be a friend.

They would need to be careful, of course. Set

boundaries and make sure that neither of them played a tug of war with Ell-rom.

He needed them both in different ways.

"When do you want to do this?" Jasmine asked, deliberately steering the conversation back to safer ground. "Question my father, I mean."

"The sooner the better," Kian said. "But if you want to be there, you need to get a little stronger. You've just woken up from a ten-day coma yesterday."

Ell-rom shifted beside her. "Maybe we could lure him to come closer to us so Jasmine doesn't need to travel?"

"That's an option," Kian agreed. "Jasmine, does your father travel for business?"

She thought for a moment. "Rarely. He's an insurance broker, and they sometimes have conventions. He goes hunting, though, and he has a cabin in the mountains. It's pretty remote—no neighbors for miles." A chill ran down her spine when she thought about how easy it could have been for him to kill her mother and hide her body out there or even leave it for the wild beasts to devour.

No. He'd loved her mother. She was convinced of that.

"What's the matter?" Ell-rom rubbed his thumb over her palm. "Are you cold?"

"No, but I had an upsetting thought that I'd

rather not say anything about in front of the little one."

Kian nodded. "I get what you mean. When you feel up to it, call your father and ask him if he's going on any hunting trips in the near future. You can tell him that you would like to stay in the cabin for a few days."

She chuckled. "He will know that for the lie it is. I hate hunting, and I have never gone there with him. It's a guys' place. He and his buddies go there and get drunk."

"Well, find a way to get it out of him. It will make our lives easier if we can catch him there instead of showing up at his home and having to deal with your stepmother as well. In the meantime, I would like William to examine that jewelry box and those tarot cards."

"I'll get them to him," Jasmine promised.

"Now that this is settled," Annani said, "who would like dessert? Ogidu has prepared something special."

Allegra perked up at the mention of dessert, abandoning her mission to feed everyone at the table. "Waffle!" she declared enthusiastically. "Sweet!"

The tension around the table dissolved, and Jasmine let out a breath.

Maybe she would finally find out if her mother had died or was still alive, understand why she had left her those particular items, and if she was still alive, why she'd disappeared without a trace and never tried to contact her again.

24

MORELLE

Back in her room, Morelle settled onto the couch beside Brandon, her mind still processing everything they'd learned about Jasmine's mother. "I think it's exciting that Syssi's vision hints at the possibility that Jasmine's mother is alive and that she might be involved with the resistance." She smiled. "Maybe Jasmine and I have more in common than I thought. We are both the daughters of rebels. What do you think?"

That would explain the affinity she felt for her brother's mate, which went beyond the gratitude for her part in rescuing them from certain death.

Brandon wrapped an arm around her shoulders. "There are still many pieces missing from the picture. We don't know why she left, what she tried to communicate to her daughter through the items she left for her, and how she found herself among the Kurdish rebels." He rubbed his hand over her arm. "If this was a plot idea I was presented with, I would return the script to the writers and tell them to make it make sense."

"You mean to make it realistic."

He nodded. "People are willing to suspend disbelief, but they still expect the story to follow a certain logic. I have a feeling that the story will make much more sense once we have at least some of the missing pieces after talking with Jasmine's father."

"I don't like the idea of Ell-rom leaving the village," Morelle admitted. "I know that nobody on Earth is seeking to harm him, but I'm so used to us having to hide that it makes me uncomfortable. I still marvel at the feeling of the sun on my face every time I leave this house."

"I've noticed." He kissed the top of her head. "But you are fighting against the ingrained fear and winning. You are a warrior."

"That's how I was raised. Well, I was raised to become a priestess, but even the priestesses are taught how to fight. Ell-rom and I practiced hand-to-hand combat daily, and we had weapons training every other day." She turned to look at him. "I can't believe that these Kurdish women have to fight for their freedom. What kind of a society do they live in?"

"Unfortunately, many places on Earth are far from enlightened," Brandon said. "The Kurdish women are remarkable because they've taken up arms not just for their own freedom, but for their entire people."

"I would like to meet them and hear their stories." She straightened. "Tell me more about them."

"I don't know much," he said. "They fight alongside their male counterparts but maintain separate command structures. They've been pivotal in many battles, especially against extremist groups who believe being killed by a woman denies them paradise."

"Just for saying that, they deserve to be killed by women." Morelle felt a smile tug at her lips. "That's the sort of fight the head priestess would have approved of even for a servant of the Mother of All Life. She would have called it divine justice against the enemies of the Mother's chosen. When I'm at full strength, I would like to help these Kurdish women. They could use someone like me, who is hard to kill."

Brandon lifted a brow. "Is that a note of approval for the head priestess I hear? I thought you didn't like her?"

"I didn't," Morelle admitted. "But I could still appreciate her wisdom and her viciousness. Both traits are highly praised in the Kra-ell society."

Brandon chuckled, the sound reverberating through his chest where she leaned against him. "I don't know why I find your viciousness so attractive, but I do. Only I don't think of it as viciousness. It's fearsomeness and a strong moral compass. You have no problem differentiating between good and evil."

"Isn't that true of everyone? It's not hard to do."

"You'd be surprised how easily humans can inverse the two in their minds. As I told you before, the gods are at fault for that. They made humans highly susceptible to influence, and that susceptibility is exploited by those who know how to manipulate it for their own evil agendas."

"You should find them and eliminate them." Her words lacked the vehemence she'd intended because she was too tired to feel extreme emotions. The lack of energy and physical vulnerability was irritating her, and she wished she could speed up her recovery. "I mean not you personally, but the clan. It's easier to cut off the head of the *diagara* than keep fighting the offspring she spawns."

Amusement danced in Brandon's eyes. "What's a *diagara*?"

He wouldn't be so amused if he ever encountered it in the forests of her home planet. "It's a huge multi-legged creature that devours everything in its path. She first injects her prey with poison, making it incapable of resisting, and then she eats it piece by piece while it is still alive. Once she's eaten enough, she finds a place to hide and spawn."

He pretended to shiver in disgust. "Now that could make a good script for a horror movie."

Weren't movies supposed to be about made-up things? Did he think that she invented the *diagara*?

"But it's real."

"I know, sweetheart." His fingers tightened on her shoulder. "The best fiction is based on reality."

The warmth of his body and the steady rhythm of his heartbeat made her both aroused and sleepy, which were contradictory reactions, but her body wasn't behaving as it should.

Morelle stifled a yawn and snuggled closer to Brandon.

"I should head home. You need rest." He sounded like that was the last thing he wanted.

"Stay. I don't want you to go."

He usually waited until she fell asleep, but she didn't want him to leave at all. She wanted him to share her bed.

After a moment, he nodded. "I'll be on the couch until you fall asleep."

"Not tonight." She pushed to her feet. "I want you to stay."

He swallowed. "I don't have anything with me. Not even a toothbrush."

"There are several new toothbrushes in the bathroom." She leaned to kiss his forehead. "I'll be right back. Don't you dare go anywhere."

He smiled. "Yes, ma'am."

After a quick shower, Morelle put on a nightgown and dabbed some perfume on her neck the way Gertrude had shown her. When she emerged, she found Brandon sitting on the couch and reading something on his phone.

As he looked up at her, his eyes were glowing, and she smiled, knowing that he was aroused by her. The nightgown was made from a shiny and clingy material that outlined every contour of her breasts, and she wondered if that was what had caused him to react the way he did or if it was the perfume.

Gertrude had told her that both were meant to entice.

Well, that was her plan, wasn't it? She wanted to entice Brandon to stop holding back so much and show her a little more of the pleasures her mother had spoken of in her dream.

"Come join me?" she asked as she slipped under the covers.

Brandon rose to his feet, toed off his shoes, and lay down on top of the covers, fully clothed, impersonating a stiff board of wood.

She turned on her side. "You can't sleep like that. Take off your clothes."

She had a feeling that her own eyes were

glowing just from the anticipation of finally seeing Brandon's body without anything covering it.

"I'd better not." He turned on his side as well, facing her.

"Why?"

"Staying clothed helps me maintain self-control."

"Perhaps I don't want you so controlled." She cupped his cheek. When he got that stubborn expression on his face that signaled he wasn't going to cave, she let out a breath. "Can you at least remove your shirt?"

Other than her brother, she hadn't seen any male without a shirt, and she was curious.

After a moment's hesitation, Brandon complied, opening a few buttons and then pulling the fabric over his head in one smooth motion.

Beautiful.

Her hand moved to trace the contours of his chest, feeling the way his muscles tensed under her touch. When his fangs elongated, she felt a surge of feminine pride.

She might be new to this, but her effect on him was undeniable.

"You're beautiful," she whispered, meaning it.

His glowing eyes held hers with an intensity that made her breath catch. "As are you, princess."

His skin was warm beneath her fingers, and his heartbeat accelerated when her hand trailed lower.

"Morelle." He caught her hand. "We should stop."

"Why?" She challenged even though she allowed him to still her movement.

"Because you're not ready. You are still recovering." His voice was strained. "Because when the time comes, I want it to be perfect between us."

25

BRANDON

Morelle gazed into his eyes for a long moment. "I might not have much experience in this or anything else, but striving for perfection is never a good thing. It's paralyzing. The head priestess used to say that only the Mother of All Life was perfect and that mortals should be satisfied with just doing their very best."

"The priestess was a wise female, but given that we are immortal, that does not apply to us. We can strive for perfection and achieve it."

Why was he even arguing the point when he actually agreed with Morelle and her teacher?

Maybe because she was right, saying that the quest for perfection was paralyzing. He was waiting for her to get better, for them to get to know each other, and for their relationship to deepen because he was afraid that without all of these conditions fulfilled, he would disappoint her.

It wasn't a baseless fear, though.

She was a virgin in the truest sense of the word. She'd never been touched or caressed in a sexual way, and he'd been the first male she'd kissed. Jumping ahead all the way to sex was premature, even if she was pushing for it. She needed time to grow, to get accustomed to being touched and touching, so the progression was natural and not forced.

Just as Brandon thought that Morelle was going to rebut his statement, she cupped his face in her hands and kissed him, pressing her tongue through his lips and wrapping it around one of his elongated fangs.

All Brandon's carefully maintained control threatened to shatter as a bolt of arousal erupted from his fang and shot straight to his groin. He knew that he should pull away to maintain the boundaries he'd set, but when her hands moved to the back of his neck and pulled him closer, he felt helpless to resist.

"Princess," he murmured against her lips. "You should stop."

"Why?" She pulled back just enough to look into his eyes. "I'm not as fragile as you think I am, and I know what I want."

The conviction in her voice and the fire in her eyes made it even more difficult for him to resist, but he knew he was right, and if he succumbed to her demands, they were both going to regret it later.

I love you, he wanted to say. *I've loved you since I first saw you.* But saying those words was as premature as consummating their love. Instead, he kissed her, pouring all his love and longing into it.

She responded with equal passion, her hands exploring his bare chest.

Perhaps it was time to move to second base, as the teenagers liked to say. It was a dangerous idea because it would stoke the fire already raging through his veins, but Morelle needed a gradual progression in her introduction to intimacy.

His hand wandered over the exposed back of her nightgown, down the length of her spine, and as he cupped her bottom, she arched into him, pressing her mound to his straining erection.

Letting go of her mouth, he trailed kisses down the side of her face until his lips found her neck, and he nipped at the sensitive skin beneath her ears before dragging his teeth down, his fangs gently scraping but not breaking the skin.

She shivered, but it wasn't from fear or pain.

The slight danger excited her.

When she slid her hand down his front, aiming for the bulge in his pants, he wanted to let her grip him, yearning for her touch, but what if it proved too much and he couldn't stop?

What finally convinced him was the realization

that Morelle needed to explore and that, eventually, he would have to let her touch him, and it wouldn't be on the same night he took her virginity.

When her hand made contact with his erection over his pants, he breathed hard against her neck and then kissed her again. She didn't move her hand, which he was thankful for because he would have erupted in his trousers if she had.

Still kissing her, he pulled the shoulder straps of her nightgown down, and as he cupped her perfect breasts, they both hissed. When she pushed on his chest, he thought she wanted him to stop touching her, but he was wrong.

Moving as fast as any immortal, she straddled his lap, with her nightgown bunched up around her narrow waist and her beautiful breasts with their needy little nipples exposed.

"Touch me more like this." She lifted both his hands and put them on her breasts while grinding her center over his erection.

"I'll do better than that." He wrapped his arms around her and pushed up against the pillows so that his mouth was in the perfect position to close his lips around one of those ripe berries.

Soon, he was suckling, kissing, and gently nibbling, and she was furiously grinding against his length while moaning and groaning so loudly he was thankful for the state-of-the-art soundproofing in the village.

When he switched to her other breast, sucking her nipple deep into his mouth, Morelle got bolder, driving her hand between their bodies and below the waistband of his pants.

Right as her fingers brushed against the sensitive head, he let go of her nipple and gripped her wrist before she could continue any further.

"Not tonight, sweetheart," he hissed before resuming his assault on her abandoned nipple. "Tonight is about you."

She murmured some incoherent objection, but he was having none of that.

Slipping his hand beneath her bunched-up nightgown, he rubbed his finger over the gusset of her panties, nearly exploding when he found it soaked through.

"You are so wet for me," he murmured against her nipple.

"I want you," she hissed. "Give me what I want."

He chuckled. "So bossy, Princess." He kept rubbing her over her panties, collecting moisture before dragging his fingers up and pressing his thumb to her clit. Circling it gently, he let go of her breast and moved to the other, repeating the suckling, nibbling, and kissing.

"Brandon," she pleaded.

As he tugged aside her panties, her breath hitched in her throat, and when he pressed his thumb directly over her clit, she threw her head back and moaned loudly again.

He found her entrance and lingered, circling it with his fingers.

"Please," she whispered.

He wondered if she knew what she was asking for and was acting on instinct or if someone had given her the Kra-ell equivalent of the birds and the bees story.

He slid his finger just past her entrance, afraid of going any deeper and hurting her, when as she moaned and rocked her hips, his finger slid a little further. He used his other hand to grip her ass and keep her from moving, but then Morelle suddenly shuddered, threw her head back, and released a keening moan that nearly sent him over as well.

26

MORELLE

As Morelle lay on top of Brandon, her body still tingling from the waves of pleasure that had crashed through her, she thought about her mother and how right she'd been to urge her to wake up and experience what life had to offer.

The physical sensations were incredible, but even more amazing was the emotional connection she felt with Brandon following those moments of intimacy.

There were only two things missing from what should have been a perfect completion.

Brandon hadn't reached his own release, and he hadn't bitten her.

She'd expected the bite, had yearned for it even, knowing it was supposed to be the ultimate pleasure to be had with an immortal male or god. It wasn't anything she had learned from the head priestess, of course, but she'd managed to have a couple of discreet talks with Annani when Brandon had been otherwise occupied.

The head priestess had exalted the merits of biting, which was mutual between Kra-ell males and females, and she had told Morelle on more than one occasion that she was lucky to be a celibate priestess because her lack of fangs would have prevented her from deriving any sexual pleasure during the dominance games the Kra-ell engaged in.

In contrast, Annani had explained that only male immortals and gods had fangs and females didn't and that the venom bite was one of the best parts of the sexual act.

Brandon's hand ran up and down her back, and she regretted having the nightgown still on, bunched up around her middle and creating a barrier that Brandon's hand had to skip over to get from her back to her ass.

"Are you okay?" he asked quietly.

"I'm more than okay," she said, still catching her breath. "I'm liquefied, and I can't move."

He chuckled. "Stay as long as you want to. I love being your cushion."

She lifted her head. "You are not soft enough to be a good cushion, but you are warm." She put her head down on his chest. "Thank you," she murmured, wondering if it was okay to say that.

Her talk with Annani didn't cover intimate conversation etiquette.

Brandon kissed her temple. "You don't need to thank me, sweetheart. Bringing you pleasure was the greatest gift. As far as I'm concerned, this was the best night of my life."

She lifted her head again to look at him. "You didn't get to culminate." The words came out more accusatory than she'd intended. "And you didn't bite me. How can you say it was the best night of your life when you denied yourself both? Denied us both?"

"Because watching you come apart in my arms was all I needed." His blue eyes were so sincere that she almost believed him. Almost.

"I don't need coddling, Brandon. I want you to tell me the truth just like I'm telling you the truth. I loved every moment of the incredible pleasure you gave me, but I regret it being one-sided and missing out on the venom bite." The lingering effects of her pleasure made it difficult to maintain her indignation. "Still, after what you just gave me, I can't complain. Just know that next time will be about your pleasure."

He chuckled, the sound vibrating through both their chests. "We'll see about that."

"No." She rolled off of him and pushed up on one elbow to look at him. "There will not be a next time unless you achieve completion first. That's not negotiable."

His laughter grew stronger, and he wrapped his arm around her waist, trying to pull her back to him. "Put your head on my chest, Princess."

She resisted, keeping her position. "I'm serious, Brandon."

"I know that." His expression sobered, though amusement still danced in his eyes. "That's exactly why I'm laughing. I love how assertive you are, how you know what you want and aren't afraid to demand it. But you need to understand something —you can't force me to do anything that I believe is not good for you."

Morelle opened her mouth to argue, then closed it again. She hadn't considered it from that perspective. They were different people, and each had their own wants, desires, and preferences. Neither of them should be forcing the other to do anything.

"We need to learn to compromise," she said. "Though I suppose it's mostly me who needs to learn. You already know how to do that." She settled against his chest, letting out a long breath. "I'm still like a child in so many ways, learning how to interact with people in this world."

His hand stroked up and down her arm in a soothing rhythm. "We have more in common than you think. We are both entering new phases in our lives, trying to find our footing."

She tilted her head and frowned at him. "What do you mean? You've lived here your entire life."

"I've been producing movies and television series for so long that I barely know how to do anything else." His voice held a note of uncertainty she'd never heard before. "I've studied the effects of media on society, but I'm not sure how to actually create meaningful change anymore."

"I hate to repeat myself, but what do you mean?"

He shifted slightly, getting more comfortable. "The world is changing faster than ever. Traditional media doesn't have the same impact it used to. That's why I've been focusing on the InstaTock project."

"You mentioned that before," she said, remembering fragments from when she'd been trapped in twilight. "While I was sleeping. But the details are hazy."

His hand continued its soothing motion on her arm. "The idea is to create content that helps young humans develop critical thinking skills. I want to teach them how to distinguish fact from fiction and how to question what they're told instead of just accepting it, but the problem is their nearly nonexistent attention span and their gravitation toward the nastiest content. I refuse to fight nastiness with more nastiness, but I don't know how to reach them."

"It's like the Kra-ell teaching their young to recognize weakness in an opponent."

He chuckled. "Similar concept, different application. Instead of physical weaknesses, we want them to recognize logical fallacies, manipulation tactics, the ways people try to influence their thoughts, beliefs, and actions."

"Because the gods made humans susceptible to influence." She remembered him saying that earlier.

"Exactly. But it's not enough to just tell them that. We need to make it engaging, make them want to learn these skills." His voice grew more animated as he explained. "That's where InstaTock comes in. I'm working on developing interactive content, challenges, games—all designed to make critical thinking fun and rewarding, but I'm not sure any of it will draw enough engagement."

"I wish I could help you, but I know almost nothing about humans, young or old. I need to start learning." She stifled a yawn. "Can you give me an example?"

He chuckled. "I'm sorry. This is definitely not the kind of talk a couple should have after a wonderful intimate moment."

"I like hearing you talk about things you are passionate about," she murmured against his chest.

"Well, in that case, one of the ideas is to present scenarios where participants have to identify different types of manipulation tactics. Another is..." His voice faded into a gentle murmur as sleep claimed her, his steady heartbeat under her ear becoming her lullaby.

27

ARU

"Everything has healed remarkably well," Merlin said as he put large Band-Aids on both of Marcus's arms. "Keep the area clean, and if it itches, rub this cream over it." He handed him a tube. "I don't expect you to experience any other side effects from these immunizations, but if you do, give me a call." He handed the guy an old-fashioned business card. "Program your phone with my number."

The guy flexed his arm, frowning at the Band-Aid. "What did you say these were?"

"Immunizations," Aru said, while reinforcing the word with a thrall. "You need them for where you are traveling. It's just additional protection."

The three men nodded, their eyes slightly glazed over as the new memories settled into place, replacing any recollection of the tracker implantation procedure.

The one from Anumati was so small that they couldn't feel it even if they rubbed their arms. The one William's team had made was slightly larger, so they might feel a small bump, but they would think it was from the immunization shot.

"Remember to keep the injection sites clean," Merlin repeated. "And if you experience any unusual reactions, contact the number I provided."

"Will do, doc." Marcus grinned, his attention shifting to Hildegard. "Thanks for taking such good care of us, sweetheart."

Hildegard had spent the night with Marcus, and Dagor had to redirect the surveillance drone attached to the guy to give them privacy. Other than that, the drones had kept the men constant company since they had left the keep's clinic the day before, and Dagor had reported that they had not done or said anything suspicious.

"All part of the service." Hildegard gave him a light peck on the cheek. "Have a good time in Tibet."

As the men gathered their backpacks, which were stuffed with their newly purchased supplies, Aru escorted them outside through the lobby, where a Lyft was waiting for them to take them to the airport. It wasn't an actual Lyft, of course, or a human driver behind the wheel. It was a Guardian, who would not only get them to the airport but would also thrall them to forget where they had come from and make sure that they boarded the plane.

When the three loaded their belongings in the trunk and got inside, Aru allowed himself to feel actual relief for the first time.

The trackers had been successfully transferred, the hosts were none the wiser, and soon he and his teammates would be free to join their mates in the village.

"I can't believe we've actually pulled this off," Dagor said once Aru returned to the penthouse.

"Time to celebrate?" He walked over to the bar.

"It's barely past noon," Negal pointed out, but he was already reaching for glasses.

"Where are Merlin and Hildegard?" Aru asked. "They are our ride to the village."

"Down in the clinic," Negal said. "Cleaning up and making a list of supplies they need to order."

Aru accepted a glass, feeling the smooth crystal against his palm. It seemed surreal that, after all this time, they were finally free to stop pretending to search for pods that would likely never be found.

"To our freedom," he proposed, raising his glass.

"To our mates," Negal added.

"To the village," Dagor concluded, and they clinked their glasses together.

The whiskey burned pleasantly, going down, warming Aru's chest. He savored the sensation, knowing it would be one of his last memories in this place that had been their base of operations for so long.

It had been lovely, but according to Gabi, the village was even lovelier.

"We should start packing," Negal said after emptying his glass. "Margo's waiting for me to get there to choose our house. She's been sending me pictures of potentials all morning, but to be frank, they all kind of look the same and not nearly as nice as this place. I'm not complaining, though, especially since we are getting them rent-free."

"Yeah, that's an important factor, given that our budget is significantly diminished now that we are paying our replacements and covering their expenses. I hope we all can get jobs in the village and earn an income."

Negal waved a dismissive hand. "Stop worrying so much about finances, Aru. Toven said he's going to help us if we need it."

Aru winced. "I'd rather not accept charity when I can work."

He also hoped Kian wouldn't demand the rest of their Anumatian tech as payment. They needed it in case someone came for them. It was possible that the commander would call and announce that they were about to get picked up.

The chances of that happening were slim but not negligible.

In addition to the trackers that had to be moved, their Anumatian communicators had to be rigged with a gadget that William had come up with, and although it had worked when they had tested it, there was always a chance the commander would notice that there was something wonky about the signal.

Dagor put his glass down and headed to his and Frankie's room. "Do you know if we are supposed to clean up before we leave?"

Aru shrugged. "No one said anything about it, but we should leave the place in a decent state. Making the beds and putting the dishes in the dishwasher should do it. Kian will probably send a cleaning crew to do a more thorough job."

"Then why bother?" Negal asked.

"Because that's the decent thing to do after enjoying the guy's hospitality and getting to stay here for free."

Negal grumbled something under his breath before heading to his room.

When Aru closed the door behind him, he didn't start packing right away, though. He stretched out on his bed, which he had already made, and closed his eyes.

Reaching out with his mind to his sister, he waited until the familiar sensation of connecting with her washed over him.

He could feel Aria's joy through the tether connecting them.

Hello, Aru, she greeted warmly. *I was just thinking about you.*

I was thinking of you, too. I have good news. The transfer of the trackers was successful; the humans are on their way to begin the search for the pods, and we are moving to the village today.

Her excitement bubbled through their link. *I'm so happy for you all. You can finally start your life in the village. Did you have any problem with the transfer? Tell me everything!*

Everything went smoothly, he shared, sending her mental images of the three men. *They are former Special Forces—disciplined, discreet, and eager to travel. They think they are on a long-term assignment that just happens to pay very well.*

Clever. He felt her satisfaction mix with a touch of wistfulness. *I wish I could see the village. See you and Gabi in your new home.*

I wish you could. The thought of his twin being unable to share in this new chapter of his life brought a familiar ache. *I will send you a mental image once I get there. Gabi is already in the village, celebrating Jasmine's transition into immortality with her friends.*

Give her my love. Aria's mental touch was gentle.

Thank you, I will. He poured all his love for her into the thought. *One day, we will find a way for you to visit and see it all for yourself.* Maybe even move in.

It was an impossible dream, but they were immortal gods, and no one knew what the future would bring. Besides, there was no harm in dreaming.

One day, she agreed. *For now, live well and prosper, my brother. Make the most of your freedom.*

As their connection faded, Aru opened his eyes to stare at the ceiling of the room he'd called home for so long.

Soon, it would be just another memory.

28

MORELLE

"Keep your core engaged," Gertrude instructed as Morelle completed another set of exercises on the Pilates Reformer. "Perfect form. You're getting stronger every day."

Morelle could feel the difference in her muscles already. The machine that had initially seemed like a torture device was proving remarkably effective at rebuilding her strength.

"Good news," Gertrude announced as Morelle finished her final repetition. "We're moving the Reformer to the gym tomorrow. You will continue your rehabilitation there."

"Thank the Mother," Jasmine said from where she waited for her turn. "I'll be very happy not to come here anymore." She smiled apologetically at Gertrude. "I love you, so don't take it personally. I just don't like feeling like a patient. I'd rather feel like a pampered lady who gets private exercise sessions."

Morelle nodded in agreement. "I feel the same."

Gertrude didn't seem to be offended. "You'll be happy to know that I will continue to be your instructor. I will have a dedicated room for the Reformer." Gertrude helped Jasmine get positioned on the machine. "I could even offer private sessions to others now that I'm an expert on this thing. But not right away. I'm too busy enjoying my new boyfriend to take on students."

They didn't need to ask who the guy was.

Like clockwork, Rob arrived every day with lunch for Gertrude, and the way the two looked at each other didn't leave room for misinterpretation.

They were in love.

A dreamy expression crossed Gertrude's face. "Rob is so awesome. I've never enjoyed a male's company as much as I enjoy his. He's smart and funny, and he actually listens to what I have to say."

Jasmine chuckled as she began her exercises. "We noticed. The two of you are like a couple of school kids in love, and I couldn't be happier for you. Rob deserves someone who appreciates him, especially after what happened to him."

"What happened?" Morelle asked.

"Ah, it was just awful," Jasmine said, maintaining her form as she spoke. "Rob was engaged to this woman who was just using him. She had an affair with her former boyfriend right before the wedding, and when he confronted her about it, she spewed hurtful things at him, saying how he was so boring she could barely tolerate him."

Gertrude huffed in indignation. "That's so untrue. Rob is the opposite of boring. We talk nonstop about every subject under the sun."

"It was despicable of his former partner to hurt him like that," Morelle said.

"Are you already planning her annihilation?" Jasmine asked with a knowing smile.

Morelle frowned. "What she did was deceitful and cruel, but it doesn't deserve death. I'm not that bloodthirsty." She paused, studying Jasmine's expression. "Is that what people think of me?"

"I've only been awake for three days." Jasmine completed another repetition. "I don't know what others think of you. It's just my impression that you have no mercy and that you believe in ruthless retribution."

Morelle narrowed her eyes at Jasmine. "Somehow, I don't believe you. Did Ell-rom tell you things about me?"

Her brother claimed not to remember much about his life on their home planet. He didn't really know the old her, and she hoped that wasn't the impression he got from getting to know the new her.

"He spoke of you with love," Jasmine said. "He doesn't remember much from before."

"All done," Gertrude told Jasmine.

"Thank you." Jasmine got off the Reformer. "Let's get out of these clothes."

Since they were heading straight from the clinic to Ella's house, they had brought a change of clothes, and even though Pilates wasn't a particularly sweat-inducing activity, they were going to shower in their former patient rooms.

The truth was that Morelle wasn't sure why she'd been invited to Jasmine's transition party, but she was glad to join in the celebration. She needed friends, and she also needed some distance from Brandon, especially after last night.

She was still processing it, torn between how wonderful the experience had been and how much better it could have been if Brandon wasn't such a stubborn male.

Ella and Julian's house wasn't far from the clinic, and when Morelle and Jasmine arrived, the others were already there, gathered around a table laden with snacks and a pitcher of something called a margarita.

"Finally!" Margo exclaimed, pulling Morelle into a hug before she could stiffen. She was still getting used to the immortals' casual displays of physical affection. "We were about to start drinking without you."

"Can't start the party without the guest of honor," Frankie said, raising her glass toward Jasmine.

Gabi poured drinks for everyone. "To successful transitions and new beginnings."

The margarita was surprisingly pleasant, tart and sweet at the same time, and after her second glass, Morelle felt warmth spreading through her limbs and loosening her tongue.

"Can I ask you all something?" she said, running her finger along the salted rim of her glass. "It's about males." She licked it off her finger.

"Oh, this should be good." Margo leaned forward. "What do you want to know?"

Morelle took another sip. "Brandon is being difficult."

Ella snorted, nearly splattering her drink over everyone. "Difficult, how?"

"He's too restrained," Morelle admitted. "He thinks that because I'm inexperienced, I'm breakable, and he refuses to give me what I want."

"Ah," Frankie nodded sagely, but Morelle could tell that she was stifling laughter. "The classic 'I'm so noble' type of restraint. It could be worse. Personally, I prefer that to the guys who want in your pants on day one and get angry when you demand to get to know them better first."

Morelle frowned. "Why would they want to wear your pants? Is that an Earth courting ritual?"

Margo laughed so hard that her hand shook, and her drink spilled on the table. "I love these little lost-in-translation miscommunications.

When a guy wants in your pants, it means that he wants to take them off and have sex with you."

Morelle frowned. "Don't they wait for an invitation from the female?"

Frankie shook her head. "In that, Earth customs are a little different. It's usually the guy who initiates and invites the woman to his bed. She can accept or refuse, but sometimes men are not as polite as they should be and pressure the woman to say yes. In worst-case scenarios, they force her. In this country, it is considered a severe crime and carries a long jail sentence, but there are countries where women have no rights, and if they are violated, they are the ones punished, often sentenced to death."

Morelle grimaced. "So I've heard. Kurdish women are fighting for their rights."

Her answer seemed to surprise Frankie. "Well, yes, but they are not the only ones."

"Ladies." Jasmine waved a hand. "Depressing subjects are not allowed at my party. Let's get back to Morelle's problem with Brandon and help her overcome his stubbornness."

"He's probably got the whole thing planned out like one of his movie scripts," Ella said. "I've worked with him on a project, and he is a perfectionist."

Morelle nodded. "He said he wants it to be perfect between us. I tried to tell him that striving for perfection is not a good thing, but he only partially listened, and he wasn't willing to budge." She crossed her arms over her chest. "I want to return the pleasure he's given me, and I want the venom bite. Is that too much to ask for?"

"Males love a challenge," Frankie said. "But they also need to feel like they're in control sometimes."

"The trick is to make them think they're in control while actually getting exactly what you want," Margo said with a wink.

Morelle shook her head. "I don't like trickery, and I don't want Brandon to be in control."

"Do you want to be the one in control?" Gabi asked.

She wanted to say yes, that she wanted to be the one who decided, but she then realized that if she insisted on dictating the rules, she would be just as bad as Brandon.

"Can't we both be in control? After all, it's a shared experience."

Margo lifted the pitcher and refilled her glass. "Yes and no. In my experience, it's better to take turns. Otherwise, it's like two people trying to drive a car. They will drive it off the cliff."

Morelle wasn't sure she understood the reference, but taking turns sounded fair. "So how do I do that? I mean, take turns."

The women exchanged knowing looks before launching into various suggestions, each talking over the other in their enthusiasm to help.

"Start slow—"

"Wear something sexy—"

"Just jump him—"

"Stop, stop!" Ella raised her hands, laughing. "You're confusing Morelle."

"The important thing," Gabi said once everyone had settled down, "is to communicate. Tell him what you want, but also listen to his concerns."

"I tried that," Morelle sighed. "He says he won't do anything he thinks isn't good for me."

"That's actually sweet," Jasmine said. "He cares about your comfort and well-being."

"Too much," Morelle grumbled, but there was no real heat in it. The margaritas had mellowed her frustration into something softer. "But you are right. It was kind of sweet of him to say that."

"Give him time," Margo advised. "Brandon is probably just as nervous as you are, even if he doesn't show it."

"Nervous?" Morelle frowned. "Why would he be nervous? He's experienced. I'm not."

"That's why he's nervous," Frankie said. "I bet he's never been with a virgin. Talk about pressure. He wants to make sure that your first time is memorable in a good way and not something to cringe about." She scrunched her nose and took a sip of her margarita. "Take it from someone who would rather forget her first miserable time."

As the others shared their memories of their first times, laughing and commiserating, Morelle felt a warm glow that had nothing to do with the margaritas. These females had accepted her so easily into their circle, and it felt wonderful to have friends.

Suddenly, a new realization dawned on her.

She no longer felt like there was no point to life and that it was all about misery. Meaningful connections with others made life worth living.

29

KIAN

Jade settled into the chair across from Kian, her posture rigid as always. "You wanted to see me."

"Yes. I have a proposition that involves Drova."

Jade's expression remained neutral, but her eyes sharpened. "Has she done something else I should know about?"

"Not at all. Actually, this is about giving her an opportunity at redemption that she might appreciate more than the stack of books she was assigned to read." Kian leaned forward, resting his forearms on the desk. "I assume you are aware of the new division we are creating in the Guardian force."

She nodded. "I've heard the force is splitting into two divisions, one to be called the Saviors and the other the Avengers."

"That's right. The Saviors will continue the rescue of trafficking victims, and the Avengers will go after even more sinister players. The pedophile rings."

"The end users," Jade said.

"Exactly. Lately, our operations have been encountering more and more young children, which has prompted us to investigate who is placing the orders. After all, the traffickers are not operating in a vacuum. They are supplying what's in demand. We asked Roni to conduct a preliminary search, and what he uncovered was staggering. This isn't just about the end users anymore. There's a whole layer of middlemen, the brokers who connect buyers with suppliers, and we believe that there are other trafficking rings that specialize in kids."

Jade's expression turned menacing, and her eyes flashed red. "Point me in the right direction, and I will take them out."

Kian chuckled. "I had a feeling that would be your reaction. But there is more. We have reason to suspect that those pimps of kids are collecting blackmail material on their clients, specifically politicians, actors, and wealthy businessmen. That fits the Doomers' modus operandi. Since blackmailing those in power with evidence of them using drugs or prostitutes is no longer as effective as it used to be, they've moved to pedophilia because that still carries a social stigma, and people in power would do anything to avoid such devastating exposure."

Jade tilted her head. "I see the logic, but the Doomers are not the only players who use those kinds of tactics. I could name several others just from casual browsing of news around the world. The patterns are there for all to see."

"True, but we need to be prepared for the possibility that we will come across Doomers. Drova's ability to compel immortals could be very useful in such encounters and reduce the risk of the children we are trying to save getting hurt, not to mention our Guardians."

Jade shook her head. "I'm surprised at you, Kian. Drova has just turned seventeen, which is not too young by Kra-ell standards, but it is by yours, and she's a female. I know that you don't even allow Kri to participate in operations that involve Doomers."

"Kri is not a compeller, and I don't expect to encounter entire Doomer teams. One or two at the most is what the Brotherhood would assign to a ring, and they'd use thralled humans or just rotten ones to do the rest of their dirty work. Drova can participate in missions and continue her education in her off hours." He smiled. "I can free her from the punishment that her former victims demanded, but she still needs to study for her high school equivalency test. That's not negotiable."

Jade shifted on the chair. "How can you trust

her with something this important after what she did?"

Kian had expected this question. "Her compulsion ability could be invaluable against Doomers. And frankly, this could be exactly what she needs—a constructive outlet for her abilities and a chance to prove herself."

"Or a chance to escape."

"The Guardians will all be wearing filtering earpieces, so they will stop her if she tries. It would also be an excellent test of her loyalty. Better to know now if she'll try to run than wait until she's stronger and more experienced."

Jade considered this, her fingers drumming once on the armrest before going still. "She would jump at the chance, if only to escape her current punishment. But that doesn't mean she's ready for such responsibility."

"You told me that she is a formidable fighter. You weren't even sure that you could overpower her to bring her to justice."

"True." Jade sighed. "But skill does not equate to maturity, and regrettably, she is still quite childish. I should have been stricter with her."

Kian wasn't sure that would have been the right approach with the rebellious teenager. Besides, knowing Jade, she'd been strict enough.

"Peter is assembling his team now," he said. "He'll likely include some of the Kra-ell trainees in the backup team. If you agree to her participation, she should meet with him while he is still choosing team members."

Jade's shoulders tensed. "If you're considering putting her on Peter's direct assault team, I'd want at least one other Kra-ell fighter with her."

"I agree. Having another Kra-ell on the team would make her more comfortable." It would also make Jade less afraid for her daughter.

"I need someone to keep an eye on her," Jade added. "With all due respect to Peter, I want to know how my daughter is doing from an objective source that will not try to sugarcoat things for me."

Kian wanted to say that no one would have done that, but he understood Jade's need to have one of her own to hold responsible for her daughter's safety and to restrain her if needed.

"I will tell Peter that's your wish. So, is it a yes?"

She nodded. "I think this will be good for her. She needs to feel useful and contribute. Maybe it would quiet the unrest inside of her."

"Precisely. I will arrange a meeting with Peter, you, and Drova at the training center."

"I know she will say yes," Jade said. "The real question is whether she's mature enough to handle it."

"That's what the meeting with Peter will determine." Kian leaned back in his chair. "He needs to be confident in every member of his team. One weak link could endanger everyone."

"And if he decides she's not ready?"

"Then she can join the training and wait until she is ready, if that's what she wishes to do, of course." Kian spread his hands. "Either way, it gives her a goal to work toward and something meaningful to focus on."

"What does Onegus think of this idea?"

"He's cautiously optimistic. He recognizes the potential value of having a strong compeller on the team." Kian's expression hardened. "Especially if we are indeed dealing with Doomers."

Jade rose to her feet. "I'll speak with her today." She paused at the door. "If Drova betrays our trust and tries to run, the consequences will need to be severe."

"I know. But let's hope it doesn't come to that."

30

BRANDON

Brandon sat at his usual table in the village café, watching the afternoon sunlight filter through the tree branches while he waited for his teenage consultants to arrive from school.

He wanted to jot down a few ideas before they got there, but his mind kept drifting back to the previous night with Morelle—the sounds she'd made, the way she'd come apart in his arms, the perfect weight of her against his chest afterward.

Heat coursed through him at the memory. Maybe he was being too cautious with the physical progression of their relationship. The way she had responded and her fierce demands were clear signs that she was ready for more.

No. He shook his head. He was right to wait.

They hadn't even exchanged words of love yet, though the emotion grew stronger in his chest with each passing day. He wanted to tell her, had almost let it slip several times, but it was also too soon for that.

He wasn't a young male who got swept away by his feelings.

He was a mature immortal with centuries of experience, and this relationship was too important to rush. If he made the wrong move and somehow alienated Morelle, he would never forgive himself.

The Fates might have brought them together, but it was up to him to make it work, especially given Morelle's lack of experience in any kind of interpersonal relationship. The female had never had anyone other than her twin brother—no friends, no other relatives, and certainly no love interests.

He was so glad that Ella had invited her to the celebration in honor of Jasmine's successful transition. Morelle needed to make friends even more than she needed to fall in love.

Oh, wow. Fall in love.

Now, that was a concept that was as new to him as it was to her.

He'd offered to let her move in with him, but they'd gotten distracted before she could answer, and that was for the best, too. These things needed a natural progression to feel right. There was wisdom in the old customs of both humans and gods, even if modern society seemed to sneer at them.

In all his years producing movies and television, he'd learned what resonated with audiences and what fell flat. People might live the hookup life and might claim they were beyond traditional romances, but they didn't want to see that in their entertainment. Movies were about ideals, about love overcoming all obstacles, and about building something lasting and beautiful.

If anyone needed proof that hookups were not the way to go, that was it.

For some, though, there was nothing more. He'd spent his life living that unsatisfying lifestyle and trying to make the most of it.

"You look deep in thought," Wonder said as she refreshed his coffee. "Plotting your next blockbuster?"

Brandon smiled. "Something like that. Though these days, I'm more focused on social media than Hollywood."

"Ah, yes, the InstaTock project." She tilted her head. "How's that coming along?"

"It's a work in progress. I'm meeting with my consultants soon." He glanced at the glass pavilion, expecting his guests to appear at any moment now. "I'm waiting for Lisa, Parker, and Cheryl to come back from school."

"Oh, yeah. Those three are sharp." She leaned

closer. "Parker is helping me with my studies. He's a smart guy."

"So I've heard. I was also told that Cheryl is an expert on InstaTock."

"I heard that too." Wonder straightened up. "Good luck with your endeavors."

"Thank you. Can I bother you by ordering cappuccinos and sandwiches for my guests?"

"It's no bother." She smiled before walking over to the next table.

The next time Brandon turned to look at the pavilion's door, he saw his consultants approaching, and as they spotted him in the café, they headed over.

"Hi," Parker said, dropping his backpack on the floor and sitting down.

The two girls followed suit.

"Thanks for coming." He gave each one of them a friendly smile. "I ordered drinks and sandwiches for everyone. I hope turkey clubs are okay?"

"Perfect," Lisa said, while Parker and Cheryl nodded in agreement.

"So." Cheryl leaned forward. "What amazing ideas do you have for us to tear apart today?"

Brandon chuckled. These kids were not going to pull their punches, which was exactly why he wanted their input.

Wonder arrived with their sandwiches and drinks, and they began eating. Brandon used the pause to organize his thoughts.

"Alright," he said once they'd made some progress with their food. "Here's what I'm thinking for InstaTock. Instead of just presenting facts and asking users to verify them, we create games and scenarios—"

"Like role-playing games?" Cheryl interrupted, her eyes lighting up.

"Similar, yes. But with real-world applications." He pulled out his tablet and opened his notes. "For example, one scenario might involve a user seeing a viral post about a new health supplement. They'd have to navigate through various information sources, identify red flags, and make decisions about what to believe."

"Boring," Parker declared around a mouthful of sandwich.

"What if instead of health supplements, it was about something more relevant?" Lisa suggested. "Like dating app scams?"

"That's a great idea, but I need a way to engage people in all topics, not just the latest thing." Brandon made a note of what she'd suggested. "Still, what other topics would engage your age group?"

The teenagers exchanged looks before launching into a rapid-fire list:

"Cryptocurrency schemes—"

"Fake designer goods—"

"College admission scams—"

"Those stupid get-rich-quick YouTube gurus—"

Brandon's fingers flew across the tablet, trying to keep up. "Those are all great examples. But how do we make investigating them fun rather than feeling like homework?"

"Points system and prizes," Parker said immediately. "Like, you get points for identifying different types of manipulation tactics."

"And badges," Cheryl added. "People love collecting badges."

"What about team challenges?" Lisa suggested. "Like, you and your friends work together to investigate something, and you get to pool your knowledge."

Brandon nodded, continuing to type. This was exactly the kind of insight he needed. "What about the format? Should it be text-based, video, interactive—"

"All of it," Cheryl said. "Different people learn differently. Plus, it's more engaging if you mix it up."

"And it needs to be fast paced," Parker added. "No one wants to spend twenty minutes researching a thing. Maybe there should be a vetted resource site where people could find answers without putting too much effort into it."

"That's dangerous." Brandon put his tablet down. "When there is one resource that everyone is told to trust, it can be easily manipulated. The whole idea is to teach young people how to mine for truth."

Parker's eyes lit up. "Like mining for crypto. No one can hack the blockchain, or rather I should say that it's extremely difficult to do. What if there was a way to do the same with data? An AI could be trained to seek the impartial truth, and the code to train it would be available for everyone to see but not to manipulate. Still, anyone who can find holes in artificial intelligence programming and prove that it is not impartial can post it and have others check the validity of the claim. As long as the blockchain's AI lack of bias remains uncontested, it will be the best source of truth that is easily accessible and incorruptible."

Brandon tried to find fault in Parker's logic, but the idea was so brilliant that the only difficulty he could see in creating such a resource was the computing power required. He was no expert on AI or the blockchain, but he knew that both required massive infrastructure. Bitcoin miners were incentivized by the Bitcoin they produced, but that would not be the case with an information blockchain as Parker was proposing.

"That's genius, Parker," Cheryl said. "Now you just need to figure out how to implement your brilliant idea."

He chuckled and lifted his hand in the air. "I'm the idea man. Someone else will need to figure out the how."

"I'll run it by William," Brandon said. "If that can be done, it would be a game changer. But we still need to come up with more ideas for engaging young people."

"Challenges," Lisa agreed. "Like those 'spot the difference' games, but instead it's 'spot the manipulation.' Everyone wants to prove that they are smart."

"That's a good one," Parker said. "It can even be a part of the 'find out your intelligence score' schemes. People love those, too."

Brandon sat back, watching them bounce ideas off each other. Their enthusiasm was infectious, reminding him why he'd gotten into entertainment in the first place—the desire to reach people, to make them think while they were being entertained.

"What about rewards?" he asked. "Besides points and badges?"

"Real-world applications," Cheryl said. "Like, if you score enough points, you will be considered for some internships or mentoring programs."

"Or scholarships," Lisa added.

"Now you're thinking like producers," Brandon said approvingly. "Always looking for ways to make the project sustainable."

"Speaking of sustainable," Parker leaned forward, "how are you going to keep people engaged long-term? These kinds of apps usually die out after the novelty wears off."

It was a good question. "That's where the community aspect comes in. Users need to feel like they are making the world a better place instead of just venting their frustrations and criticizing everyone. I think there is a thirst for positivity that is lacking from current social media."

Cheryl nodded. "I like it."

"You'll need moderators," Lisa pointed out. "Lots of them. And they'll need training."

Brandon made more notes, impressed by his young consultants' enthusiasm and, at the same time, awareness of potential problems. "These are all excellent points. What would make you want to be part of something like this? Not just as users, but as content creators or moderators?"

"Money or recognition," Cheryl said finally. "Or both. Not just within the app but in the real world. Like being able to put it on college applications or resumes."

"Training," Lisa added. "Real skills that we can use later."

"A voice," Parker said quietly. "The chance to actually make a difference. We see what's happening in the world. We see how information gets twisted and how people get manipulated. We want to do something about it and not wait until we finish college to take part in reshaping the world. We are skilled and capable enough as we are."

The others nodded in agreement.

Brandon set down his tablet. "That's exactly why I wanted your input on this. You understand the problem better than most adults because you're living it every day."

"So, make that part of the platform," Cheryl suggested. "Let us help design it, help run it. Make it ours as much as yours."

"Yeah." Lisa brightened. "Like, different user levels could have different responsibilities. The more skills you master, the more input you have in how things run."

"A meritocracy," Parker said. "Without age discrimination."

Lisa lifted her cappuccino. "I'll drink to that. Power to the young!"

31

KIAN

Kian checked his watch as he stood in the parking lot beside the large "Welcome to the Village" banner that Amanda had commissioned a long time ago. It had served multiple arrivals before and would hopefully serve many more in the days and years ahead.

The gods would arrive any minute, and he was grateful he'd managed to make it despite the chaotic day.

The investigation into the pedophile rings had uncovered more disturbing evidence, and he'd spent hours in meetings with Onegus discussing strategy. But this was a celebration, and he refused to let the darkness of his work cast shadows over such a joyous occasion.

Syssi squeezed his hand. "Stop thinking about work," she whispered. "I can feel the tension radiating off you." She tilted her face up to look at him.

"Think about Allegra with your mother. Sometimes I wonder who the stronger personality is."

That got a chuckle out of him, and he lifted their conjoined hands to plant a kiss on the back of hers. "You always know what to say to make me feel better."

"What, it wasn't the balloons?" she teased.

Margo, Gabi, and Frankie were juggling an assortment of colorful balloons, which Amanda had also provided from her growing stash of decorations.

They had been visiting the village regularly, but today they were moving in officially and joining the community with their mates.

Good times.

Kian collected them like gems to add to his collection. As someone who had lived for over two thousand years, he knew how rare and precious days like these were.

Although, to be frank, every day had been a good day since first Syssi had come into his life and then Allegra.

"Do you think they remembered to pack everything?" Margo asked Frankie. "I bet Negal forgot to pack up the bathroom. All my makeup is there—"

"I'm sure he remembered," Frankie said. "And if he didn't, we can get it later." She turned to Kian. "Right? Are we getting clan cars anytime soon?"

"Soon," he confirmed. "For starters, each couple

will get one vehicle, but we are getting a new shipment in a month, and then you'll each get a car."

Frankie grinned. "I can't believe that everything is free. I kind of feel bad about it."

"How is your cousin Angelica doing with Edgar?" Syssi asked. "Did he tell her already about her potential?"

Frankie winced. "I think he's scared. Getting dumped by Jasmine did a number on him. He wants to be sure that Angelica is in love with him before he tells her. The problem is she has some baggage too and is afraid to commit."

The sound of the car lift engaging drew their attention, and a few moments later the first car appeared, with Hildegard at the wheel and Dagor sitting beside her. The lift engaged again, and while Dagor and Frankie celebrated their reunion, the other car emerged with Merlin at the wheel, Aru sitting beside him, and Negal in the back.

"Negal!" Margo launched herself at her mate the moment he stepped out of the car, sending her balloons flying up to the ceiling.

Kian watched with a smile as Gabi wrapped her arms around Aru's neck while he lifted her off her feet.

Frankie and Dagor were still in a lip lock, kissing as if they hadn't seen each other in weeks rather than this morning.

"Welcome to your new home," Kian said,

extending his hand to Aru once Gabi had released him.

The god's eyes were suspiciously bright as he shook Kian's hand. "Thank you, Kian. I'm so grateful for everything you have done for us."

"You've done a lot for us as well."

Aru chuckled. "Yeah, brought you bad news."

"You helped us find Ell-rom and Morelle. My mother is overjoyed to have her brother and sister." And a connection to her grandmother, but that wasn't something Kian could mention in public. Negal and Dagor didn't know that Aru was on a secret mission and that he could communicate telepathically with his twin sister on Anumati.

Naturally, Margo and Frankie didn't know that either.

Once the gods collected their belongings from the trunks of both cars, they all made their way to the elevators, with Margo and Frankie chattering excitedly about the homes they had chosen to settle in.

Gabi didn't say much and seemed content to have her arm threaded through Aru's.

As the group spilled out into the glass pavilion, Kian was glad to see the way the gods gazed at the village vista that stretched out before them. The setting sun painted everything in soft hues, making the carefully maintained greenery and paths look almost magical.

"My mother has prepared a welcome dinner,"

Kian said, "but first, let's get you settled in your new homes." He gestured to the two waiting golf carts.

"We chose three homes that are right next to each other," Gabi said. "Frankie and Margo wanted to be next to Mia like they had dreamt of doing since they were little girls, but that area was full. The good news is that our homes are in the original phase of the village, so we get to be close to the café and the village square, and that's where everything is happening."

"As long as I'm with you, I don't really care where we live." Aru pressed a kiss to her temple. "But I have to admit that this place is even nicer than I imagined."

"It's no more than ten minutes' walk," Kian said after the bags had been loaded into the back of the carts. "But since we have the carts here and we need to get to my mother's later, I suggest that we all hop on."

Merlin and Hildegard said their goodbyes, and then the rest of them got on board, with Kian driving one and Gabi the other.

As they wound through the village paths, Kian couldn't help but notice how the gods were taking everything in, and he felt a sense of pride at what he'd created. The question was whether this place would sustain his people down the line or whether they would need to find a new location that was better hidden.

He'd been thinking about it a lot lately, but he was reluctant to accept that the village might be too small or too vulnerable despite the current abundance of houses and their best efforts at keeping it hidden.

As they pulled up to the first house, Gabi hopped off the cart. "This one is ours," she told Aru, practically bouncing with excitement.

As they headed toward the front door, Kian noticed several curtains twitching in nearby houses. News traveled fast in the village, and everyone was curious about their new neighbors, even though they had all met them during the cruise.

"Let me give you a tour," Gabi said, taking Aru's hand and leading him up the front steps. The god followed, looking around and grinning like someone who had just won the lottery.

Well, he had.

Finding his true love mate on Earth was like winning a galactic lottery, and then being able to move into their community was a boon on top of that.

The house was similar to most of the homes in this part of the village in terms of its floor plan and amenities. Its exterior sported one of the handful of specs finishes that the architect and Ingrid had put together. Similarly, it had Ingrid's interior design touches that varied a little for this model, making it both elegant and homey. None of the homes in the village, Kalugal's being the exception, were nearly as high-end as the penthouses the gods had just vacated.

Still, Aru seemed happy, and the other two couples who had joined them for the house tour were commenting excitedly about how nice everything was.

The tour of Dagor and Frankie's house next door went similarly, though with considerably more squealing from Frankie as she showed off every feature. Then, it was Margo and Negal's turn.

"We should head to my mother's," Kian said after they'd completed the final tour. "She's eager to welcome you properly, and the Odus have been cooking all day to prepare a feast for you."

"Will Ell-rom and Jasmine be there?" Margo asked.

"Of course," Syssi said. "And Morelle and Brandon. For now, they are still staying in the Clan Mother's house, but I expect them to move out soon. Morelle will probably move in with Brandon, and Ell-rom and Jasmine will need to choose a home."

Kian wondered if Brandon would be willing to host the other couple. The twins would most likely want to live right next door to each other, and there were no more vacant homes in their part of the village.

32

MORELLE

The world had taken on a pleasantly fuzzy quality as Morelle followed Brandon into Annani's living room. Her limbs felt lighter than usual, and warm contentment had settled over her—aftereffects, she assumed, of the delicious drink called margarita that she'd shared with her new friends.

She would definitely need to ask Annani's Odus if they knew how to make it. The combination of tart and sweet, with that interesting salty rim, had been utterly fascinating. She'd never tasted anything like it before.

As Morelle settled onto the couch beside Brandon, she noticed that Jasmine seemed far less affected by the drinks despite having consumed just as many. Her brother's mate was radiating excitement that was somehow contagious even through Morelle's pleasant haze.

"I can't wait for you to meet these three fabulous gods." Jasmine settled onto a large armchair with Ell-rom. "They helped me find your pod. Without them, it wouldn't have been possible, even with my scrying stick." She chuckled. "Negal carried me on his back most of the way because I somehow managed to twist my ankle." She smiled at Ell-rom. "I was never the outdoor type."

Morelle frowned, old suspicions rising through the margarita-induced warmth. The head priestess's warnings about the duplicitous nature of gods echoed in her mind, but then these gods were mated to Margo, Frankie, and Gabi, so they couldn't be too bad. Maybe they were rebels like her father and his followers. "I'm missing parts of the story, and it just occurred to me that I don't know why these gods wanted to find the Kra-ell settlers."

Brandon's hand found hers, his thumb rubbing soothing circles on her palm. "Perhaps we should start at the beginning. Aru and his friends only arrived on Earth five years ago."

It suddenly occurred to her that Kian had said something about the gods arriving only recently from Anumati and reporting about the progress there, but later, she'd learned that there had been no contact with Anumati for thousands of years.

"How did they get here?" She turned to look at him. "You said that communication with Anumati was severed a long time ago."

"To most Anumatians, that was true." Annani turned to face her. "But the Eternal King secretly sent patrol ships to this sector from time to time, and small scouting teams were sent to check whether the missing settler ship arrived. Aru's team was the last one, and they found Kra-ell settlers, but only those who had already awakened from stasis on their own. They found us only after we freed those Kra-ell from Igor's oppression."

What Annani had just said made little sense to Morelle.

"Who is Igor?" she asked.

Ell-rom leaned forward. "Our mother wasn't the only one who smuggled people on the ship. The Eternal King smuggled Kra-ell assassins, who were supposed to kill our father and the other gods who supported him, but since the ship was lost in space, he kept sending scouts to find out whether it had arrived on Earth. Aru and his friends are the last such team, and they discovered that the ship had finally arrived, but it exploded. It managed to release all its life pods beforehand, but only a few of them opened, and not at the same time. Several groups of Kra-ell woke up from stasis and tried to make sense of what happened to them and survive. Igor was in one of those pods that opened, and he was one of those assassins. When he realized that Ahn and the gods were gone, he decided to become the king of the Kra-ell, and since he was a powerful compeller, he forced his pod mates to obey him, get rid of the males of the other pods, and take the females. His goal was to change the normal ratio of Kra-ell males to females and equalize it."

"That's absurd." Morelle waved a dismissive hand. "That's how nature made the Kra-ell. Was he a scientist? Did he know how to manipulate genes like the gods?"

"No," Brandon said. "He was just trying to reverse the natural order of the Kra-ell and subjugate the females to the males. He was a bad male who had no regard for honor or life."

The room seemed to tilt slightly, and Morelle wasn't sure if it was the margaritas or the horror of what she was hearing. "How did he find the others? How did he know when they awakened?"

"Trackers," Jasmine said. "All the settlers had trackers implanted in their bodies. They were only activated when they woke up from stasis."

"We don't have them," Ell-rom said quickly. "Mother made sure of that when she smuggled us onto the ship at the last moment. I assume that we took the place of two Kra-ell who were supposed to be there."

Brandon's arm tightened around her shoulders, drawing her closer, and she gladly leaned against his solid warmth.

Morelle took a deep breath, trying to organize

her slightly scattered thoughts. The margaritas weren't helping her usual mental clarity. "So, Aru and his team were searching for the other pods, trying to find more survivors before the evil Igor could get to them?"

"Yes," Jasmine nodded. "They couldn't help the Kra-ell he subjugated because they were not allowed to interfere, but they kept searching for the others."

"How did the Kra-ell find the clan? Was it because of the gods?" She broke off as voices drifted in from the entryway, followed by the sound of footsteps.

"Speaking of Aru's team," Jasmine rose gracefully to her feet, "they're here."

As they entered, Morelle knew right away who was who by their mates.

Aru was with Gabi, Negal was with Margo, and Dagor was with Frankie. She heard their names mentioned countless times during the celebration of Jasmine's transition, but seeing them in person was a reminder of how perfect the gods were, even in comparison to the immortals.

"Princess Morelle." Gabi's mate approached her with a warm smile. "We've heard much about you from your brother."

The god's smile seemed genuine, his manner open and friendly, but years of conditioning had made her wary.

Morelle rose to her feet. "Thank you for helping find our pod and saving our lives."

"We couldn't have done it without Jasmine. If you want to thank anyone, you should thank her."

"I've already thanked her, but I wish to thank you and your teammates as well."

"You are welcome." Aru dipped his head.

Next, Negal and Dagor introduced themselves, and then it was time to adjourn to the dining room.

These gods seemed like good people and nothing like the duplicitous creatures the head priestess had claimed gods were.

As conversations flowed around her, Morelle tried to reconcile everything she was learning. The gods who had helped save them had been implanted with trackers themselves, and that was why they couldn't come live in the village until now. They had to find a way to transfer their trackers into humans who would take up the search for the pods in their stead. It was a lot to process, especially with her head still spinning from the drinks she had earlier.

She made a mental note to ask more about Igor when she was feeling clearer. Anyone who could control Kra-ell warriors through compulsion was a threat worth understanding, even if he was no longer a danger.

What had they done with him? Was he dead?

"I heard that you discovered your talent," Aru said, passing a dish of something that smelled wonderful. "A nullifier—that's quite rare."

Morelle accepted the dish, though her appetite was diminished. "So I've been told. Though I'm still learning how it works."

33

BRANDON

Brandon listened to the conversation around the table, but he was only paying superficial attention to it. His mind kept circling back to Morelle's declaration from the previous night about returning the pleasure he'd given her.

The determination in her eyes had been both arousing and terrifying, and he didn't have the option of escaping to his house because she now demanded that he share her bed.

He'd packed an overnight bag, including silk pajamas he'd never worn because he preferred sleeping in the nude. The thought of wearing them tonight made him feel ridiculous, but he was going to, nonetheless.

Maybe he could pretend to fall asleep early?

The thought was so absurd that he stifled the urge to snort. The immortal legendary Hollywood producer who'd had countless lovers was acting like a damn virgin.

If Morelle wanted to explore, he should just let her.

She was a grown woman, perfectly capable of making her own decisions. But she was also completely inexperienced. Would she even know what to do?

His princess didn't even have the benefit of watching movies or reading books that would have given her an idea of how to go about pleasuring a male, and as he thought about teaching her, he got hard. Worse, everyone around the table could probably smell his arousal.

"Brandon?" Morelle turned to him with a frown. "Is something wrong?"

Crap. Well, he hadn't spent years writing scripts and hanging around actors for nothing. He could put on a good act.

Smiling confidently, he wrapped his arm over the back of her chair. "Just thinking about the humans who are on their way to Tibet to search for the missing pods. What if they actually find one?"

Across the table, Aru set down his wine glass. "That's very unlikely. My teammates and I followed every rumor of anything suspicious in the area, and we found nothing."

"Where could the pods be?" Morelle asked. "We

were told that they are indestructible, so they must be somewhere."

Kian leaned forward. "We've theorized about this extensively. Some must have ended up in the Arctic Ocean, and the currents there could have carried them deep under the ice. Others might have created impact craters that have since been covered by vegetation, although given that they landed not so long ago, not enough time has passed to allow for complete coverage."

"Earth is mostly water," Dagor said. "The odds of pods landing in the ocean are much higher than them landing on land."

Syssi chuckled. "Or maybe they've already been found and are hidden away in some government facility like Area 51."

"Area 51?" Morelle turned to Brandon. "What is that?"

Brandon welcomed the distraction of explaining, even as part of his mind remained acutely aware of her thigh pressing against his under the table. "It's a highly classified military installation in Nevada. There are all sorts of conspiracy theories about it housing alien technology, and even about experiments being conducted on extraterrestrial life forms."

"Which isn't entirely implausible," Syssi pointed out. "Most humans might think that's a conspiracy theory, but we know better." She turned to Kian. "Did the clan ever investigate the place?"

"We didn't have a reason to." Kian put his wine glass down. "Our ancestors were in Sumer, not America, and the Kra-ell settler ship exploded over Russia. I don't expect the US government to have anything overly interesting in there. They are probably working on experimental technology that is unrelated to aliens."

Brandon had seen several scripts for movies about Area 51, and he'd even considered one of them for production, but the head of the studio had decided against it, and Brandon hadn't put up too much of a fight to make it happen. The script had been a fun idea, and the movie would have probably made good money, but it hadn't promoted any of the ideals the clan was interested in.

He was about to share this with the others when Morelle's hand casually rested on his knee and robbed him of his thinking faculties.

"I think you should investigate it." Morelle's fingers traced patterns on his thigh.

"I suppose it might be worth looking into eventually," Kian said. "Roni could probably hack their systems without too much trouble, and perhaps Andrew can find out a thing or two about the place."

Syssi shook her head. "I asked him. He doesn't have access to that kind of information. It's all compartmentalized."

As the conversation drifted to what the government might be hiding and where, and circled back to the missing pods, Brandon was completely distracted by Morelle's casual touches. She seemed unaware of the effect she was having on him, continuing to participate in the discussion while her fingers drew circles of fire on his thigh.

"The Himalayas are still a good place to look for the pods," Negal was saying. "That's where we found yours, so it makes sense that there might be more buried out there. That's why we sent the humans to Tibet."

"The Himalayas surprised me," Margo said. "I actually had a good time out there, but that's probably because I didn't have to hike the terrain. Jasmine and the guys did all the hard work."

"I would have enjoyed it much more if I hadn't twisted my ankle." Jasmine smiled at Negal. "I owe you several dinners for carrying me on your back. I can't wait for Ell-rom and me to have our own house so I can cook and invite you all."

Annani sighed. "I hope that you will stay here for a little longer. I am enjoying having my sister and brother and their mates living with me."

Brandon swallowed.

Was he Morelle's official mate?

Glancing her way, he was afraid to see her shaking her head, but she was smiling at Annani.

"We can come every day. If it is possible, though, I would love to have a house of my own. I've never even had a room to myself before this one." Morelle waved her other hand in the direction of the hallway.

"Would my house do?" Brandon asked. "Or do you want an entire place to yourself?"

Her hand had stilled on his thigh. "I guess we can move into your place."

"Nonsense," Annani protested. "You are still recuperating, and here you have the Odus to prepare and serve you meals. Who is going to cook for you at Brandon's?" The Clan Mother leveled her gaze at him. "Can you cook, or are you planning to feed my sister sandwiches from the café?"

"I can make eggs and toast, but that's the extent of my culinary expertise. I can learn, though."

The conversation turned to food delivery options, and as the Odus served dessert, Brandon remained hyper-aware of Morelle beside him. Every movement, every casual touch sent sparks through his body, and he was both dreading and anticipating their return to her room later.

He needed to stop overthinking everything and just let whatever happened happen. He should trust Morelle to know her own desires and himself to be what she needed.

"Brandon?" Morelle's voice drew him back to the present. "Are you sure you're alright?"

"Yes, sweetheart." He lifted her hand to his lips and brushed them over her knuckles. "I'm just thinking about how grateful I am to the Fates for bringing you into my life. I also wish that I could have been there in the Himalayan mountains, searching for you."

Jasmine snorted. "Count yourself lucky that you weren't. These two looked like skeletons. It wasn't a pretty picture."

Ell-rom leaned to plant a kiss on Jasmine's cheek. "And yet you stayed by my side."

"Of course. I knew you were fated to me, my prince."

34

MORELLE

Brandon radiated nervous energy as they entered her room, his usual graceful confidence replaced by an endearing uncertainty that made Morelle's heart squeeze.

He had lived for centuries and had been with countless females, so the only reason he might look anxious was because he didn't want to do anything that would be less than perfect for her.

"Brandon." She took his hand. "I don't want to pressure you into doing anything that you are not comfortable with. If all you want to do tonight is hold me while I sleep, that's perfectly fine."

The relief that flooded his features made her feel slightly guilty about her true intentions but not guilty enough to abandon her plans of seduction.

"I'm glad you decided to follow my advice and take it slow."

"Slow. Yes." Ella had told her to make her moves slow and deliberate. "I will take things slow." She waved a hand toward the bathroom door. "Go ahead and use it first. I need to arrange a few things in the closet."

"Are you sure? I can wait until you are done."

"No, you go first. I insist."

Brandon regarded her with a questioning look but then nodded, grabbed his overnight bag, and headed toward the bathroom. "Thank you. I won't be long."

As soon as the door closed behind him, Morelle retrieved the borrowed nightgown from where she'd hidden it in her dresser drawer. The fabric was soft and delicate, similar to that of the two nightdresses that Brandon's shopper had gotten for her. But unlike those which were floor length, this one was short.

Morelle held it up against her body, studying her reflection in the full-length mirror. Ella was a small female, considerably shorter than her, which could be a problem. The hem would definitely sit higher on Morelle's longer frame, but as long as it covered her bottom, it would do just fine. She was still very thin, so the width shouldn't be an issue.

According to Ella, the garment would make Morelle irresistible to Brandon, and that was what she wanted. Her storyteller was overthinking their intimacy, perhaps telling himself stories about fragile princesses who needed to be treated with care or they would fall apart.

She wasn't that type of princess, and maybe this alluring nightdress would help her rewrite Brandon's story.

When he emerged from the bathroom, Morelle's eyes widened appreciatively.

Was he trying to emulate her plan and make himself irresistible to her?

He needn't have made the effort because she already couldn't resist him, but he looked incredible in the loose black pants and matching shirt. The fabric draped perfectly over his broad shoulders, and even though it was loose, she could still appreciate the definition of his muscles underneath.

"Is this common night attire for males on Earth?" she asked.

Brandon chuckled, running a hand through his slightly damp hair. "Actually, I usually sleep naked," he admitted. "I got this set as a gift a long time ago, and I thought I should dress fancy for you tonight."

Or modest. She knew precisely why he was wearing it to her bed.

Silly, sweet male.

"You look very handsome," she said. The black, shiny fabric suited him perfectly, making his blue eyes seem even more striking.

Gathering her borrowed nightgown, she

headed for the bathroom. "Don't fall asleep until I'm out. I won't be long."

"I won't." He got in bed and lay down over the covers.

She hoped he didn't intend to spend the night like that, but right now, she was enjoying the view. It would be better if he removed the shirt as he had done last night, and she planned to ask him to do it once she was out of the bathroom.

Once in the shower, Morelle washed her body and the fuzz on her head with the liquid soap that smelled so good. She stood under the warm spray a little longer than was needed to wash away the soap because she enjoyed how it felt, and there was no reason to rush through things that gave her pleasure.

It was a new concept that she was still adapting to.

In the temple, everything had been austere, and things had been done quickly and efficiently without any regard for enjoyment. The water she'd washed with hadn't even been warmed up. Here, everything seemed to be about pleasing the senses —the soft fabrics her clothing was made of that seemed to caress her body, the food that was delicious in addition to being nutritious, the soap that smelled sweet and flowery and was not just meant to clean but to soothe and perfume. Even the bedding was like an intimate caress.

Drying off quickly, she slipped the borrowed

nightgown over her head. The material felt amazing against her skin, almost liquid, cool, and sensual. As she'd suspected, the hem barely covered her bottom, but the width was fine, maybe even a little loose across her still-too-thin frame.

Looking in the mirror, Morelle was happy with how the garment made her look. The nightgown was a pale pink that made her skin glow, and the short length made her legs look long. Her hair was growing back, just enough to create a soft, dark fuzz that somehow made her features look more feminine rather than harsh.

With one last look in the mirror, she opened the bathroom door and stepped out.

Brandon's sharp intake of breath was exactly the reaction she'd hoped for, and as his eyes traveled from her face down the length of her body, lingering on her legs, they started to glow.

"Where did you get that nightdress?" His voice was husky. "It wasn't among the ones Melinda chose for you."

"It's borrowed." She smoothed her hands along the sides. "I wanted something more alluring."

His eyes narrowed as understanding dawned. "So, when you said you'd be satisfied with me holding you as you slept, that was a lie."

"Not exactly." She sauntered toward the bed with an extra sway in her hips, as Ella had demonstrated. "I was just hoping for more."

The nightgown swished around her thighs as

she moved, and she was acutely aware of Brandon's gaze following her every movement.

Still, despite her show of confidence, her heart was racing.

This was all new territory for her, and it was so exciting. Seduction, desire, and the art of tempting a male resonated with something deep and primal within her. This wasn't nearly as foreign as she'd thought it would be.

"You're playing a dangerous game, Princess," he said, his voice low and rough.

Climbing onto the bed on her knees, she let the nightgown ride up just enough to give Brandon a glimpse of more thigh, and the way his breathing hitched was deeply satisfying.

"I'm just getting ready for bed in my borrowed nightgown," she said, feigning innocence and wondering whether his earpieces were translating her tone as well as her words.

His laugh sounded strained even through her earpieces, so maybe they were doing as good of a job of transmitting her inflections.

"You know exactly what you're doing," he said.

She did, and the power of it was intoxicating, the freedom of it exhilarating.

The fact that Brandon was obviously affected only made it better. His usual controlled demeanor was cracking, revealing the passion he'd struggled so hard to conceal. All she had to do was push a little more, and maybe tonight, he would finally let go of some of his cherished restraint.

As he shifted against the pillows, placing his arms behind his head, she'd still caught the evidence of his arousal before he hid it by crossing his legs at the ankles.

"I want to touch you," she said as she moved one knee over and straddled him.

35

BRANDON

Brandon could barely breathe.

Morelle was straddling his thighs, wearing that skimpy nightgown that was nearly sheer, her core pressed against his erection.

He had to allow her to explore, but his hands had to stay tucked under his head. Letting her do this and not responding was going to be torture, but he had to power through it for her.

"I'm yours, Princess," he murmured. "Do with me as you please."

Her feral smile was a promise and a warning wrapped in sex and tied with a ribbon of gotcha. "Remember you said that." She leaned down and pressed a kiss to his neck, then started on the buttons of his pajama top.

She kissed each inch of skin she revealed, and when the last button was undone, she parted the two halves of his pajama top and leaned back to look at his chest.

"You are very nicely put together, Brandon," she said with a crooked smile. "And I love the way your skin tastes." She leaned over him once more and pressed a kiss near his nipple.

When she closed her lips around it, Brandon couldn't help but arch his hips and press his erection against her center, and when she flicked her tongue across it, he saw stars.

"You are killing me, Princess," he hissed.

Morelle laughed, pressed a soft kiss to the nipple she'd been licking, and then moved to the other one.

Keeping his hands behind his head was becoming a struggle.

All he wanted to do was grip her hips, flip them over, and dive between those long legs of hers to where the intoxicating scent of her arousal was coming from.

Was she naked under that skimpy nightdress?

He could feel the outline of her lower lips on his shaft, but with the fabric of his pants between them, he couldn't tell for sure.

It would be so easy to find out...

She grazed his nipple with her blunt front teeth, and he wished she'd inherited fangs from her Kra-ell mother so she could bite him, suck his blood—

No, no, no, that was absolutely the worst image

he could conjure right now when he was moments from soiling his pajama bottoms.

Moments? Who was he kidding? He wouldn't even last one more moment of this.

Thankfully, her mouth left his nipple, and when she pressed soft kisses to his ribs, he had a short moment of respite, but as the kisses trailed down his belly, he guessed her intentions, and the moment was gone.

"Morelle, don't."

She tilted her head to look at him. "You said I can do whatever I please to you."

He hadn't expected a virgin to be so bold. "I did, but not this. I should please you that way first."

She tilted her head sideways. "Is there a rule book that dictates such things?"

Well, yeah, there was—a gentleman pleased his lady first—but even in his own head, it sounded chauvinistic.

What about her inexperience?

He could use that.

"I know about carnal pleasures more than you do. I should be the one to teach you."

She laughed, which was the last thing he had expected. "I don't have the same equipment, so I doubt you can teach me how to please you."

When her fingers curled on the waistband of his pajama bottoms, and she pulled, he had no choice but to lift himself up and let her tug them down his hips.

"Oh, wow." She leaned back. "I didn't expect it to be this big."

There wasn't even an iota of fear in her tone, but Brandon didn't trust the earpieces to transmit her reaction accurately.

"Perhaps it was too early for the reveal." Finally letting his hands leave his head, he reached down and tugged on the waistband.

She put her hand over his to stop him. "You are perfect all over, Brandon, and now that I have had a moment to adjust my expectations, I will continue with my explorations." She took both of his hands and returned them over his head. "I think they should stay there."

He was speechless.

None of the females he'd been with had been so assertive with him, and they had been experienced.

His bossy princess was damn sexy.

Tucking his hands under his head, he lifted his legs when she pulled the pants all the way off him. "I hope you know what you're doing, Morelle. I'm very close to erupting, and I don't think you are ready for that."

She leaned up on her knees and laid a finger on his lips. "I know everything there is to know in theory, and now I'm implementing what I've learned." She removed her finger, replacing it with her lips.

When she slid her tongue into his mouth, he

didn't allow her to wrap it around his fangs and instead pushed it back and entered her mouth.

If she touched his fangs, it would be game over.

She leaned away, and the challenge in her expression should have prepared him for what she was about to do, but he once again underestimated her boldness.

Gripping the lacy hem of her nightdress, she lifted it over her head in one swift motion and threw it behind her.

Her breasts were just as he remembered them from last night, small but perfect and topped with dark nipples that stood erect and begged to be sucked.

He hadn't gotten nearly enough of them last night.

Before he could decide what to do next, Morelle cupped her breasts and started undulating her hips, her panty-covered lower lips rubbing over his exposed erection and coating it with the moisture that soaked through the fabric.

"I'm warning you, Princess. You are playing with a volcano that is about to erupt."

She let out a throaty laugh, scooted back, and let go of one of her breasts to run her hand over his shaft. "I love the way you feel. Hard and soft at the same time." She closed her fingers around it. "You are so thick and long. I wonder how you are going to fit inside of me."

"Very carefully," he hissed from between his fully elongated fangs.

"I want to taste you." She dipped her head and flicked her tongue over the head, lapping up the drop of moisture that had gathered there.

He bucked, imploring his rising seed to recede and allow him a few more moments of this excruciating pleasure.

Morelle licked him again and then lowered her mouth over the tip.

Brandon's eyes rolled back in his head, and when she took more of him into her mouth, he had an out-of-body experience.

"Princess, I'm about to come in your mouth."

He expected her to back off, but instead, she sucked him hard and, at the same time, squeezed the base of his shaft with her hand.

He exploded, his fangs dripping venom as he spilled down her throat.

She swallowed as he came, and when he was spent, she licked him as if she was hungry for every last drop.

He didn't give her a chance, gripping her waist and flipping them over. He needed to bite her, and he couldn't wait, even though the sequence was all wrong.

Smiling, Morelle tilted her head to the side and exposed her neck. "Do it. Bite me, Brandon."

36

MORELLE

When Brandon's fangs pierced Morelle's neck, pleasure unlike anything she'd ever experienced flooded her system. The venom flowed through her veins like liquid starlight, and suddenly, she was floating, drifting through a kaleidoscope of colors and sensations.

She saw herself as a child in the temple, but instead of the strict environment she remembered, the walls were covered in flowering vines. Her younger self danced free and unveiled through corridors that sparkled with rainbow light, her laughter echoing off the crystal walls. The head priestess's severe robes transformed into butterfly wings, and she soared away into an aurora-lit sky.

The scene shifted, and she was running through the village streets, but they were paved with stardust. Every house she passed glowed with warmth, and she could see the love between mates as visible threads of golden light connecting them.

Time seemed meaningless as she floated through these visions. She saw Ell-rom and Jasmine surrounded by children with her brother's blue eyes. She watched Annani reunite with Khiann in a garden where the flowers sang, and the trees danced. She glimpsed her mother, young and beautiful, weaving protective spells of rainbow light around her and Ell-rom's pods.

Then the visions grew more abstract—fractals of light that twisted into impossible shapes, colors that had no names, music she could see, and light she could taste. Through it all, she felt Brandon's presence like a tether, keeping her from drifting too far into these spectacular worlds.

When she finally opened her eyes, she found herself cradled in Brandon's arms, her body relaxed, and her mind peaceful in a way she had never experienced before.

The room was filled with early morning light, and they were both dressed in their night clothes, which meant that Brandon had put her nightgown on her while she was soaring on the wings of fantasy.

"Welcome back, Princess," he murmured, brushing a kiss across her forehead. "How was your trip?"

She smiled dreamily, the echoes of those magnificent visions swimming through her mind and leaving her languid. "Indescribable. Margo and Frankie and the others told me about their trips, but mine was nothing like theirs."

"What did you see?"

As she described her visions, he listened with a smile on his face, and when she told him about her mother's rainbow spells, she could still see traces of that magical light when she closed her eyes.

"I've heard many descriptions of venom trips, and yours was more vivid and unusual than all of them."

"Maybe it's because I'm part goddess?" She settled more comfortably against him, feeling deeply satisfied.

"Maybe." He pressed a gentle kiss to the top of her head. "Or maybe you're just special."

Morelle smiled, remembering how the venom had made her feel completely connected to everything—past, present, and future, all existing simultaneously in a beautiful dance of light and love. "Thank you for not fighting me off too hard and showing me this."

His arms tightened around her. "I should be the one thanking you. You've given me pleasure without asking for anything other than a bite."

She closed her eyes, savoring the perfect contentment of the moment.

Back on her home planet, she'd never imagined that simple physical contact could carry so much meaning and make her feel so complete.

"What are you thinking about?" Brandon murmured against her temple, his hands tracing soothing patterns along her spine.

"How different everything is here." She pressed closer, breathing in his familiar scent. "I don't need to tell you what I was taught about sex back home. You have Kra-ell living among you."

His arms tightened around her. "I'm not privy to their practices, but I heard it's brutal." He chuckled. "It's not something I want to be talking about while enjoying this moment with you."

"You're right." Morelle smiled, remembering her mother's words in her dream. "Mother told me to wake up and live. To experience everything life has to offer." Her hands traced the contours of his chest, feeling his heart racing beneath her palm. "This is what she meant, and she was right about it being worth living for."

"Your mother was a wise female. She wanted you to know love, to feel a connection, to experience joy."

"Is that what this is?" Morelle asked. "Love?"

Instead of answering, Brandon kissed her with such tenderness that tears pricked at her eyes. This wasn't just desire or passion—this was something deeper, more profound.

When he finally pulled back, his eyes held a vulnerability she'd never seen before. "I want to tell you that I love you, Morelle, and that I've loved you since I first saw you, but it's too early, and I don't want to overwhelm you, so let's pretend that I didn't say anything yet."

It was such a silly thing to do, but at the same time, Morelle knew exactly what he meant.

She wanted to tell him that she loved him too, but it felt premature, and she wanted him to know how she felt about him without fully committing to it yet.

Love was a big deal between immortals and gods. It meant literally forever, and they should be completely and irrevocably sure that was what they were feeling before promising it to each other.

"I want to tell you that I love you too, but I also want to wait to be sure that what I feel is forever."

"My smart, beautiful princess." He lifted her hand and kissed her fingers, one at a time.

She leaned in and pressed a kiss over his heart. "The Mother of All Life or the Fates guided me to you. You are the best thing to ever happen to me."

"I feel the same." As he lowered his mouth to hers again, Morelle gave herself over to the sensations.

It felt like coming home.

37

BRANDON

"This is incredible," Morelle breathed as she took in William's sprawling laboratory complex, her hand squeezing Brandon's in excitement.

Her blue eyes were wide with wonder as she scanned the rows of gleaming equipment, the wall-mounted screens, and the various setups scattered throughout the space.

William practically preened at the praise. "Most of this is custom-built," he said, gesturing at a particularly complex array of machinery. "We develop most of the tech ourselves."

"Standard human technology doesn't quite meet our needs," Kaia said as she rose to her feet and extended her hand to Morelle with a bright smile. "I'm Kaia, William's mate, but that's not why I'm here. I'm a researcher, and I just use William's space to do my work."

Brandon appreciated that Kaia hadn't explained what kind of a researcher she was. He doubted that Morelle would have understood what a bioinformatician was.

The truth was that he hadn't known about that field of study before Kaia joined the clan, and he still didn't understand exactly what she did. He wasn't in the least scientifically inclined.

"What do you research?" Morelle asked as she shook Kaia's hand.

Well, so much for that.

He knew what Kaia was researching, but most clan members were under the impression that Kaia was working with Bridget to find the secret to what made them immortals. Only the council members and Annani's family knew that she was working on deciphering Okidu's journals. If she succeeded, the clan would know how to build more cyborgs like the Odus and, as a side bonus, discover how to turn any human immortal.

Those were lofty goals that Brandon wasn't sure how to feel about. Both offered remarkable benefits but also could lead to catastrophic results.

"I'm a special type of medical researcher," Kaia said. "I combine biology, computer science, and statistics to analyze large biological data sets and use that to solve various problems in healthcare and research."

Morelle smiled and nodded, but Brandon had a

feeling she understood very little of the description. "It sounds exciting," she said.

"It is." Kaia returned her smile. "Would you like a tour? I can show you where we're assembling the Perfect Match machines, which is what everyone is most excited about seeing, and I can also show you some of our other innovative projects."

Morelle glanced at Brandon. "I would love that. Do you want to come?"

"I've already seen all that, but you go ahead. I need to discuss Parker's ideas with William."

"Oh, that." She waved a dismissive hand. "I didn't understand most of it the first time you told me about it, and I doubt I'll understand more the second time around. I'd rather go with Kaia."

"Have fun." He kissed her cheek and then watched her go.

"So," William said. "I'm curious to hear Parker's ideas."

As Brandon outlined Parker's concept for the blockchain-secured, AI-driven truth verification system, he could see William's expression shifting from interest to concern to outright skepticism.

"It's an interesting idea," William said, running a hand through his perpetually disheveled hair. "But there are some serious challenges to consider."

"I figured as much." Brandon leaned against a nearby workbench. "Walk me through them in as simple terms as you can manage?"

William nodded thoughtfully. "First, let's talk

about the fundamental concept of a centralized truth repository. Even with blockchain security, you're creating a single point of failure—not in terms of tech, but in terms of authority. Who decides what constitutes truth?"

"The AI would be programmed to be impartial," Brandon said, playing devil's advocate even though he deferred to William's expertise.

"And there's problem number two." William leaned against an untidy desk and crossed his arms over his chest. "Training an AI to be truly impartial is practically impossible. Every dataset we use would carry inherent biases. Even if we make the training data and algorithms completely transparent, we can't eliminate bias entirely."

"Parker suggested having the community verify the AI's impartiality."

"Which brings us to problem number three." William lifted his finger to push his antiglare glasses up his nose. "Who is this community? How do we ensure they have the expertise to evaluate AI systems? How do we prevent bad actors from gaming the verification process?" He shook his head. "Look at what happens with cryptocurrency. The technology is solid, but human nature finds ways to corrupt even the most secure systems."

"So, you're saying it's impossible?"

"Not impossible," William corrected. "Just impractical with current technology. The computational power required to run a blockchain system on that scale would be enormous. And that's before we even get into the philosophical questions about what constitutes truth in situations where facts are open to interpretation."

Brandon's enthusiasm for the idea was fading fast. "What if we started with something smaller and focused on specific types of verifiable facts? Things that are less susceptible to misinterpretation?"

William's expression turned thoughtful. "That might be more manageable. We could start with easily verifiable data points like statistics, historical dates, and scientific facts and build up from there. The blockchain could work for that scale, especially if we limit the initial scope. But frankly, that's not economically viable for the purpose you intend it for."

"There must be a way to supply verified information to help young humans develop critical thinking skills," Brandon said. "If we give them tools to recognize manipulation and misinformation, we will safeguard the world from tyranny. There is tremendous value in that."

William rubbed his chin for several long moments. "No matter how noble a goal is, if it doesn't have real-world commercial use, it will not secure funding. But what you want to achieve does not require an ultimate arbiter of truth. It would have been nice to have that, but it's just not feasible currently." William shifted and crossed his legs at the ankles. "We could develop a system that is trained to flag manipulation tactics, provide context for claims, and show how information can be verified independently."

"You just said that an ultimate arbiter of truth is not possible."

"It's not." William grimaced. "But even what I suggested needs significant computing power. The AI wouldn't need to determine truth, just identify patterns of manipulation and provide tools for users to investigate claims themselves. The final analysis would remain the responsibility of the truth seeker."

How many would bother?

Too few to make it worth the effort.

It was much easier to defer to the various so-called experts or rather influencers. Social media had revived the old snake oil salesmanship with a twist and much larger audiences.

It was a goldmine for those who knew how to use it.

Still, Brandon wasn't ready to give up yet.

"What if we combined Parker's basic concept with social elements?" he suggested. "Create a platform where users can collaborate to investigate claims, with AI assistance but not AI judgment?"

"That has potential." William drummed his fingers on the desk. "We could use blockchain to secure the investigation process itself—verifying sources, tracking changes, preventing tampering.

The AI would act more like a research assistant than a judge. Still, it will require a lot of computing power that cannot be justified by even the most successful social platform." He smiled apologetically. "I'm sorry that I don't have better news for you."

"That's the nature of truth, right? Often, it is not what we want to hear, but we'd better listen instead of doing something stupid."

"True." William nodded.

Brandon pushed away from the bench he'd been leaning against. "Now for the other reason I brought Morelle over. She needs a phone and laptop like the one you provided for Ell-rom. The one with an artificial intelligence English teacher."

"Of course." William's expression brightened. "I've made some improvements to the AI teacher program since then. The language acquisition algorithms are even better now." He walked over to another desk and started opening drawers. "I've had both devices ready to be delivered for days, but I forgot about them. You did well by coming over and reminding me."

As Morelle and Kaia rejoined them, Morelle immediately launched into an enthusiastic description of everything she'd seen. "The Perfect Match machines are terrifying, with that big helmet thing that comes over the head, but Kaia said that the experience is amazing and that I should try it. She said that they have a new adventure that's called The World Tour. In three hours, I can visit most of Earth's greatest attractions, but it will feel as if I'm spending weeks on a guided tour."

Brandon hadn't been aware of that new adventure, but the truth was that he didn't like the idea of letting a machine take over his mind and put fake memories in there. "Sounds great, but I'll pass. On another note, William's going to set you up with your own phone and laptop," he told her. "Complete with an AI teacher to help you master English."

Morelle's initial disappointment at his lack of enthusiasm for trying the Perfect Match experience was replaced with excitement. "Like Ellrom's?"

"Even better," William said. "The new version is more advanced and adapts better to your learning style and pace. Let me show you."

38

MORELLE

Brandon's lack of enthusiasm for Perfect Match was puzzling. It was the kind of technology that the gods on Anumati might possess, but no Kra-ell had ever enjoyed.

Maybe things had changed since she'd left the home planet, and the Kra-ell had more access to the wonders of the gods, but back then they had lived quite primitively, even compared to how the humans on Earth lived now.

Was it thanks to Annani's drip-feeding of the gods' tech to the human world?

Would they have advanced as much on their own without the immortals' help?

The answers to these questions were important to her because if humans could achieve so much on their own, why hadn't the Kra-ell?

They had complained that the gods hadn't allowed them access to education, but then humans didn't study in the gods' institutions of higher learning either. They had developed their own.

Or maybe not.

Maybe it had been started by the rebel gods and then continued by Annani, who had undertaken her father's mission.

"Would you like to see the Perfect Match machines at work?" Kaia asked. "We have an entire section of the old village dedicated to the enterprise. I can continue the tour there."

"Can you?" Morelle's interest was piqued. "I'd love to see them, but I don't want to keep you from your important work."

Kaia waved a dismissive hand. "I need a break." She smiled at her mate. "Am I right to assume that you don't want to join us?"

William shook his head. "I wish I could, love, but you go ahead."

Kaia blew him an air kiss and headed toward the elevators. "Two houses contain the machines themselves, one in each bedroom. The third house serves as office space. Toven and Mia work there, along with their ever-expanding crew. Now that Margo and Frankie have moved to the village, they've joined the Perfect Match team. Soon, we will need to dedicate another house to the enterprise."

"Or build a new office building," Brandon grumbled. "The village already looks like a patchwork of unplanned communities. Kian's vision for the place didn't anticipate Kalugal and his crew joining us, then the Kra-ell, and then Toven deciding that he wanted to buy Perfect Match and run it from the village. We should probably start looking for a new location."

Morelle wondered if his sudden sour mood was because of what he'd talked with William about while she was touring the lab with Kaia, or because she was excited about trying out a Perfect Match adventure while he seemed reluctant to do so.

After last night, she'd expected him to be walking on a cloud, and in the morning he had been, but now he seemed to be walking underneath it, and instead of a fluffy white one, it was dark and gloomy.

Morelle didn't like it.

It made her stomach feel uneasy as if she was expecting something bad to happen.

Was that normal?

Was it natural for couples to be so sensitive to each other's moods?

Brandon's frown deepened. "We don't have much time. Morelle has an appointment with Gertrude at the gym at one o'clock this afternoon."

"The whole tour won't take more than an hour," Kaia assured him. "We'll even have time for lunch at the café before that."

Morelle touched Brandon's arm. "I'd really like to see the Perfect Match operation. Margo,

Frankie, and Jasmine talked about it so much during Jasmine's party."

He softened immediately under her touch, as she'd known he would. "Whatever pleases you, my princess."

His smile and term of endearment immediately resolved the knot of anxiety in her stomach, and even though it was a relief not to feel it, she didn't like that he had such a strong effect on her.

It shouldn't be like that.

As they stepped out of the glass pavilion, Brandon started toward one of the carts parked in the front, but Kaia shook her head. "It's a five-minute walk."

"Morelle is still recuperating." He continued to the vehicle.

"I'd rather walk." Morelle stayed next to Kaia. "It's a beautiful day, and I feel strong."

She loved walking through the village, feeling the sun and the breeze on her face. Brandon had insisted on taking the cart from Annani's house earlier, and while the open-air ride had been pleasant enough, she preferred using her own legs.

Soon, Morelle hoped to be strong enough to run. She'd seen people running through the village path just to enjoy the activity, and not because they needed to get somewhere fast or get away from something in a rush.

The idea appealed to her, and she wanted to try it.

There were so many things she wanted to try, and she wouldn't let anything or anyone stand in her way.

She was proud of how she'd managed to break through Brandon's stubborn resistance last night and give him pleasure as he'd given her.

And then that bite...

The pleasure of it...

The euphoria...

Her body tingled, remembering it. She couldn't wait to experience another venom-induced trip.

"What's that smile about?" Brandon took her hand.

"Nothing," she said innocently, but her smile gave her away, and his knowing look sent warmth spreading through her chest.

When they arrived at the first Perfect Match house, an immortal female rose to her feet and walked over to greet them.

"Councilman Brandon, Princess Morelle, and Kaia. To what do I owe the honor of your visit?"

"The princess wanted to tour the Perfect Match operation," Kaia said. "She's heard a lot about it from Margo, Frankie, and Jasmine."

Morelle wanted to ask everyone to stop calling her a princess and just call her Morelle, but then she noticed that the female didn't have translating earpieces.

Fortunately, she'd planned ahead for the possibility that some people didn't have them and brought the teardrop with her.

She pulled it out of her purse, hung the string around her neck, and activated the device.

"Please, call me Morelle. I'm not really a princess."

"Welcome, Morelle. I'm Sarah," the woman said. "What would you like to know about the Perfect Match experience?"

"If someone wants to go on an adventure, what's the process?"

"Everything starts with our comprehensive questionnaire. It not only helps us find ideal matches for participants but also allows us to customize each virtual experience to the participant's specific desires and comfort level." She smiled. "Some people are risk averse, while others are adrenaline junkies. Imagine how difficult it is to match an adventure for a couple when one wants nothing more exciting than a cozy mystery, while the other wants *Jurassic Park*."

Morelle didn't know what either of those things were, but she could imagine one was timid and the other not. "How do you resolve the conflict?"

"I don't," Sarah grinned. "Thankfully, it is all done by the algorithm. All I have to do is check whether the questionnaire was completed and help the participants choose an avatar." She leaned to whisper conspiratorially. "You can choose to be someone else entirely. We have a mer adventure that happens underwater so you will get a fishtail, or a futuristic world adventure where people choose all kinds of physical enhancements. Wings are, of course, the most popular."

"Of course," Morelle parroted.

She wouldn't have minded trying on wings. It sounded like fun.

"Let's sit down." Sarah led them to a seating area. "We have brochures you can leaf through and get a feel for the kind of adventure that appeals to you." She continued to give more detail about couples' adventures, solo adventures, and training modules, and she finished by explaining why the service was called Perfect Match. "The main purpose of the service is to find people who match each other perfectly. That's why we have such a detailed questionnaire."

"Could I see it?" Morelle asked.

Brandon tensed beside her. "It's in English. You won't be able to read it."

"Then it will be excellent motivation to learn quickly." She turned to Sarah. "Do you have one you can spare?"

The female smiled. "I can send you a link so you can download it. All I need is your email address."

Morelle cast a helpless glance at Brandon. "Do I have something like that?"

He let out a breath and pulled her new laptop

out of his bag. "This belongs to Morelle. You can airdrop the questionnaire."

Sarah nodded, took the laptop, and did something with her phone that Morelle assumed had to do with the questionnaire. "It is quite extensive," Sarah said. "And some of the questions are quite intrusive. Take your time with it."

Morelle chuckled. "Given that I need to learn English first, it will take a while."

On her other side, Kaia cleared her throat. "Not really. You don't have to wait. You can ask the AI to translate the questions for you, you can tell it your answers, and it will fill them in for you."

Morelle's heart fluttered as the prospect of experiencing a Perfect Match adventure seemed within reach. "Thank you. That's awesome. I'll probably get to it this evening."

This time, Brandon was the one to clear his throat. "Amanda is coming over to conduct more tests."

"Right. Then I'll get to it tomorrow." Morelle rose to her feet. "Thank you, Sarah."

"Take some brochures." Sarah handed her a bunch. "I know you can't read them, but you can look at the pictures."

When they stepped outside into the sunshine, Kaia chuckled. "I didn't want to embarrass Sarah, but you can easily read the brochures with the help of your laptop. I'll show you how when we get to the café."

As they continued to the house where the offices were located, Morelle noticed that Brandon's frown hadn't gone anywhere and had only gotten worse.

"What's wrong?"

He ran a hand through his hair. "Do you need the algorithm to tell you whether we are a perfect match or not?"

The question was so unexpected that it made Morelle laugh, but she immediately regretted it when she saw the flash of hurt across his face. "Oh, Brandon, no! That's not why I wanted to fill out the questionnaire."

"Then why?"

"Because I want to try a Perfect Match adventure." She squeezed his hand. "I'll go solo if you don't want to share it with me. There seem to be endless possibilities, and I'm so excited to try out as many of them as I can."

His mouth twisted in a wince. "You want to do it all without me?"

Something in his tone made her feel uneasy. "Being a couple doesn't mean we have to do everything together or enjoy all the same things, right?" She shook her head, feeling like this was such an obvious thing that any reasonable adult should realize it. "You're supposed to be the experienced one. You should know that."

Kaia let out a small laugh. "Should I give you two some privacy for your first couple's spat?"

"We're not having a spat," Brandon protested. "It was just a misunderstanding."

"In what way?" Morelle arched an eyebrow at him. "To me, it seemed like you got upset because I wanted to try something on my own."

He let out a long breath. "I'm not upset. I just worry about you."

"Why? The machines are perfectly safe, right?" She looked to Kaia for confirmation.

"Completely safe," Kaia assured them. "And all experiences are carefully calibrated to each participant's comfort level. That's what the questionnaire is for."

Brandon's expression remained troubled. "It's not about safety, exactly. I know these things are supposed to be safe, but I don't like the idea of a machine taking over my mind and planting false memories in my brain. I don't understand why more people are not concerned about that. It's naive to put so much trust in those machines. I've just spent an hour listening to William explain how it was impossible to keep information clean of corruption. Do we really want to run the risk that the corruption will spread to our brains?"

Morelle sighed. "I might not understand much about it, but if thousands of people have tried it and nothing happened to them, I'm willing to risk it. You might be more risk-averse than I am, and that's fine. I will not force you to do anything you are not comfortable with."

He chuckled. "But you will do everything you can to coerce me out of my comfort zone."

"I might." She took his hand. "And you can stubbornly refuse to leave it, and I promise not to get angry."

Kaia cleared her throat. "This is sweet and all, but we should probably continue the tour if we want to make it to lunch before your Pilates session."

"Lead on. Unless..." She looked at Brandon. "Are we still having a spat?"

He cracked a smile. "It was not a spat."

"Just a misunderstanding. Got it." She stretched up to kiss his cheek. "Now, shall we see the rest of the operation?"

As they followed Kaia toward the second house, Morelle felt a surge of affection for Brandon. He might be centuries old, but in some ways, he was still learning too—learning to trust her judgment, to let her explore, and to accept that they would not always agree on everything.

39

BRANDON

Brandon's favorite spot in the village café was under the limbs of a massive oak tree that provided shade over the somewhat secluded table. He wasn't the only one who favored the spot, though, and he'd been lucky to have snagged it after escorting Morelle to her Pilates session.

The afternoon crowd had thinned out, leaving only a few other patrons scattered among the tables—mostly clan members who liked to work there and a couple of Kra-ell hybrids who preferred human food.

From his position, he had a clear view of the glass pavilion about a hundred feet away, where the elevators would bring Morelle up from the underground complex. The structure gleamed in the sunshine, and its modern architecture was in stark contrast to the more traditional styling of the residences in the village.

He'd approved the building plans along with the other council members, so he couldn't complain about the mismatching of styles, but if they ever decided to move somewhere else, he promised himself to pay more attention to what he was putting his signature on.

Before, he hadn't cared because he had not intended to spend much time in the village, but now...

Well, that depended on whether he managed not to blow things with Morelle. If she dumped him, which was starting to seem likely, he would go back to his condo in the city.

Brandon looked down at his untouched cappuccino and the patterns created by the shifting breeze on its surface—he then lifted his head and gazed at the open laptop and the notes about InstaTock displayed on the screen. He'd intended to work on incorporating William's suggestions, but his mind kept circling back to his behavior earlier that day and the damn tantrum he'd thrown.

There was no other word for it. It had been a carefully controlled, outwardly calm tantrum, but a tantrum nonetheless, all because Morelle had wanted to try something he wasn't a fan of.

Brandon ran a hand through his hair, catching

his reflection in his darkened tablet screen. The truth was this shouldn't have surprised him. He'd always been this way—controlling, demanding, absolutely certain that his way was the right way.

The only way.

After all, his reputation as a Hollywood shark had been well-earned. He hadn't gotten that nickname by being nice, mellow, and accommodating. He'd earned it by bulldozing over any opposition to his creative vision and being utterly confident that he knew better than anyone else what worked and what didn't.

During Morelle's coma and her initial recovery, his protective instincts had surfaced, overshadowing his other tendencies, so all she had seen was the gentle side of him, the nurturing side that he hadn't been aware of having. He'd been focused solely on her well-being and providing whatever she needed.

His usual controlling inclinations had lain dormant.

But now that she was recovering her strength and demonstrating her resilience, she was starting to assert her independence. Well, the shark was swimming back to the surface.

"Asshole," he muttered into his cooling cappuccino, though he supposed the more fashionable term these days was alpha-hole.

Either way, he needed to do better.

Much better.

If he didn't learn to compromise—and fast—he might lose her.

The thought sent a chill through him despite the warm California day. Morelle wasn't some Hollywood executive who could be intimidated into compliance or an actor who could be charmed or coerced into following his vision to the letter. She had her own mind and her own vision of how she wanted to lead her life, and if he tried to stifle her independence and her drive, she might choose to walk away instead of fighting for what she wanted.

"Can I get you anything else?" Marina appeared at his elbow, coffee pot in hand.

"No, thanks." He gestured at his full cup. "Still working on this one."

She gave him a knowing look. "How is Princess Morelle doing?"

"Getting stronger in every way."

"I'm glad to hear that." She moved on to the next table.

Brandon turned his attention back to the glass pavilion, and a movement caught his eye. Morelle emerged from the elevator, her lithe silhouette moving with a sensual sway of her hips. Her stride was growing more confident with each passing day.

When she walked out the pavilion doors, he

stood and smiled as she approached his table. "Had a good session?"

"Yes." She stretched, and his mouth went dry at the graceful movement. "Gertrude says I'm making excellent progress."

"You are. Would you like a cup of coffee? Something to eat?"

She chuckled. "We had lunch less than an hour ago. We should head back."

He cleared his throat. "Would you like to stop on the way at my house? It's not far from Annani's."

Her eyes lit up. "Yes, of course, I would."

They walked toward the waiting cart they'd used that morning. Brandon was sure she was tired, but he wasn't going to take anything for granted anymore.

"If you prefer, we can walk. Someone else will take the cart."

"I would," she smiled. "I might need a rest or two on the way, but we have plenty of time before Amanda is due to show up at Annani's with more tests for me."

He hesitated. "You are already tired, and after the long walk, you will be exhausted. Do you really want to push yourself like that before attempting to use your power again?"

Morelle let out a breath. "You're right. I don't want my performance to be compromised. Let's take the cart."

His relief for having gotten such a minor

concession out of Morelle was too great, but it was proof that she was reasonable and willing to listen.

After helping her to the cart, he drove over the village paths, going slower than usual due to the pedestrians who were out in force this time of day.

"It's busy out here," Morelle commented. "Where is everyone going?"

"The gym, the café, to visit other people. Most of those who work from home are done by this time. Immortals are much faster than humans and get more done in the same time frame."

"Interesting." Morelle smiled and waved back at someone.

When they reached his home, he helped her down from the cart, and for a long moment, she just looked at the front yard and the house's façade.

"It's beautiful," she said.

He chuckled. "You don't have to say that. My house is almost identical to Annani's."

"Her house is beautiful as well." Morelle took the hand he offered and let him lead her to the front door and then inside. "It's so big." She turned to look at him. "And you live here all alone?"

He nodded. "For now. I hope that soon you will join me."

"It's large even for two people."

Morelle hadn't said no, and relief flooded him. She was open to the idea of moving in with him.

"Do you want me to show you the rooms?"

She nodded.

As they toured the four bedroom suites, she checked out every bathroom and walk-in closet, and when they were done, she stopped in the middle of the hallway. "Would you consider having Ell-rom and Jasmine move in with us? Your house is huge, and I would like to have my brother close by."

Brandon's initial reaction was an immediate, visceral no. He'd lived alone for centuries and was so used to having privacy that the idea of sharing his home with anyone who wasn't his mate made him acutely uncomfortable.

But then he remembered his earlier resolution. This was exactly the kind of situation where he needed to compromise to accommodate the wishes of his mate. If he wanted to enjoy the bliss of matehood, he had to give up some of the privileges of bachelorhood.

As the saying goes, he couldn't have his cake and eat it too.

"That could work," he said, trying to inject enthusiasm into his voice. "There's certainly enough room, but weren't you concerned about living with Jasmine and having to share your brother with her?"

Morelle shrugged. "I like Jasmine. She's okay. Besides, someone will need to cook, and I assume it's not going to be you."

He laughed. "Good point, but don't say that to

Jasmine. She will think that you are only inviting her and Ell-rom to stay with us because of that."

"She said so herself. I'm just repeating her offer to you to sweeten the deal."

Chuckling, he pulled her into his arms. "It seems that I've been outmaneuvered."

40

DROVA

Drova ran the polishing cloth over her boots for what must have been the hundredth time that day, studying her reflection in the gleaming black leather. The boots were identical to the ones her mother wore, which was why she'd almost never worn them, but they were what the Guardian force used, and she wanted to look the part.

"Drova!" Her mother's voice carried through the house. "We need to leave in five minutes."

She glanced at her watch. The meeting was in half an hour, and it took no more than ten minutes to get to the training center, but her mother believed in arriving early rather than risking being late.

Tardiness implied disrespect in her mother's rulebook.

"Coming!" Drova gave the boots one final swipe before pulling them on.

The all-black outfit she'd chosen might also seem like an attempt to impersonate a Guardian, but that was what she and Jade usually wore. Now that Drova was the same height as her mother, she often took clothes from her closet.

Jade didn't mind.

Glancing at her reflection in the glass doors of her bedroom, Drova took a deep breath, smoothed her hand over her ponytail, and turned to walk out the door.

This meeting with Onegus and Peter could change everything for her. There would be no more endless hours of studying human history, no more being treated like a kid by the older Kra-ell and a suspect by everyone else.

But first, Onegus and Peter had to accept her.

"These boots never looked shinier," Phinas said, his tone teasing. "But if you keep it up, you'll make a hole in them."

"I won't." She cast her mother's mate a smile. "Wish me luck."

"Good luck, Drova." He clapped her back. "But you need to remember that it's just a preliminary meeting, and there is no guarantee you'll get in. They're only going to assess you."

She nodded. "I want this, Phinas. This could be my chance to actually do something meaningful. To prove myself."

His expression softened. "We spend our lives proving ourselves. It's not a sprint, it's a marathon, and if you don't get this assignment, there will be others. You are a capable fighter, you are smart, and you are a damn powerful compeller. They need you."

"I know, but they think of me as the troublemaker who can't be trusted."

He shrugged. "Actions have consequences, kid. That's life."

Drova let out a breath. "Even my mother doesn't trust me."

"Drova." Jade walked into the living room. "We need to be out the door right now."

"Time to go." Phinas clapped her back again. "Remember to be honest about your abilities and your willingness to learn. That's all they're looking for."

Easy for him to say. He wasn't the one who had to convince the clan's leadership that she could be trusted on a mission outside the village.

Dear Mother of All Life, how she wanted the opportunity to prove herself.

Jade opened the front door, her expression neutral, but Drova knew her mother was anxious. If she messed up or said something stupid, it would reflect badly on Jade.

Already, the stunt she had pulled with the teenagers was undermining her mother's position as the leader of the Kra-ell. Pavel had told her that people were gossiping, saying that Jade was unfit to lead them because she couldn't even keep her own daughter under control.

Control was everything to the Kra-ell, and the idiots should realize that she had the ultimate power to control them all if she so pleased. Once she took over from her mother, they wouldn't be able to even think those nasty thoughts, let alone say them.

Only that was far into the future because Drova was too young to lead, and Jade was too young to quit and pass the role to someone else. The idiots should count their blessings for having her mother as their leader. Jade was just the right combination of strict and moderate, and she listened to their stupid grievances.

Igor would have just squashed them under his boot like the bugs they were.

A shiver ran down her spine as the image of his face appeared in her mind. He had been more of a machine than the damned Odus. There had been no life in those dead eyes of his. He'd never gotten angry, but he'd never been happy either. She'd never seen him smiling a genuine smile.

Not at her anyway.

Igor could rot in that stasis coffin for all she cared. He'd never been a father to her, and she'd only realized that having one was nice when Phinas had mated her mother.

Not that he pretended to be her father or asked her to call him Dad or anything. But he was there when she needed him, and he was a pleasant presence in their house, which Drova couldn't even say about her own mother.

As they passed the administration building, the front door opened, and Kian emerged.

"Good afternoon." He fell into step beside them.

"Good afternoon," Jade said.

Drova dipped her head. "Thank you for giving me this opportunity."

"Don't thank me yet," Kian replied. "This meeting is just a brainstorming session to see how your unique talents can be utilized for the new types of missions we have in mind. There are many factors that need to be considered, and your natural ability is just one of them."

Drova had no problem reading between the lines.

They could use her compulsion ability, maybe even her fighting skills, but she hadn't trained with the Guardians, and she was considered unreliable.

It was a huge surprise that Kian had even thought of her for those new missions, whatever they might be. They would want to assess her ability to follow orders without question.

As they entered the pavilion and her mother called up the elevator, Drova's heartbeat accelerated.

This was where she belonged, not buried in books. She was a warrior, like her mother, like all their people. She just needed the chance to prove it.

41

PETER

Peter leaned against one of the desks in the classroom that Onegus had chosen for this interview, trying to find a diplomatic way to tell Kian that he was out of his mind.

Drova? On his team? The same Drova who had used her compulsion ability to manipulate others for her own amusement, who was wearing a location cuff because they had to restrict her movement so she couldn't compel anyone else?

Furthermore, ever since becoming the victim of Emmett's compulsion, Peter had preferred to stay away from compellers. He'd made his peace with Emmett, but that didn't mean that he liked spending time with the guy.

He watched as the young Kra-ell sat ramrod straight in her chair, dressed in tactical-style black clothing that made her look like she was cosplaying as a Guardian.

There was a hardness to her and a determination that showed potential, but she had only recently turned seventeen, which was too young to even enter the Guardian training program, let alone go on missions.

"Let's be clear about what we're discussing," he said carefully, making sure that he sounded measured and respectful. "You want me to consider adding an untrained seventeen-year-old to a team that's going after some of the vilest predators on Earth?"

Kian met his gaze steadily. "Her ability to compel immortals could be invaluable if we encounter Doomers."

"If," Peter emphasized. "And that's assuming she can control her ability under pressure and direct it at the enemy instead of targeting her teammates. Assuming she can follow orders. Assuming she has the maturity to handle what we're going to encounter and not fall apart." He shook his head. "That's a lot of assumptions to risk Guardian lives on."

Jade shifted in her chair but remained silent.

Peter could read the conflict in her expression—pride in her daughter's potential being acknowledged by Kian and Onegus warring with concern for her safety.

Onegus, who had been quietly observing from where he was leaning against another desk, folded his arms over his chest. "Drova's compulsion ability is stronger than Toven's. If properly directed, it could be an indispensable asset. I understand your reservations but try to imagine for a moment that you could take Toven with you on every mission. Wouldn't you be thrilled to have such a weapon in your arsenal? We couldn't have taken Igor's compound down without him."

It was probably not smart to contradict the chief, but as a newly minted Head Guardian, Peter was allowed more leeway than the rest of the rank and file. "I agree that Toven was invaluable to that mission, but his role was to infiltrate and gather information. He wasn't needed for the actual attack on the compound. Compulsion, unless it can be used as a blanket over the enemy, is not a good tactical weapon."

Kian shook his head. "You forget that the Kra-ell are resistant to all types of mind manipulation, which was why Toven's compulsion was useless in the attack on the compound. But if those were Doomers, he would have been a great help. Except for the rare immune, whoever heard Toven's voice would have been compelled to obey his commands."

Peter would have liked to forget how it felt to be the victim of compulsion, and he would have preferred not to work with the vile power if he didn't have to.

"We're going on our first mission Tuesday night. I can't risk taking an inexperienced girl."

He was getting married on Sunday, and he planned on taking Monday off to celebrate with his bride. He didn't have time to train a greenhorn.

A knock at the door signaled Pavel's arrival. Peter had asked the young Kra-ell to join the discussion because he was assigned to the backup team of the first Avenger mission, and he knew Drova well.

After she'd compelled him to eat dirt, he shouldn't have the best opinion about her.

"Come in, Pavel," Peter called out.

"Did you invite him to come?" Jade asked.

He nodded. "Pavel is going out on the first Avenger mission. I wanted his opinion on Drova."

When Pavel entered, he took up a position near Drova but maintained a professional distance, or maybe he was just still wary of her.

"Hi," he said to her.

To Peter's surprise, the girl blushed and smiled. "Hi."

"I invited you to hear your opinion of Drova," Peter said. "Onegus and Kian think that her compulsion ability might be useful on our missions because we suspect Doomers are involved in this vile trade. Personally, I think she is much too young and lacks experience."

Hopefully, the young Kra-ell would understand what Peter wanted him to say and not try to be a wise guy.

"Drova is one of the best fighters I've ever

trained with," Pavel said. "She was trained by Jade since she was old enough to hold a stick, and her combat skills are exceptional, even by Kra-ell standards. I have no problem with her joining our team."

Damn. That wasn't what Peter had wanted him to say.

"Combat skills aren't the issue." Peter shifted on the desk. "This isn't just about fighting ability. We're going to be dealing with situations that would challenge even experienced warriors psychologically, and Drova has lived a sheltered life. I know it wasn't easy in Igor's compound, but as his daughter, I'm sure she didn't suffer as much as the others."

"I didn't get any preferential treatment, sir," Drova interjected. "I'm tough, and I can handle myself."

Peter studied her for a moment. The girl had spirit. He'd give her that. But spirit without discipline was dangerous. "You lack the discipline this kind of work requires. I cannot and will not put my team in jeopardy by adding a loose cannon to the mix."

"I'm not—" Drova started to protest, but Peter cut her off.

"You need training."

"Despite the pranks she pulled, I think that Drova has a lot of self-control, and she's a good person, and her heart is in the right place." Pavel paused. "Still, we should probably tell her what we are going up against first."

After Peter nodded, Pavel told Drova about the pedophile rings, and he didn't mince words. He gave her an unedited version that would have turned the stomachs of most adults.

At first, Drova's eyes flashed red, and then her fangs elongated. "I'll tear them apart with my bare fangs and drain their blood."

The vehemence in her voice was scary, and everyone in the room, save for Jade and Pavel, was taken aback.

Jade beamed with pride, and Pavel smiled as if his best friend had just proven herself to be a badass.

Well, she had.

These Kra-ell were wonderfully vicious, which made them the perfect Avengers. Perhaps Peter needed to rethink future team compositions and make them mostly Kra-ell.

"I appreciate the sentiment," he said. "Still, Tuesday's operation is too soon. Everyone on the team knows their roles, their positions, and their responsibilities. I can't introduce a new variable at this stage."

"What if she observes only?" Kian suggested. "No direct involvement, just surveillance from a safe distance, let's say, the surveillance equipment van. It would give her a chance to see how the team operates, expose her to the filth, and give you a chance to evaluate her potential under real conditions."

Peter considered this. Having Drova observe wouldn't compromise the operation, and it would give him a chance to see how she handled herself in a high-stress situation, even if it was from a distance.

"She would need a Guardian to watch over her and ensure she stays in position and doesn't try to involve herself if things go wrong."

"I'll do it," Pavel volunteered.

"No." Peter shook his head. "You're needed on the perimeter team. The Guardian manning the surveillance will suffice."

"I don't need a babysitter," Drova protested.

"You need to be observed and evaluated," Peter said bluntly. "This is a test to see how you handle taking orders, staying in position, and dealing with the stress of watching without acting. All of that will factor into whether I consider you for future operations."

Kian nodded. "Agreed." He looked at Drova. "Those terms are non-negotiable."

"I accept the terms, sir." The girl was practically vibrating with barely contained energy, but she was making a visible effort to appear professional.

Maybe the idea of putting Drova on an Avengers team wasn't as crazy as Peter had initially thought.

Nevertheless, he still wasn't happy about it.

42

MORELLE

The delicious aromas wafting from the kitchen made Morelle's stomach rumble, but she was more focused on the warmth of Annani's hand in hers as they sat together on the couch. She wondered if her sister was getting tired of hosting dinner guests almost every evening.

The Odus did all the work, but it was still exhausting. At least for Morelle, but then she had spent her life in the temple in near isolation, and she wasn't used to being surrounded by people all the time.

Annani, on the other hand, loved company.

Over the last two days, Morelle had started to yearn for a little alone time. She loved having Brandon around, always ready to help her with whatever she needed, but she would have liked a little time away from him as well.

She just wanted to sit outside in Annani's backyard, close her eyes, lift her face to the sun, and enjoy the quiet.

"It must be tiring to have to entertain guests all day long," she told Annani.

Her sister squeezed her hand. "Not at all. I love having people over, especially close family. I entertain a lot wherever I am, whether it is here in the village, in my sanctuary in the snow, or at my daughter Sari's castle in Scotland. It is part of my job as the Clan Mother."

Annani had told her about her wondrous sanctuary, and the plan was for Morelle and Ell-rom and their mates to visit, but first, things needed to calm down, and the investigation of her and Ell-rom's special talents had to be completed.

It was important to find out the extent of their abilities and take appropriate precautions.

Across from them, Jasmine sat curled in an armchair, her forehead creased as she frowned at her laptop screen. Ell-rom, on Annani's other side, was equally absorbed in his own research about a place called Kurdistan, occasionally exchanging observations with Jasmine and sharing information.

They were both consumed with learning everything they could about the region where Syssi's vision had placed the woman they suspected was Jasmine's mother.

From the little tidbits of information Morelle had gathered listening to Jasmine and Ell-rom sharing what they were finding out, she felt sorry for the Kurdish people and empathized with their struggle. Multiple countries had conquered their lands long ago, and these invaders were still working to erase their culture and very existence.

Compared to their suffering, the ongoing conflict between gods and Kra-ell seemed almost civilized, which, given how offended any Kra-ell would be at being called anything other than savage, was quite a statement.

Brandon was also busy with his laptop, sitting in the other armchair, his fingers flying over his keyboard as he worked on something for his Insta-Tock project.

The sight of everyone absorbed in their screens made Morelle's fingers itch to explore her own new device. The English lessons William had installed were waiting for her, not to mention that intriguing Perfect Match questionnaire. If it weren't for Amanda's imminent arrival with more tests for her nullifying ability, she might have sneaked away to her room to start exploring the wonders stored inside the machine.

Another reason for her restlessness was the prospect of moving into Brandon's house. She still hadn't figured out how to tell Annani. The thought of leaving her sister made her chest tight with guilt, especially in moments like this when Annani's energy wrapped around her like the warm embrace of love.

As the doorbell's chime interrupted her thoughts, Ogidu emerged from the kitchen and rushed over to the front door.

Morelle heard him welcoming each guest by name: Amanda and Dalhu with little Evie and Syssi and Kian with Allegra, who immediately spotted Morelle and made a beeline for her with arms outstretched.

"Illy!" the little girl demanded, and Morelle gladly scooped her up, settling her between herself and Annani.

Two more couples entered behind them, and she rose to her feet to greet them.

Arwel she recognized from their previous testing session, but his mate Jin was new to her. She was a tall, striking woman with long dark hair and a mischievous smile. The other couple was no less impressive. Yamanu was a massive male with Kra-ell coloring and hair but with typical gorgeous immortal features and light eyes. His mate Mey, who was Jin's sister, was just as striking as Jin, if not more so.

There was something different about them, both in their looks and the energy they exuded.

"Jin and Mey are part Kra-ell and part immortal," Amanda explained. "They have some unique talents of their own, and they also run a clothing company specializing in fashion for tall women."

Something bloomed in Morelle's chest, and she felt an immediate kinship with the sisters. Two females who, like her, straddled two different worlds.

"I'm still learning about Earth fashion," Morelle said, grateful to see that both were wearing translation earpieces.

Jin's smile was warm. "We'd love to show you our designs sometime." She gave Morelle a thorough look-over. "Although you could make do with regular-sized clothing."

She chuckled. "Where I come from, clothing is still made to order. I mean on the Kra-ell side of the planet. The gods are big on mass production of goods like humans seem to be."

"Speaking of clothes," Amanda interjected, "do you have an evening dress for the wedding on Sunday?"

"I think so." Morelle tried to remember what Brandon had told her about each garment and what occasion it was appropriate for.

"Melinda got Morelle several options," Brandon said.

"Well, if you'd like to try something different, you're welcome to shop in my closet," Amanda offered with a wink. "We have a similar build, and I have quite a collection."

"That's very kind of you, Amanda, but I'm sure that what's hanging in my closet will do. Brandon's personal shopper did a great job picking out my clothing."

"Let's sort out dresses later," Syssi suggested.

"First, we should see if Morelle can nullify Jin and Mey's abilities. Their talents are quite different from what we've tested before."

"What are your talents?" Morelle asked the sisters.

"I can tether a string of my consciousness to anyone I touch," Jin said. "And once I'm connected, I can see and hear everything they hear and see in real-time. I make the perfect spy."

Morelle's eyes were peeled wide. "That's probably the most amazing talent I've heard about so far. And here I thought that Cassandra's ability to blow things up was astonishing."

Jin chuckled. "Wait until you hear what Mey can do."

Mey waved a dismissive hand. "My talent is not nearly as unique or useful as my sister's. I can hear echoes of conversations embedded in walls. Usually, only emotionally charged events leave echoes, and the more charged they are, the stronger the echo."

"Fascinating," Morelle said, already wondering how her nullifying ability would interact with such different powers.

She turned to Amanda. "How do you want to test it?"

"Hold on." Amanda waved over Mey's impressive mate. "Yamanu also has a unique talent. He can shroud and thrall entire cities. The problem is that he can only affect humans, so we can't really test your ability on him. I just wanted to introduce him properly."

Morelle dipped her head. "I'm duly impressed."

He cast her a bright smile.

"Dinner is ready," Annani said. "We should eat first."

43

DROVA

Drova could barely contain her excitement as she and Pavel headed for the door.

She was in!

Well, sort of.

Being relegated to observation wasn't exactly what she'd hoped for, but it was a foot in the door.

"If we encounter any Doomers," she said, practically bouncing on her toes, "I can freeze them in place. Or better yet, make them eat dirt." She winked at him.

Pavel snorted. "Or their dirty socks."

Even Peter, who was gathering his materials from the desk, cracked a smile at that. "Pavel, why don't you show Drova around the facility and introduce her to the team? Her training starts now."

Wow. She was really in.

"Let's go," Pavel said.

His professional demeanor was back in place, all hints of joking and familiarity gone. She needed to adapt her expectations now that they were working together, and she needed to get over her crush. Maybe in a few years, when she was over twenty and part of the Guardian force, he would start regarding her as a desirable female.

Or so she hoped.

She was still Igor's daughter and a powerful compeller, and who wanted a partner like that?

The thought dampened her exuberant mood over being provisionally accepted into the force. There was a good chance that she was destined to be shunned by all the males in the village, and if she ever wanted to get any action, she would have to do it the Kra-ell's old-fashioned way and issue an official invitation to the males she desired.

She wouldn't issue it to Pavel, though. Never. She would never want him to just service her as an obligation. With Pavel, Drova wanted everything. She wanted what her mother had with Phinas and what Vanessa had with Mo-red. They were proof that even purebloaded Kra-ell could form loving, exclusive relationships, but she would be the first to do so with one of her own and not an immortal.

It might not be fair because there were far more males than females, and if everyone paired up, many males would remain without partners, but that was a worry for another day. Perhaps the immortals would find a way to change the Kra-ell genetics and even out the birthrate ratio of males to females.

"This level has most of the classrooms," Pavel explained, pointing out various rooms as they passed. "Combat training, tactical planning, weapons instruction, explosive materials, and everything else a soldier needs to know."

"When do I start classes?" She sounded eager, but she couldn't help it.

Pavel's expression softened slightly, reminding her more of the friend who came to study with her and shared drinks with her, than the official Avenger. "There is a hand-to-hand class later this evening, and you are welcome to join. Before that, we can work out in the gym."

They descended another level, and the sound of gunfire reached her ears.

"That's the firing range," Pavel said, slipping back into instructor mode. "We train with both traditional weapons and some special accessories that William's team has developed."

Through a glass partition, Drova could see several Guardians practicing with what looked like standard-issue firearms. But as she watched, one of them picked up something that definitely wasn't store-bought and attached it to the gun.

"What is that?"

"A range enhancer," Pavel explained. When she leaned forward for a better look, he added, "You'll need extensive training before touching any of the advanced equipment."

They moved on to a large breakroom, complete with comfortable seating areas and a row of vending machines. "This is where the Guardians decompress between lectures and training sessions and sometimes after missions." Pavel walked over to one of the machines. "We even have one for our kind. It dispenses small packets of synthetic blood."

"It's cool," she said, taking it all in.

Drova wanted desperately to belong here, to be one of the warriors.

Then she remembered what he'd told her about their missions and the kind of monsters they would be hunting, and her eyes flooded with a red haze and her fangs elongated.

"What's wrong?" Pavel asked, his tone shifting from professional to concerned friend.

"I thought about what you told me about the missions." Her hands clenched into fists. "I want to tear those pedophiles apart with my bare fangs and claws. Make them suffer."

Pavel's expression hardened. "I understand how you feel. Believe me, we all do. But that's not how the clan operates. Our orders are to capture them for interrogation."

"Why bother?" With an effort, she forced her fangs to retract. "Why not just thrall them and be done with it? Any immortal could rip the information right out of the humans' heads."

"It's not that simple." Pavel guided her to one of the comfortable couches. "Thralling only accesses recent memories and then only the visuals. We need deeper information—account passwords, contact lists, Bitcoin wallets. The kind of stuff that requires more intensive questioning."

"Torture, you mean." She wasn't bothered by the concept. These monsters deserved whatever they got.

"The clan prefers to call it enhanced interrogation." His lips twisted slightly. "But yeah. The idea is to take their money, their resources, and everything they have and use it to help rehabilitate their victims. It's not just about punishment. It's about justice and recovery."

Put that way, it made sense. "That's actually smart."

"The clan's been fighting trafficking for a long time, so they know what they are doing. The new division is going to deal with the end users and the intermediaries, so adaptations will be required, but they are not starting from scratch." He rubbed his jaw, suddenly looking less sure of himself. "I've been going out on missions only as a backup, and I can't wait to be in the forward team."

"Are you ever scared?" Drova asked quietly.

"I'm scared of messing up. I'm not scared of confronting Doomers. We are stronger than they are, and they can't infiltrate our minds, but they do have weapons, so we should always proceed with caution."

"Yes, definitely."

Drova had no idea what it meant to proceed with caution when being fired on, but she assumed that was what training and Kevlar vests were for.

"Come on." Pavel stood up. "I'll introduce you to the rest of the team."

44

MORELLE

Throughout dinner, Morelle kept catching herself rubbing her hand where she'd shaken Jin's. Had Jin attached a tether to her during that brief contact, or was she just being paranoid because of Jin's mischievous and irreverent vibe?

As Jin launched into a long story about her first and only significant mission for the clan, Morelle studied her more carefully. There was something about the tilt of her lips and the amusement dancing in her eyes that suggested a natural troublemaker. How did someone as mellow and sweet as Arwel handle such a mate?

Margo had said something about opposite personalities being attracted to one another, but Gabi had qualified that statement by pointing out that it was crucial for a couple to have at least some things in common and that their differences should provide a little spice to the relationship but not define it.

It was all so confusing, and completely unknown territory to Morelle. What she'd been told about Kra-ell interactions was centered on loyalty to the tribe, respecting the pecking order, and honoring the Kra-ell traditions. The head priestess had never talked about the intricacies of one-on-one relationships because they were foreign to the Kra-ell culture.

"...so there I was," Jin was saying, her hands painting pictures in the air, "finally having tethered Kalugal when all mayhem broke loose."

Morelle tensed again, rubbing her hand, but Brandon seemed unconcerned, and he had shaken Jin's hand as well.

"A human shows up with a gun," Jin continued, her eyes sparkling with excitement. "We all ducked as bullets started flying, and then I saw Arwel soaring over the crowd like Superman and landing over the shooter, taking him down to the floor." She looked lovingly at her mate. "You were incredible."

"I was terrified that he was going to hurt you." Arwel clasped her hand.

"And that's how Kalugal realized that Arwel was an immortal," Jin continued, "used his compulsion to freeze everyone other than Jacki, who is immune, and caught himself a Head Guardian."

The tale grew more complex with each passing

minute, so full of twists and turns that Morelle glanced at Brandon. "You should write this into a script for one of your movies."

His laugh seemed a little forced. "It would be too fantastical for people to suspend disbelief. As the saying goes, reality is stranger than fiction, and most people don't realize how true that is."

By the time Jin approached the culmination of her story, the Odus were serving tea and coffee along with a freshly baked chocolate cake that made Morelle's mouth water.

Back home, the food she'd been given was meant to nourish her, but it had been mostly fruits and some vegetables that were somehow sneaked into the temple.

She'd never tasted anything as decadent as chocolate, and the scent of it mixed with coffee was intoxicating.

"So that's how Kalugal ended up in the village," Jin finished with a flourish. "A prime example of the Fates at work."

Morelle nodded, thinking of her own journey. "The way Ell-rom and I were found is another example of that. If Jasmine hadn't accepted her criminal boyfriend's invitation to spend a vacation with him at the same hotel where Margo was attending her brother's soon-to-be former mate's party, she wouldn't have been found by the clan, and without her scrying ability, Ell-rom and I wouldn't have been found and would have probably died."

"Fates forbid." Brandon squeezed her hand.

She smiled at him. "The Fates brought us together."

"Yes, they did." His smile was the first genuine one she'd seen all day, making her wonder if he was still upset about her interest in trying Perfect Match adventures with or without him. His mood had improved considerably after she'd agreed to move into his house, though she still hadn't found the right opportunity to tell Annani about that decision.

"Your turn." Jin waved an elegant hand at her sister. "You should tell them about your talent and how you used it to find me."

Mey's story was also entertaining and filled with tense moments, carrying them through coffee, tea, and several pieces of that amazing chocolate cake. Morelle was just reaching for another small slice when Amanda cleared her throat.

"I could keep eating this cake until I burst, but I think it's time for testing."

That was apparently the signal for everyone to thank the Clan Mother and rise from their seats.

"We'll start with Jin," Amanda announced, motioning for the younger sister to approach. "Try to attach your tether to Brandon." She turned to

Morelle. "Your job is to prevent her from doing that."

Morelle frowned. "What if I can't stop Jin? Will Brandon stay tethered to her?"

Jin's laugh was light and careless. "I'll snap the connection, silly. It's not like I enjoy being a peeping Tom and observing someone else's life." She leaned in closer to Morelle. "I'll let you in on a secret. Most of the time, it's incredibly boring, and sometimes it's also embarrassing."

Morelle could imagine private moments that should never be observed by another person, even a loved one.

"I wonder if this is going to feel different," Amanda said. "Cassandra's explosion ability is straightforward but unique. Somehow, she manages to influence with her mind the molecular structure of the object she wants to blow up, and she doesn't even know how she does it. In that respect, Jin's mental tether almost seems simpler, but it implies that consciousness is not bound to the body and, under certain circumstances, can be independent of it."

"I could have told you that," Syssi said. "How do you think I access visions? Consciousness is also not bound by time and space, which is why I can see into the past, the future, and even other planets."

For some reason, the explanation eased Morelle's mind about the test. It made Jin's power sound more like science with a tinge of spirituality than magic.

Looking at Brandon's face, she could tell that he shared some of her reservations about Jin's ability, and she couldn't blame him. No one wanted someone else's mind inside their own or even just hitching a ride on their optic and auditory systems.

45

BRANDON

Brandon tensed involuntarily as Jin's hand came to rest on his shoulder. He knew intellectually that she couldn't read his thoughts, could only see what he saw and hear what he heard, but the idea of someone latching onto his consciousness was deeply unsettling.

Across the room, Morelle watched Jin with a frown, her large blue eyes focused on Jin with laser-like intensity. Brandon had no idea if whatever she was attempting was working. Jin's tether was weightless, and there was no visible sign of Morelle's nullifying ability, so there was no way to tell if she was successfully preventing Jin from establishing her ethereal tether.

Something about this whole setup bothered him. Jin and Mey had freely shared details about their abilities during dinner before Morelle had even attempted to nullify them. Either Amanda had forgotten to instruct them to keep their talents secret for testing purposes, or she had something else in mind.

Amanda wasn't the type to forget such details.

The feather-light pressure of Jin's hand lifted, and Brandon fought the urge to step away from her.

"Well?" Amanda asked, tablet poised to record the results. "What's your verdict?"

Jin grinned. "It's like we thought—"

Amanda's raised hand cut her off. She turned to Morelle instead. "How did you stop her?"

"I concentrated and imagined snipping the tether." Morelle demonstrated the action of cutting with her fingers.

"Where exactly did you place your scissors?" Amanda pressed. "At the source, meaning Jin, or the destination, meaning Brandon?"

"The source. I imagined snipping the tether extending from Jin's mind."

Amanda's satisfied smile suggested this was the answer she'd been expecting. She waved a hand at Jin. "Now, you can explain."

"With pleasure." Jin turned to Morelle. "Before coming here this evening, I tethered Mey, Arwel, and Yamanu. I held on to those three tethers during dinner and checked on them occasionally to make sure that they were still there and that you didn't nullify them unintentionally. Then, when I attempted to tether Brandon, I not only couldn't establish the connection but also lost the other three." She appraised Morelle with her brown, expressive eyes. "You didn't know I was tethering anyone else, right?"

"I didn't." Alarm flashed across Morelle's face. "Did I destroy your ability to do that?"

Jin didn't look worried. "Let's test it." She turned toward Arwel and then frowned, looking worried. "I can't establish a new connection."

"Step outside," Amanda instructed. "Try it out in the backyard away from Morelle. Distance matters with her nullifying power."

"I'm not actively doing it anymore." Morelle sounded stressed. "I don't know how to turn it off."

Brandon wrapped his arm around her waist. "I think it just needs time to fade."

When Jin and Arwel returned a few minutes later, they both looked relieved. "It worked outside," Jin said.

Tension visibly drained from Morelle's shoulders. "Thank the Mother."

"Yes." Amanda smiled at Jin. "Thank the merciful Fates. We don't want to lose a valuable talent like that."

Jin chuckled. "I hope to only use it for entertainment. I really don't want to be a spy."

Arwel took her hand. "We will never ask you to do something that goes against your conscience. You know that."

"Mey?" Amanda turned to the other sister. "You're next."

Mey shifted uncomfortably. "I'd rather not listen to the echoes here. The house is new, so the conversations would be recent. I don't want to intrude on the Clan Mother's privacy."

Brandon tried to think of other places in the village where it would be okay to listen to echoes of past conversations. "I suggest the grand assembly hall," he said. "A lot of spirited and emotionally laden discussions have been carried on there, but none were private. We can try it there."

"That's a good idea," Kian said. "But we should save it for another day. It's getting late, and Allegra needs to go to bed soon."

Brandon heard the relieved breath Morelle had released, but he doubted anyone else had noticed. He should have realized that she was drained.

"We could test with Arwel again," Amanda suggested. "I have a few ideas about different variations we can try."

"We should call it a day," Brandon said. "Morelle is tired."

The stiffening of Morelle's shoulders made him immediately regret speaking for her. He had promised himself to ease up and be less controlling. And he shouldn't have spoken up for her, but he couldn't help his protective instincts.

"I think I'm good for a few more tests," she said

with a measured tone, but he could sense the annoyance she was trying to hide. "Unlike Allegra, I'm old enough to realize when it's time for me to go to bed."

Ouch. He was so in the doghouse.

"I'm sorry. I shouldn't have spoken for you, but your well-being is important to me, and I'm not willing to compromise on that."

"Brandon's right," Amanda conceded before Morelle could argue. "None of this is urgent, and we can take our time exploring the limits of your ability." She smiled. "From our experience in the university, paranormal abilities diminish with repetition, so performing when you are tired will affect the results."

The tension bled from Morelle's shoulders. "You are the expert, Amanda."

Brandon thanked the merciful Fates and Amanda's diplomatic approach. Perhaps he was saved from the proverbial doghouse tonight.

He'd promised to work on his controlling tendencies, but the line between care and control was a fine one.

46

MORELLE

Being part of a couple was completely foreign territory. Morelle had no reference points, no examples to follow or emulate. In the temple, relationships had been clinical topics in theoretical discussions, not living, breathing things that required constant navigation, and even those had dealt with tribal dynamics and had little bearing on her situation with Brandon.

How was she supposed to balance her wishes and desires when they didn't align with Brandon's?

How was it possible to merge two lives without losing one's individuality in the process?

Brandon knew how these things worked, or at least he should know, given that he lived in a society where people paired up and were supposed to spend the rest of their lives together, loving and supporting each other.

Morelle relied on him to lead her in the right direction, but the problem was that she wasn't the type who followed anyone's lead, not even his, and that was despite her feelings for him that were growing stronger with each passing day.

It went against every fiber of her being.

She might not be a real princess in title, but she was by birth, and those genes she'd inherited from her mother and her father made her a leader and not a follower.

She could pretend for a little while, but she knew it would only get her in more trouble. She'd tried to stifle those instincts to get along with the head priestess, but it had always ended in a major blow-up between them, with Morelle being punished and spending several nights sleeping on a floor in a windowless room away from Ell-rom.

Brandon wasn't the head priestess, though. He was willing to compromise because he had deep feelings for her and wanted what was best for her.

As she and Brandon said their goodnights and entered her bedroom, Morelle sat on the couch and patted the space beside her. "Come sit with me?"

"Always." He sat down and wrapped his arm around her shoulders.

"I need a manual," she murmured.

"For what?"

"A step-by-step guide on how to be part of a

couple." She was only slightly joking. "I need to know the rules and expectations. Where I come from, they didn't teach that. I'm surprised that Ellrom seems to be doing so well. Jasmine must be a good teacher."

"And I'm not?" Brandon said quietly.

She lifted her head to look at him and smiled to counter his dejected expression. "You are great, but we haven't been together as long as they have, and I'm not as patient as my brother. I want a shortcut."

His chuckle was warm and affectionate. "Is that why you want to go on a Perfect Match adventure? Is that your idea of a shortcut?"

"No." She shook her head. "Well, yes, but it's a different shortcut. I want to see this world, learn about its different peoples, history, politics, and cultures, and I can do that much faster with the Perfect Match machine. It can literally just load all that information into my brain."

She was also curious about the questionnaire and hoped it would help her understand herself better.

Figure out what she wanted.

For some reason, Morelle didn't want to share this particular motive with Brandon. He might say that this wasn't the best way to do it and that she needed to experience real life to learn about herself, but she believed that she would learn a lot from answering guided questions, and if not, no harm would be done. She would use it to feed the Perfect Match machine and have it design a wonderful adventure for her.

There was no downside to filling out the questionnaire other than upsetting Brandon.

"That's exactly the part I don't like," Brandon said. "I want my memories to be real, not implanted by a computer program."

She tilted her head. "Does it matter how you acquire your memories as long as you can distinguish between the real ones and the computer-generated ones? It's just a faster way to learn and experience things."

His smile was a little condescending. "We are immortal, Morelle. What's the point of rushing anything? We should savor real experiences and prolong them as much as we can instead of cramming them into a three-hour session. It makes sense for humans but not for us." He took her hand and kissed her knuckles. "And the best part about being mated immortals is living forever together and experiencing everything as a couple."

She looked up at him. "Are couples supposed to do everything together? I mean, we are not the same person, and we might enjoy different activities. Do we have to give up the things that the other person doesn't like and only engage in activities that we both enjoy?"

A shadow crossed his face. "Are you tired of my

company, Princess? Do you need some space? I could sleep at my house tonight and give you some breathing room."

Morelle felt torn.

The truth was, she wasn't used to sharing every waking moment with another person, even Brandon, who she cared for deeply. But how could she explain that need for space without hurting his feelings?

"I didn't ask these questions to hint that I want to be alone. I don't. I truly need answers."

His shoulders relaxed. "Couples should not do everything together, and no one should give up what they enjoy doing just because their partner doesn't. If you want to go on Perfect Match adventures, go. You don't need me to come with you."

Morelle smiled, happy with the answer he'd given her. "But I would like you to join me, at least from time to time. Is there a chance I could change your mind?"

He groaned. "I'll think about it."

That was progress.

She lifted her head and kissed his cheek. "Thank you. That's much better than a flat-out no."

He looked at her from under lowered lashes. "Are you sure you don't want me to leave? I seem to have annoyed you today, and I don't want to become the annoying guy who doesn't know when to back off."

"I don't want you to leave," she said. "But I would like to take a long, relaxing bath."

One hour of solitude was all she needed. It would recharge her.

He nodded, though something in his eyes suggested he understood she was asking for more than just bath time. "Do you need help filling it up?"

The offer made her laugh. She leaned in to kiss him softly. "Speaking of backing off, my dear. You need to give me some room to breathe."

"I'm sorry." He ran a hand through his hair. "I know I can be overbearing, controlling. I've spent most of my life telling people what to do and expecting immediate compliance. I know it's not the right way to handle a relationship, but old habits are hard to break."

"Don't apologize." She cupped his cheek. "I know that you care about me and that you mean well. When your controlling tendencies bother me, I promise to let you know. We're both learning how to do this, how to be together." She rose to her feet.

He shook his head. "Fated Mates should fit together perfectly. Otherwise, the bond won't snap in place."

The words sent an unexpected chill through her chest and froze her in place.

Fated mates? Was that what everyone meant

when they said that their encounter had been fated?

She desperately needed to talk to Jasmine, Margo, and the others to find out if everything had been perfect between them and their mates from the start.

What if she and Brandon weren't fated for each other? What if the connection she felt with Brandon, powerful as it was, didn't go as deep as that?

The thought made her feel ill.

Morelle forced a smile. "We have plenty of time to discover whether we're fated mates or not. As you said, we are immortals, and we are not in a rush, right?" She leaned over him and kissed his forehead. "Are you going to be okay here while I soak in the bathtub?"

He nodded, but his expression was still troubled as she ducked into the bathroom and closed the door behind her.

Leaning against it, Morelle let out a shaky breath.

Fated mates. The phrase echoed in her mind as she started the water running. Did it really mean a perfect fit?

Everyone seemed to expect some magical, instantaneous perfection. What if she and Brandon didn't live up to that standard?

The steam from the filling tub began to fog the mirror, obscuring her reflection. Appropriate, she thought wryly, given how unclear everything felt right now.

Adding some of the bath oils Annani had given her, Morelle breathed in the calming scent and closed her eyes.

Maybe she was overthinking everything.

Maybe fated didn't mean perfect and devoid of challenges.

47

ROB

At six in the morning the gym was already humming with activity, and as Rob headed toward his favorite station by the punching bag, he was glad that no one had taken it yet.

He'd quickly fallen into a comfortable new routine—an hour of training in the morning, shower, head to the lab and go over all the things William wanted him to learn before he started the actual job, lunch with Gertrude, back to the lab, then another two hours in the gym before spending his evenings with his girlfriend.

Sometimes, Margo and Negal joined them, along with the other gods who had recently moved to the village.

Rob smiled to himself as he wrapped his hands, still amazed at how his life had changed. If someone had told him a few months ago that he'd be spending his evenings casually hanging out with gods and immortals, he would have questioned their sanity. Yet here he was, preparing to train in a state-of-the-art facility built into a mountain, surrounded by beings straight out of mythology or science fiction or both.

And the most amazing part was that he felt more at home in this village than he had ever felt in the human world.

For the first time in years, Rob felt genuinely happy.

There was one more hurdle he had to overcome before this dream could become his permanent reality, and that was the dreaded induction ceremony and the transition that followed.

He wasn't afraid of getting bitten by an immortal, nor was he anxious about surviving the transition, but he didn't want to embarrass himself, and by extension, his sister and her mate, by doing poorly in the ring.

His form had improved considerably since he had started training. The basics of boxing were becoming more natural, and he was learning various sparring techniques so he could hold his own for a few moments in the ring and put up a decent show.

As he approached the heavy bag, it occurred to him that he no longer attacked it with barely contained rage, venting his anger at Lynda. The pain she'd caused him and the profound feeling of unfairness had fueled his aggression. Now that the anger had dissipated and optimism about his future took root, his strikes were controlled and focused.

Life was great when you loved the right woman, and she loved you back. It was difficult to hold on to anger.

Rob hadn't actually told Gertrude he loved her yet, though. He was waiting until after his transition, wanting to promise her forever when forever actually meant something.

The thought made his next punch a bit harder.

"Your left hook is improving."

Rob turned to find Arwel behind him, his arms folded across his chest and a smile tilting up his lips.

"Thanks." Rob steadied the bag. "What's up, Arwel?"

The Guardian leaned slightly forward. "We should schedule the induction ceremony. You are more than ready."

That caught Rob off guard. "I'm not in a rush," he said, wiping sweat from his forehead. "It's not like my residency status in the village depends on it. I'm a confirmed Dormant."

Arwel shook his head. "It's time, Rob. You're human, so you could train for years and still not last more than a minute in the ring with me. I'm a Guardian, and I've been training for centuries. There's no point in waiting. It needs to be done."

Rob's stomach tightened. "When do you want to do this?"

"I suggest we do it this Saturday evening."

Rob's gut twisted as anxiety took hold.

"Where? And how does it work exactly? I've never actually been told all the details." Or any at all.

People must have assumed that he knew, or maybe they were waiting for him to ask, but he'd been too much of a chicken to do so.

"It's usually done right here in the gym." Arwel leaned against the wall. "In the sparring ring. I'll put up a notice on the clan's bulletin board so people can attend if they want to. Kian needs to be informed since he's the leader of this community and the master of ceremonies, and you should make sure your sister, Gertrude, and your other friends come to cheer you on."

Another wave of anxiety washed over Rob, more powerful than the first. "What else is involved in the ceremony? I mean, apart from the match itself?"

"Nothing too elaborate." Arwel shifted his weight. "Kian says a few words, and his butler distributes ceremonial wine in tiny cups. He'll ask if you accept me as your mentor, then he will ask me if I accept responsibility for you, and lastly, he will ask if anyone objects to our match." He lifted a finger. "Oh, I forgot that he will ask who is presenting you and vouching for your worthiness.

Mia and Toven can be your presenters. Then we fight in the ring, the crowd cheers you on, I take you down to the mat, bite you, and you're out for a few minutes or longer. An hour at the most."

"And then?"

"Hopefully, the transition will start the next day or two days later. If it doesn't, you might need another round, probably with someone else." Arwel scratched his chin thoughtfully. "Toven would be your best bet since he is a god, and you can't ask for more potent venom. Or you could ask Negal. Actually, maybe you should just go with one of the gods as your inducer in the first place. There's nothing like a god's venom to ensure a smooth transition. I have no problem stepping aside."

"No." Rob's response was immediate and firm. "I want you as my inducer. Unless you've changed your mind about doing it?"

"Not at all." Arwel clapped him on the shoulder. "I'd be honored. Just wanted you to be aware of your options. If it doesn't work, Negal would be a solid backup plan."

Rob nodded, turning back to the heavy bag to hide his relief. Having Arwel as his inducer felt right. The Guardian had been helping him train and offering guidance both in and out of the ring. Plus, there was something reassuring about his steady presence. Maybe it was his empathic ability and his friendly demeanor, but Rob had felt comfortable with him from day one.

"Saturday," Rob said, testing the word. "That's soon."

"Too soon?" Arwel asked.

"No." Rob threw a combination at the bag, his form better than ever. "It's just getting real, real fast."

48

ANNANI

Diffused by the marine layer, the morning light streamed through the dining room windows as Annani watched her brother and sister and their mates gather for breakfast. These morning meals had become precious moments, opportunities to observe her newly found siblings settling into their new lives. The Odus moved around them, serving coffee and fresh pastries.

"I plan on visiting Roni today," Jasmine said, accepting a cup of coffee from Ogidu. "I want to go over the information he's gathered about my family. I just wish he had time to dig into the rebellion in Kurdistan and find some clues for us, but he is busy with a big project, so he only has a few minutes to spare."

Ell-rom's wince meant that her brother was well aware of what was occupying the hacker's time these days. Roni was hacking into the pedo networks, as Kian referred to them, and preparing for the Avengers' first mission on Tuesday. The closer they came to activating the new division, the closer Ell-rom came to testing his deadly ability on actual humans, and the thought troubled him deeply.

Annani needed to change the subject to disperse the dark cloud hovering over Ell-rom's head.

"This evening, we're all invited to Syssi and Kian's for dinner. It has become something of a family tradition, their Friday dinners, though they do not always work out, and sometimes we have to gather on another day. We try to have the family together at least once a week. It is important for the children." She smiled. "And for me. This is one of the main reasons I stayed here so long instead of going back to the sanctuary or visiting Sari more. I feel a little guilty about that, but not enough to make me leave."

"At least you are getting a break from hosting today," Morelle said. "I know that you enjoy this, but it's tiring even for me, and I'm not the host."

Annani laughed. "Oh, my dear Morelle. You will get used to it. Your years of solitude are over."

Morelle nodded. "It's difficult to adjust, and sometimes it gets overwhelming, but I'm still so glad to be here." She turned to Brandon and took his hand. "I love being part of this community, and

I think it is time for me to stop being a guest and become a resident."

Annani had a feeling where Morelle was going with this, and she braced for what her sister was going to say next.

"I believe it is time Brandon and I move into his house. I'm mostly recovered, and I don't need to be taken care of. Although, I have to admit that I don't know the first thing about preparing a meal, and Brandon's culinary skills are almost as scant." She turned to Jasmine. "That's why I think you and Ellrom should move in with us. If you can spare the time, you could teach us to cook."

Jasmine grinned. "With pleasure. Frankly, I've been feeling like we were overstaying our welcome, but I was afraid to bring this up." She turned to Annani. "The last thing I want is to upset you, Clan Mother, so if you prefer that we stay longer, of course we will."

Part of Annani wanted to say yes and insist that her newly found family stay close, but she knew this was for the best. "I would love for the four of you to stay here forever, but I know that you need your own space, and I am glad that Brandon is inviting you to live in his house. No houses are available in this part of the village, and I want you all nearby." She couldn't quite resist adding, "You must visit me at least once a day, though. I insist."

"We will whenever possible," Jasmine promised. "But are you sure it's okay?"

Annani sighed. "Of course it is, my dear. I will resume the audiences with my people that I have paused during your stay, so it is not as if I will be all alone in here and bored. And if you visit me every day, you will make it up to me." She turned to Brandon. "Your life is changing drastically, Councilman Brandon. From a bachelor who barely bothered to visit the village, you have not only moved back, but you now have a mate, and you are inviting her brother and his mate to live with you. That is quite an adjustment. Are you sure you are ready for that?"

He nodded. "I am more than ready."

Morelle did not look as enthusiastic as her mate, which was not surprising. Annani had noticed that her sister was still struggling with aspects of her relationship with Brandon.

She wished Morelle would come to her for advice, but with Brandon constantly hovering, the poor girl could barely breathe.

It reminded Annani painfully of Khiann and how even their deep love had not prevented him from feeling trapped within the palace walls. That was why she had agreed to let him lead the caravan to Egypt or Kemet, as it had been called back then. It was a decision she had spent millennia regretting, believing it had led to his death.

But if her theory was correct, and her father had compelled the witnesses to falsely testify that Mortdh had murdered Khiann, then that decision had actually saved his life. If Khiann had stayed in the palace, they both would have attended the assembly where all the other gods had been killed.

Then again, if Khiann had not left, Mortdh would not have supposedly murdered him, there would have been no assembly and no bomb, and all the gods would still be around. The Eternal King's assassins couldn't have taken advantage of all the gods being assembled in one place to take them out and blame it on Mortdh in case anyone ever came from Anumati to investigate the tragedy.

So perhaps it had all been her fault after all.

"What's wrong?" Ell-rom's voice broke through her circular thoughts.

"Just giving myself a headache thinking in loops," she admitted, rubbing her temple.

"Can I help?" Morelle asked. "I have a knack for untangling complicated webs."

"That you do, my darling sister. The mental exercise I was engaged in was rather futile," Annani said, "but I don't mind sharing it. Perhaps you can help me untangle it."

She explained her thoughts about Khiann, the assembly, and the complex web of cause and effect that had led to so much tragedy. As she spoke, she watched her siblings' reactions—Ell-rom's thoughtful frown and Morelle's sharp focus.

Brandon and Jasmine shared a similar look of empathetic concern.

"It's not your fault," Morelle said firmly when Annani finished. "The Eternal King's actions and Mortdh's choices are not your responsibility."

"Everything that happened flows from them, not from your decision to let Khiann travel," Ellrom added. "You can't blame yourself for other people's evil deeds."

Their quick defense warmed her heart.

"Besides," Jasmine said softly, "if everything hadn't happened exactly as it did, none of us would be here now. We are all just threads in the Fates' tapestry."

"That is true," Annani conceded. "The Fates don't share their plans with flesh and blood creatures, and their game includes thousands if not millions of threads. It is impossible to comprehend even if those threads are shown to us. Until they are woven into the tapestry, they are meaningless."

She studied her family around the breakfast table, those precious people who had come into her life through such unlikely circumstances. Perhaps there was no point in questioning the path that had led them here.

"When do you intend to move?" she asked Morelle.

"I thought we should do it today. It's not like there is much involved. It's a few minutes' walk to Brandon's house, and all we need to do is carry our clothing there."

Jasmine winced. "That's easy for you to say. I have a lot of luggage."

"That's not a problem," Brandon said. "Once everything is packed, Ell-rom and I will take care of it. I can get us a cart, or we can just make a few trips."

Annani did not understand the rush, but she understood and appreciated her sister's decisiveness.

She was the same way. Once she made a decision, she did not wait before acting upon it.

49

GERTRUDE

The supply cabinet was organized, and Gertrude made notes on her tablet about items to reorder, even though there hadn't been enough activity in the clinic lately to deplete their stock.

Besides Morelle and Jasmine's Pilates sessions, which Gertrude conducted now in the gym, her days were quieter than she would have liked, and she was bored.

She should post an ad on the clan's virtual bulletin board about taking on more students. The Reformer was an excellent piece of equipment that shouldn't sit idle, and she was getting pretty good at teaching the Pilates technique.

Gertrude glanced at her watch for the third time since she'd started on the cabinet, but there were still fifteen minutes until lunch with Rob—the highlight of her day.

She smiled. The nights were awesome, too, now that she was spending them with Rob, and not just because he was such a giver in bed. They were hanging out with his sister and her mate and sometimes with the other gods and their ladies as well.

Poor Hildegard felt a little neglected, but she'd had no problem finding solace in the arms of one of the hybrid Kra-ell. Gertrude was crossing her fingers for that to turn into something more meaningful because she had someone great while her best friend was still alone.

She sighed as she realized that she'd lost count of the bandages and had to start over.

After what felt like an eternity, her watch finally cooperated, and she closed the supply cabinet, collected her purse, and put an Out to Lunch sign on the clinic's door. If anyone needed her urgently, they would call her number, which was posted as well.

They could also just walk over to the café or wave, and she would see them.

Her heart warmed at the sight of Rob already seated at one of the tables, their usual order arranged on a tray before him. He was looking straight at her, smiling and waving his hand, and she smiled and waved back, but even from this distance, she could read the tension in his posture.

Something was wrong.

When he stood to greet her with a kiss on the

cheek, she didn't waste time on pleasantries. "What's the matter?"

He chuckled as he pulled out a chair for her. "Why do you think there is something the matter?"

"Your shoulders are tense." She sat down.

He rotated his shoulder. "I overdid it this morning with the punching bag."

She lifted a brow. "Talk to me, Rob."

He let out a breath. "I have news, but it's nothing to be concerned about. Arwel and I scheduled my induction ceremony for this Saturday evening."

Gertrude's heart skipped several beats, and she pressed a hand to her chest. "This Saturday?" When he nodded, she asked, "Why so soon?"

Rob shrugged. "Arwel says that there is no point in me continuing my training in preparation for the ceremony. No matter how well I train or how good I get, he'll still have me face down on the mat in under a minute anyway, so there's no reason to delay."

She swallowed hard, her throat suddenly dry. "That's probably true, but I just wish we had more time."

"Time for what?"

"To be together." Her voice came out thicker than intended. "I don't want to lose you."

His expression softened, and he cupped her cheek with gentle fingers. "You're not going to lose me. You're going to gain forever with me, if you want that, of course." He leaned closer, his breath warm against her ear. "Don't you want to feel the venom bite? I hear that the experience is incomparable."

Heat flooded through her at his words and the promise they held. Of course, she wanted that, and she wanted forever with him, but Rob was in his early thirties, which put him in a higher risk category for transition complications.

The thought doused her arousal like ice water.

"Bridget needs to give you a physical before the ceremony," she said firmly. "Any health issues need to be resolved before you attempt transition. I would have scheduled it earlier, but I didn't expect you to do it so soon."

He pulled back, disappointment evident in his expression that she hadn't picked up on his sexual banter. "I don't have any health issues. I had a physical less than six months ago. Everything was fine."

Gertrude waved a dismissive hand. "I know all about those so-called physicals. At your age, you are assumed healthy because statistically men your age are, so they do the bare minimum. Bridget will be much more thorough." She reached for her phone, already composing a text in her head.

His hand covered hers, stilling her movement. "What are you doing?"

"Texting Bridget."

"Don't bother her. I'm in perfect health."

She closed her eyes, drawing in a deep, stabilizing breath. "Do it for me? Please?"

His head dropped in defeat. "Fine. I'll do it for you. But just so you know, I don't appreciate being manipulated like that."

Guilt seeped through her. After everything he'd been through with Lynda, she hated using his ex's tactics, but fear made her desperate, even though logically she knew she was probably overreacting.

Rob showed no signs of illness. His color was good, there was no puffiness in his face or extremities, and he managed twice-daily intense training sessions without experiencing excessive fatigue.

She was letting her fears run wild.

"I promise never to coerce you into doing anything again," she said softly. "But I had to do this. I'm having an anxiety attack just thinking about you in that ring with Arwel and... and not waking up from his bite."

The hardness in his eyes melted away. "Has that ever happened?"

She shook her head. "It hasn't, but we've had so few adult male Dormants transition. The sample size is too small to draw any real conclusions. Anything could happen."

He squeezed her hand. "Have a little faith. The Fates brought me here for a reason, and it wasn't to die on the sparring mat."

His confidence should have been reassuring, but Gertrude knew better than to rely on statistics or the Fates. Both meant very little when someone you loved was at risk.

Love.

The word echoed in her mind, and she realized she hadn't told him yet. She'd been waiting for the right moment, but maybe there was no perfect time. Maybe she should tell him now, before the ceremony, before everything changed.

But the words stuck in her throat. What if saying it now would feel like goodbye? What if he thought she was only saying it because she was afraid?

"Hey." His voice drew her from her spiraling thoughts. "Where did you go just now?"

"Thinking about Saturday." It wasn't entirely a lie. "I just hope that Bridget can make time for you. Julian is also a good physician, but I prefer her because I have worked with her for a long time, and I know that she doesn't miss anything."

Gertrude pulled out her phone and texted Bridget.

The reply came back a couple of minutes later. *Five-thirty today*.

She showed Rob the screen, and when he nodded, she typed back a thank you, then lifted her head and smiled. "That means no afternoon training session for you."

He shrugged. "Apparently, I have no need for it." He reached for her hand. "And it means more time with you."

50

JASMINE

Jasmine clutched her mother's jewelry box to her chest as she and Ell-rom headed to William's office through his sprawling laboratory complex. The wooden box wasn't valuable in monetary terms, but along with the tarot cards, two rings, and a simple gold chain, it represented everything she had left of her mother.

"I'll take excellent care of it," William promised, noticing her white-knuckled grip on the box. "We'll start with noninvasive scanning, and if we find anything unusual, I'll consult you on how you want to proceed."

"If there is something hidden inside," Jasmine said, "I might consider taking it apart if the person doing it knows how to return it to its former condition. We could talk to someone who specializes in the restoration of things like that."

William nodded. "That's a wonderful idea."

Jasmine placed the box carefully on his cluttered desk, worried about leaving it there on top of the chaos of papers, tools, and mysterious devices.

Ell-rom glanced at his watch. "We should head over to Roni's office. He only has a few minutes for us."

"I'll take you to him," William suggested. "Roni doesn't have his own office, not because he doesn't deserve one, but rather because he doesn't want one. He enjoys working in the lab's open space." William led them toward a back section of the large room.

As William warned, Roni's space was just one station among many scattered throughout the room. The only distinctive feature was an enormous black swivel chair that dwarfed its slim occupant.

"Behold the Batman chair," William said with a grin. "Don't mock it. Roni loves this monstrosity."

The hacker was surprisingly young and slight, nothing like the imposing figure Jasmine had imagined. She'd also expected him to be surrounded by a team of assistants, given how much work he handled for the clan.

"Hello." Roni extended his hand without getting out of his chair. "It's nice to finally meet you in person." He grinned as she put her hand in his. "I saw you when you and Ell-rom arrived at the village, of course, and I feel like I know you from the background checks I did, but this is the first time that I have the pleasure of actually talking with you."

He was perfectly polite and charming, and she couldn't understand all the warnings she'd gotten about Roni being surly and abrasive.

"Thanks for the fake dossier you prepared for me ahead of the trip to Tibet, and for digging up stuff about my family."

"All in a day's work." He shifted his gaze to Ell-rom. "You're looking better than the last time I saw you, which was also during the party the Clan Mother threw in your honor."

"Thank you," Ell-rom said. "Jasmine and I appreciate you agreeing to see us when you are so busy with other projects."

"Sure thing." He started to swivel his chair toward his desk.

"Don't you have people helping you?" Jasmine blurted. "And your own office? I've heard so much about you that I was sure you had an entire floor dedicated to hacking."

It didn't make sense to her that Roni had to do everything by himself when there was so much to do. Surely, he could delegate some of the less important tasks to others.

Roni spun his chair back. "I like working alone. I used to work in isolation before the clan rescued me, and people only came to me when they needed favors. Now I enjoy being surrounded by people who leave me alone so I can work."

Jasmine tried to parse the contradictory statement—wanting company but not interaction—except she had no more time to waste on personal questions.

"We don't want to take up too much of your time," Ell-rom said, echoing her thoughts. "Can you show us what you have found so far?"

"That's what I got." Roni handed her several printed pages. "There is nothing new in there, but I thought you would like to have the supporting documents. It's your mother's student visa, the date she arrived from Iran, when she married your father, etc. The basic timeline."

Jasmine's heart sank. She'd hoped Roni had found out more, something that would suggest Syssi's vision had indeed been about her mother.

"There is one new piece of information that you might find interesting." Roni smiled, leaning back in his enormous chair, and steepling his fingers in a gesture that reminded Jasmine of villains in movies. "Kian asked me to check whether your father and your stepmother were legally married since your father couldn't prove your mother's death. Turns out that your father provided the court with notarized divorce papers that had been sent from Iran."

The implications hit Jasmine like a physical blow. "But... that would mean..."

Roni nodded. "Either the papers were forged, or your mother was alive to sign them—in Iran."

Ell-rom's grip on Jasmine's hand tightened. "Can you tell which?"

"That's where it gets complicated." Roni spun his chair toward another screen. "From what I can see, the documents appear authentic, with the proper notary seals and the required official language. If they're forgeries, they weren't cheap. The interesting part is the timing. The papers were filed several years after your mother's supposed death."

Jasmine's mind raced. "So, either my father somehow obtained forged documents that could pass scrutiny..."

"Or your mother was alive to sign them," Roni finished. "And given that the papers came from Iran..."

"She might have returned there." Jasmine struggled to keep her voice steady. "To Kurdistan, maybe? Like in Syssi's vision?"

Roni shrugged. "It's possible."

"Do you have her signature from before?" Ell-rom said. "We could compare them to see if the divorce papers were a forgery."

Roni gave him an indignant look. "Of course, I compared it to the one on the marriage certificate, and they seem close enough, but I'm not an expert. You will need a forensic document examiner, and given that we can only print out photos of the originals, I assume that comparing the signatures will be difficult."

"Can you print out the copies for me?" Jasmine asked.

"Sure thing." Roni punched a few keys, and the printer on his desk revved to life. "I can dig up some more, but it will have to wait. I'm in the middle of a huge project." He handed her the printouts.

"Thank you." Jasmine clutched them, new hope blooming in her chest. "When you have the time, let me know if you find anything more."

"I will." Roni saluted her with two fingers. "Good luck." He swiveled his chair and went back to work as if they weren't there.

Walking back through the lab, Jasmine's mind whirled with possibilities. Her mother might be alive. She might have chosen to leave them for some reason, but why would she do that?

The idea that her mother had chosen to abandon her should have hurt, but if Kyra had sacrificed her family and her own happiness to fight for her people, perhaps she could forgive her.

"Are you okay?" Ell-rom asked.

Jasmine nodded. "Roni has given me hope that Kyra is still alive, and if Syssi's vision was about her, she is fighting for her people, and I'm proud of her."

"You're not angry at her for leaving you and your father?"

Jasmine took a deep breath. "I cannot judge her until I know all the details. I bet she had a very good reason for what she did, and she either had no choice or thought to protect us." She turned to look into Ell-rom's big blue eyes. "My father holds the answers to at least some of these questions. We need to pay him a visit."

51

MORELLE

It took Morelle less than ten minutes to pack her entire wardrobe into the suitcases Brandon had brought from his house. Another five minutes in the bathroom was all she needed to collect the few toiletries that were actually hers and not what she'd found in Annani's home.

All that she owned fit inside one suitcase, and it was more than she had ever owned before. As she looked around, she realized that this room in her sister's house had become more of a home to her than anywhere she'd lived before.

Strange how a place could feel so familiar after such a short time. But then, she hadn't really lived in the temple. She'd merely existed, marking time like a prisoner counting days but with no end to her sentence in sight.

She couldn't have known that her mother

would one day smuggle her and her brother off the planet and send them across the galaxy to their father.

Morelle had believed that the temple was where she would spend the rest of her life, copying scriptures by hand and performing other mundane tasks she found boring.

In the past two weeks here on Earth, she had done more living than in all her previous years combined.

Brandon had already gathered the few belongings he'd brought to Annani's home and gone to help Ell-rom and Jasmine, who had somehow managed to fill the entire walk-in closet in their room, mostly with Jasmine's things, she'd been told.

Well, there was no comparison between her brief life on Earth and Jasmine's. Her brother's mate had a lifetime of collecting stuff, and it looked like the people of Earth enjoyed having many things.

It was nice, Morelle had to admit, to own outfits of different kinds to fit different moods. Variety added another dimension that had been lacking in her previous life. She'd had two sets of identical robes and veils, and there had been no change in her appearance from one day to the next.

Making her way to the other bedroom, she found Jasmine folding clothes on the bed, the suitcase open on the floor next to her, already half full.

"Where are Ell-rom and Brandon?" Morelle asked.

"They went to Brandon's house with what I've already packed," Jasmine explained, smoothing a wrinkle from a blouse she was folding.

"Do you need help?"

Jasmine smiled. "No, thank you. I'm very particular about how I fold my things and in what order I put them inside the luggage, but you can keep me company."

That was already one way in which Morelle was sure Jasmine and Ell-rom differed. Her brother couldn't care less about his clothing and how it was folded.

"Can I ask you something?"

Jasmine cast her a sidelong glance. "Shoot."

The word made Morelle frown. "Shoot what? I don't have a weapon."

Jasmine's laughter filled the room. "I meant talk."

"Oh." Morelle nodded, filing away yet another confusing Earth expression. "Why can't people here just say what they mean literally?"

"Language is a reflection of the culture," Jasmine said with a shrug. "Is that what you wanted to talk about?"

"No." Morelle perched on the edge of the bed, careful not to disturb Jasmine's carefully folded piles. "I wanted to ask if fated mates enjoy all the same things and agree on everything."

Jasmine's hands stilled on the shirt she was folding. "If you're asking about Ell-rom and me, we definitely don't agree on everything, and we have very different preferences. I love being around people, socializing, and getting a lot of attention. I'm a performer at heart, and the more eyes on me, the more energized I feel. Ell-rom gets exhausted if he's around people for too long. He needs his privacy, his quiet time."

Relief flooded through Morelle. So, her hunch had been right, and even Ell-rom and Jasmine, who considered themselves fated mates, weren't perfect mirrors of each other.

"I also need solitude from time to time," she said. "But Ell-rom and I differ in other ways. He is much more accommodating and pleasant than I am." She sighed. "How do you manage to bridge the differences between you and Ell-rom? Do they lead to arguments?"

"We don't argue," Jasmine said, resuming her folding. "We're aware of each other's needs, and we compromise. That's the real secret to a good relationship—finding balance. You can't be completely selfish and want everything your way, but you can't be a doormat either. The key is finding a middle ground and taking each other's preferences and limitations into account."

The advice was sound, but Morelle suspected

achieving that equilibrium would be harder for her and Brandon than it seemed to be for Ell-rom and Jasmine. Her brother and his mate were naturally more flexible and less stubborn than she and Brandon.

"Is everything okay between you and the councilman?" Jasmine asked.

"Brandon and I care deeply for each other, but we're still struggling to find that middle ground you mentioned. It's not as simple for us."

Jasmine set down the skirt she was folding. "These things take time and patience. Don't give up just because everything isn't perfect yet."

"I'm not giving up," Morelle said quickly. "But patience isn't my strong suit. I was hoping you might know of a shortcut. Maybe a manual for relationships?"

Jasmine chuckled. "We could make that a project—you and me. Interview everyone in committed relationships and compile their advice. But it'll have to wait until after I solve the mystery of my mother's disappearance."

Ell-rom and Jasmine had reported about the divorce document that her mother had sent her father. They were not sure that it was authentic, but if it was, it meant that Jasmine's mother had been alive at a time when she was supposed to be dead.

"Do you believe she's alive?" Morelle asked.

Jasmine straightened, something fierce and

determined crossing her expression. "Yeah, I do. But I'll know more after talking to my father, or rather, after having a Guardian get into his head while I question him. My father never gives me straight answers, but this time, I'll have someone pluck it straight out of his brain."

52

MARINA

Wedding jitters were the worst.

Marina nearly fell on her ass as she crouched to arrange pastries in the display case. Her balance was off, and not just physically.

Everything felt off-kilter.

Luckily, she managed to stabilize the tray so that nothing fell off.

"You should go home," Wonder said. "Your wedding is on Sunday. You should be soaking in the bathtub with a tub of ice cream and a spoon, watching romantic comedies. You're so stressed I'm afraid you'll pop a vein, and then what will become of your wedding?"

Marina shook her head, carefully arranging the pastries. "I'd rather keep busy than stay home thinking about everything that could go wrong."

And there was so much that could go wrong.

Peter's recent promotion to lead the new Avengers division should have been exciting news, and it was, but she couldn't stop worrying. Going after pedophile rings was dangerous enough when dealing with humans, but if Doomers were involved as suspected...

Immortals weren't invincible. A well-aimed bullet to the head or heart could still kill them. The thought of Peter facing armed criminals was bad enough. Adding Doomers to the mix changed the equation, making it much riskier for him.

"As you wish," Wonder said. "I offered. By the way, I love my bridesmaid dress. Good choice." She clapped Marina on the back before grabbing the coffee carafe to deliver refills.

"It was all Amanda," Marina called after her retreating form. "I only saw the pictures."

Wonder's knowing smile said she'd already known that.

The dresses were gorgeous, each in a slightly different hue of blue and varying cuts. She wondered if her bridesmaids would be willing to part with the dresses after the wedding because she wanted to keep them. She could wear them on the dates she and Peter were planning to go on as a substitute for not having a honeymoon. Peter had reserved four dinners at *By Invitation Only*, one each Wednesday following the wedding.

A heavy sigh escaped her as she watched Wonder weave between the outdoor tables. The whole wedding felt surreal as if she was playing dress-up in someone else's life. Amanda had worked her usual magic, transforming the village square into something worthy of a fairy tale, but Marina felt like Cinderella before the transformation—completely unworthy.

She was an ordinary human girl marrying an immortal, and yet a goddess was going to preside over their ceremony.

Any one of Peter's immortal friends could have officiated, maybe even the chief, and that would have been honor enough. Instead, the Clan Mother herself was going to do it, and Marina was probably going to faint.

"Hey, Marina." Lusha's voice pulled her from her spiral of anxiety. "How are you holding up?"

"I'm okay, more or less." Marina gestured toward Wonder's retreating form. "Wonder thinks I should go home and eat ice cream in the bathtub while watching romantic movies. That's her idea of relaxing. My idea is to work until I drop."

"I don't know why you're so nervous." Lusha leaned across the counter. "You're going to look like a princess in that incredible dress. Peter will grin so hard when he sees you that his face will split."

The dress had been delivered the day before, and Lusha had demanded to see Marina in it. Peter had been in a meeting, so Marina had obliged her, which had resulted in Lusha gushing for hours about the incredible masterpiece and how the dress was worthy of a princess.

It helped, Marina wasn't going to deny it, but it wasn't enough to steady her nerves.

"I'm not stressed about Peter." Marina began reorganizing the already perfectly arranged cups. "I'm stressed because a goddess is going to marry us."

"Oh." Understanding dawned in Lusha's eyes. "Just keep your eyes on Peter and ignore everyone else."

"Right." Marina rolled her eyes. "As if anyone can ignore the powerhouse that is the Clan Mother. She glows, Lusha. Actually glows."

"I know." Lusha reached for her hand, giving it a reassuring squeeze. "But this is going to be your day, and you will glow just as brightly because you're the bride." A mischievous smile crossed her face. "In fact, I got this new makeup that reflects light and makes you look like you're glowing. I'll smear it all over you."

The mental image startled a laugh from Marina. "You could also attach Christmas lights to my train. That would make me glow even brighter."

Lusha wagged a finger at her. "That's not a bad idea. Let me see if I can find any."

"Lusha!" Marina called after her retreating friend.

"Just joking," Lusha called back. "See you at home later."

Watching Lusha leave, Marina felt some of her tension ease. Her friends might not fully understand her anxiety, but they were trying to help in their own ways. Wonder with her practical suggestions, Lusha with her humor—they were doing their best to support her.

According to Bridget, Marina's test results were encouraging, and so were Lusha's, but more time was needed to figure out how much the regular exposure to venom prolonged their lives. Kaia had also been throwing around hints about the research she was conducting that could lead to a breakthrough. The scientist was positive that one day she would discover a way to turn regular humans immortal and joked about Marina being her first test subject.

She hoped Kaia would find the answer for her, and she didn't want to think about the implications for the rest of humankind. Would the discovery turn every human immortal? Would it be a good thing or terrible?

One step at a time.

Right now, she needed to survive until the wedding ceremony without having a nervous breakdown and try to enjoy the most important day in her life.

53

KIAN

Fridays were special, not just because of the family dinners that had become tradition, but because both Syssi and Amanda finished at the university earlier than usual, which meant that Kian also cut his Fridays short whenever he could.

It wasn't because Syssi needed his help to prepare dinner. Okidu handled all the cooking and setup with her guidance. But knowing his mate and daughter were home, staying at the office was difficult. He was eager to be done with his week and join them, his duties be damned.

Kian found his wife and daughter in the living room, playing with blocks on a colorful mat that Syssi had placed next to the fireplace, which was never on. The sight of them together still made his heart squeeze, even after all this time.

"Dada!" Allegra abandoned her tower-building project and ran to him.

He scooped her up, breathing in her sweet baby scent. "Hello, Princess. Building cities again?"

"Big tower!" She pointed proudly at her creation.

Syssi smiled and stood up. "I'm so glad that you managed to leave the office early. I love it when you cut your Fridays short."

"I do it whenever I can." He wrapped his other arm around her and kissed her cheek. "I have some interesting tidbits for you about the Kurdish resistance movements." He led her to the couch and sat with her leaning against his side while Allegra wiggled out of his lap and returned to her blocks.

She arched a brow. "When did you have time to look into this?"

"I asked Shai to compile a summary for me to read."

"I would love to see it," Syssi said. "I intended to read up on it during the weekend."

"I can give you the highlights. The Kurdish resistance spans several countries—Iran, Iraq, Syria, and Turkey. Each region has its own distinct movement, but they share common goals: autonomy, cultural preservation, and women's rights. The Women's Protection Units have become particularly significant in recent years."

"*Jin, Jiyan, Azadi,*" Syssi quoted. "Women, Life, Freedom."

"Exactly. It's more than just a slogan though, it's their core philosophy. These women aren't just fighting for territory, they're fighting for fundamental human rights, for the right to exist as a people and a culture."

"Hold that thought." Syssi lifted a hand. "Before you continue, would you like a cappuccino?"

He smiled. "Of course." One of his favorite things to do was to share a cup with Syssi after work.

"Dada, look!" Allegra spread her arms over the tower with pride in her eyes.

"It's beautiful. Maybe you will become an architect one day like your mommy."

Syssi laughed over at her cappuccino station. "I'm not an architect if I'm not actively working as one."

"Of course you are. Is a physician no longer a physician when she retires?"

"That's different," she said loudly over the thumping of the machine.

"I don't see how."

"I never completed my internship. I'm not licensed."

That was true, and he wondered if Syssi ever regretted her choice to pivot into working with Amanda on paranormal research. He knew that she liked the work and enjoyed his sister's company, but Syssi was also a creative person, and there wasn't much creativity in the research lab.

"Do you miss it?" he asked when she returned with the cappuccinos. "Architecture, I mean."

Syssi shrugged. "I like the design process, but frankly, I don't think I would have enjoyed working with clients. I don't regret my choices."

"Good." He let out a breath. "I don't want you to compromise on what you love doing."

"I don't." She took a sip from her cup. "Tell me more about the Kurdish women's movement before our guests arrive."

"The women's units operate in coordination with the male units." Kian took a long, grateful sip of his wife's superb cappuccino. "Some of their enemies believe that being killed by a woman denies them paradise."

"Good," Syssi said with unexpected heat. "I like it that they fear the women warriors."

Kian nodded. "The women also created a social revolution within their communities. They've established councils, educational programs, and leadership training. Young women who might have been forced into early marriages are instead becoming fighters, leaders, and teachers. They're changing the entire social fabric of their society."

"That's incredible. I bet they face a lot of opposition."

Kian nodded. "They're fighting on all fronts. Traditional tribal structures are difficult to abolish, and the governments in the area see them as a threat."

Syssi took another sip and put her cup on the coffee table. "How do they manage that? I mean, I'm not aware of women in any other region organizing themselves into independent military units."

"True. It's really a unique phenomenon. They are like the Amazons of myth. They also believe in providing education for their members in addition to combat training."

"Like we do here in the clan," Syssi said.

"Well, they are fighting for their survival and basic human rights."

"So are we." Syssi smiled sadly. "We fight for our existence. If we didn't, Navuh and his goons would have eradicated our people a long time ago."

"True." Kian sighed.

"It's remarkable," Syssi said. "These women choosing to fight not just with weapons but with education and social change. But what's more remarkable to me is how little is known about them in the West. I would think that every women's organization should have sung their praises on every channel available, and yet I didn't know anything about it until that article I read online, and I stumbled upon that by chance."

Kian leaned back. "There is no money in it. That's why you don't hear about it. No one is pushing their agenda."

She shook her head. "It's always about the money. It makes me so mad. That's why hearing about the Kurdish women's resistance makes my heart feel lighter. And maybe we will find Jasmine's mother fighting with them. I worry, though. They are going against superior forces that don't abide by any humanitarian conventions."

"The resistance has safe houses throughout the region," Kian said. "But I worry for them too."

Allegra's tower crashed, sending blocks scattering, but instead of crying, she laughed and started rebuilding.

His daughter was a true leader.

Kian got off the couch and gathered the scattered blocks, and as Syssi joined them both, Allegra's squeal of joy was priceless. These ladies were his entire existence, and he thanked the Fates daily for their blessings. If only all the women on Earth were as fortunate, happy, and safe.

"I hope they succeed in reshaping their part of the world." Syssi leaned her elbows on her knees. "Wherever women are free and respected, society as a whole flourishes, and wherever women are oppressed and devalued, the society is consumed by rot and doomed to failure."

"We're fortunate," Kian said, watching Allegra carefully place a block on top of her latest tower. "To be able to raise our daughter safely and have the luxury of choosing our battles. We owe it all to my mother and her unwavering spirit. She's been fighting for women throughout her life."

Allegra lifted her head and cast them both a

crooked smile that was slightly evil before crashing her tower. "Boom!"

"Boom indeed," he laughed, pulling her into a tickle attack that had her shrieking with delight.

The most important thing a leader could do was remember what they were fighting for—these simple moments of joy, the right of all people to live in peace and raise their children in safety.

54

MORELLE

The large dining table at Syssi and Kian's home buzzed with familiar energy, and Morelle's heart warmed as she observed her newfound family. Kalugal and Jacki secured their serious-faced little boy in his highchair, the child's solemn expression a stark contrast to Allegra's animated features as she made faces at Morelle and Jasmine from her seat beside Annani. Evie stubbornly clung to Dalhu's neck, refusing to sit in the highchair, while Alena's infant son slept peacefully in his stroller nearby.

Looking at these children, something fierce and primitive stirred in Morelle's gut, the intensity of it catching her off guard. She felt an absolute certainty that she would defend these little ones with her last breath and would destroy anyone who threatened them. The feeling was both foreign and natural, like accessing a part of herself that had always existed but lain dormant until now.

Under the tablecloth, Brandon's hand found hers. "Excited?" he asked softly.

"About what?"

"Moving in with me." He waggled his eyebrows playfully.

Her pulse quickened as she wondered if he was implying what she thought and hoped about tonight. But no, she knew her mate better by now.

Brandon had his ideas about how their physical relationship should progress, and he stuck to his plans with infuriating determination. He'd hinted at what he wanted to try next, though, and heat coursed through her body at the mere thought.

"I am excited about that," she admitted, leaning over to kiss his cheek. "I like having the primary bedroom with that huge bed. Did you have it made to your specifications?"

His laugh was rich and warm. "No, it came with the house. Ingrid, our interior designer, ordered all the furniture."

"That's somewhat disappointing." She looked at him from under lowered lashes, enjoying his intake of breath.

Brandon shifted in his chair, and Morelle felt a surge of satisfaction at successfully disturbing his carefully maintained equilibrium.

Across the table, Amanda's knowing look suggested that she hadn't missed their exchange.

"We've made good progress with your ability this week," she said. "But we need to continue testing your limits. We have exciting stuff happening over the weekend, so I'm not going to bother you with tests until Monday."

"Good." Morelle managed a tight smile. "I can use the rest to settle into my new home. We're moving into Brandon's place."

"So I've heard." Amanda grinned. "Congratulations."

"Thank you," Morelle said.

As the conversation drifted to logistics, with Amanda pondering where Jasmine and Ell-rom might live next and whether Guardians should be relocated to the original section of the village to vacate a house for them, Morelle retreated inward.

Her nullifying power was interesting, she supposed, but it was underwhelming compared to her brother's ability to kill with a thought. Deep in her bones, though, she knew there was something more significant hiding and waiting to manifest.

The frustrating part was not knowing what it might be or whether it would ever emerge.

The Mother knew Morelle had tried to access it back in the temple, desperate to prove herself to the head priestess. But it had been like chasing a half-remembered dream, always hovering just beyond her grasp.

Closing her eyes, Morelle tried to tune out the dinner conversation and peer inward. This wasn't the ideal time or place for such exploration, but something about the energy surrounding her tickled at those elusive edges of awareness.

It had something to do with her family. Their power was like a current she could feel flowing around her like invisible threads of energy that she might be able to touch, to shape into something else, something she could use.

But when she reached for that sensation, it slipped away like water through her fingers.

Opening her eyes with a frustrated sigh, Morelle told herself she was being fanciful. She wasn't really sensing their power; she couldn't actually touch or manipulate it. She was just tired from the day's activities—packing her belongings, working out with Gertrude, showering, and changing at Brandon's place before coming here.

"Are you alright?" Brandon's voice was pitched low for her ears only.

"Just thinking." She squeezed his hand under the table.

His thumb traced patterns on her palm that sent shivers up her arm. "About?"

"Everything. Nothing." She watched Allegra successfully make Evie giggle despite the girl's determination to remain serious and hide her face in her father's neck. "My family is incredible."

"That's good, right?"

"Definitely." She leaned against his shoulder.

"Though I still feel like I'm waiting for something to happen."

He tensed. "Like what?"

"Oh, I don't know. Maybe something more interesting about my nullifying ability. So far, it seems pretty useless."

Brandon didn't know about Ell-rom's talent, so she couldn't confess to him that she hoped for something equally powerful. The Mother had played a nasty trick on her and Ell-rom, giving them each powers that would have been better suited if switched.

She would have no problem killing with a thought those who deserved it, and Ell-rom would have been very happy with an ability that could stop her from doing that.

Could she stop him, though? Stifle his death ray like she'd snipped Jin's tether?

It was possible that she could do it, but testing it would be much more difficult than the other tests Amanda had come up with so far.

55

BRANDON

After dinner, the family migrated to Kian and Syssi's spacious living room, where the children were settled on a play mat near the ornate gas fireplace. Brandon regarded the elegant but impractical fixture, wondering about the wisdom of installing even a decorative hearth in Southern California's perpetually mild climate.

Morelle sat beside him on the couch, her hand warm in his, but her attention was clearly elsewhere. Though she smiled and nodded at appropriate moments in the adult conversation, her focus remained fixed on the children playing with blocks on the floor. Her body language suggested she'd rather be down there with them than participate in the discussion about where would be the best location for the clan's future settlement.

Brandon found it only mildly interesting since

he knew that Kian was not making any concrete plans, and the village was too new and too valuable to abandon anytime soon.

"You really like children, don't you?" he asked her softly.

She looked up at him, those striking blue eyes serious. "Doesn't everyone? It's hardwired into our psyche. Without children, there are no tomorrows."

He had a feeling that she was parroting what she'd learned in the temple and not what was actually going through her mind and heart.

Nevertheless, his response needed to address her statement and not what he suspected she was actually thinking. It was just one more way in which he was projecting his beliefs and preferences on her.

"We are immortal, so continuity has a different meaning for us than for the humans and even the Kra-ell, but you're right, of course." His gaze drifted to the little ones. "Children are like a story being written before your eyes. No one knows who they'll become or what they'll accomplish. It's fascinating and exciting to watch, but it's also a lot of work, which is why so many choose not to have kids these days." He paused, clarifying, "Not us. Children are valued above all in our community, but humans are having fewer children, and some populations are shrinking, especially in developed countries. It's a dangerous trend."

"How so?" Morelle asked.

Brandon hesitated, not wanting to launch into a full doomsday scenario during family time. Instead, he shrugged. "The trend could reverse at any time. With humans, it's often just a matter of what's culturally acceptable at the moment. But first, governments in affected countries need to acknowledge the problem and implement policies that incentivize families to have more children—financially, culturally, structurally."

She tilted her head in that way that always made his heart beat faster. "You said humans are very easy to influence. Why isn't your clan doing something about it? You, in particular, could do a lot by producing movies that glorify family life."

Her observation not only struck a chord but also surprised him. Morelle was a newcomer to this world, and she knew practically nothing about media apart from what he had told her, but apparently, she had been listening and absorbing more than he had thought was possible in such a short time.

Smart female.

He was so proud and happy that the Fates had sent him a mate who could not only keep up with his fast mind but could also challenge him.

The problem was that things were not so easy these days. Once upon a time, he could have steered Hollywood productions in whatever direction the clan desired without much effort, but the industry had changed dramatically.

Unless Kian and Edna approved using thralling to advance the clan's agenda—something they had never been okay with before—his charm and powers of persuasion weren't cutting it anymore.

Still, maybe he should think about Morelle's suggestion more creatively.

He turned to Kian. "What do you think about shifting some of the clan's efforts into movie production? We could start our own streaming channel and produce content that promotes families the way that was popular up until not so long ago. I think there's a real thirst amongst the public for positive messages instead of the constant focus on dysfunction."

Kian leaned forward. "That's more than just a big undertaking, it's a tectonic shift, and it would require major funding. But given the changing attitudes in your industry, maybe that's exactly what we need to do."

As if nature herself wanted to comment on the word choice, a tremor suddenly shook the house. It lasted only seconds before subsiding, but Brandon felt Morelle tense beside him.

"What was that?" She sounded alarmed.

"Nothing to worry about," he assured her. "Seismic activity is common in this area."

Kian was already reaching for the remote. "Let's check the news to see what's happening. Sometimes what we feel as a minor tremor here can be part of a larger event elsewhere."

As Kian flipped through channels seeking information, Brandon wrapped his arm around Morelle's shoulders, offering support in case she was still worried.

He wondered what kind of stories she might want to tell if given the chance. What messages would someone raised on an alien world in near isolation want to share with Earth's inhabitants?

Her perspective could be fresh and invigorating, bringing new ideas into an industry that had grown stale and endlessly recycled old stories because it was devoid of creativity.

"No reports of significant activity," Kian announced, setting down the remote. "Probably just a routine adjustment along one of the minor fault lines."

Brandon felt Morelle relax beside him, and her gaze shifted from the screen hanging over the fireplace to the children playing below it.

They hadn't even paused in their play during the brief tremor.

"We should discuss this streaming platform idea further," he said to Kian. "We could start small and build our audience organically."

"If we want to use it as a tool to influence the public, doing it small is not going to cut it." Kian leaned back and folded his arms over his chest.

"The only way to do it is going full out, and that would require significant investment."

"True, but we'd have complete creative control. No more fighting with executives who don't share our values or understand our goals."

Morelle squeezed his hand. "You could tell stories that matter."

The simple observation carried a big weight. How long had it been since he'd focused on stories that truly mattered rather than just projects that would sell?

The clan's influence had always been subtle, working within existing systems, but maybe it was time for a more direct and louder approach in a world that had gotten much too noisy, and not in a good way.

56

MORELLE

The tremor might have been minor, but Morelle still felt rattled by it long after the brief shaking had stopped. She couldn't understand how everyone else seemed so casual about it. On Anumati, there was no seismic activity that caused things to shake, but it had been covered in her temple studies as a phenomenon that plagued many of the gods' colonies. She'd read about the devastation it could cause.

The television mounted above the ornate fireplace droned on quietly, its sound muted. Two attractive humans, a female and a male, gazed steadily into the camera, their relaxed expressions suggesting nothing serious had occurred. Text scrolled across the bottom of the screen, but the English script was inaccessible to her.

Still, it bothered Morelle that the screen was

hanging directly over the heads of the children, and no one seemed bothered by it.

She leaned toward Brandon. "Shouldn't the little ones be moved to a safer area?"

He followed her gaze to the screen. "Oh, don't worry about that. It's secured with a bracket that can withstand a major earthquake. The house would fall apart before that thing gives."

Morelle didn't share his confidence, and his comment about the house itself collapsing as a result of strong seismic activity only added to her anxiety.

Returning her gaze to the children playing on the mat, something in her chest eased, and at the same time, something in her gut twisted. Their innocent vulnerability called to her on a primal level, a protectiveness that was both instinctual and learned.

Kra-ell females, as well as the males, were charged with protecting the very young who were defenseless and teaching them to protect themselves as soon as they could. She and Ell-rom had started practicing blocking stances at three years old.

These children were still too young to fend for themselves, and watching their carefree play was endearing. Allegra was carefully stacking blocks to build a tower that was about to topple at any moment, while Evie was satisfied with just watching her cousin. Kalugal's serious little boy had moved closer to the fireplace, studying the ornate stonework with solemn eyes that seemed too old for his face.

Almost unconsciously, Morelle found herself reaching out with senses she didn't fully understand, drawing on the energy that seemed to pulse from everyone in the room. Logically, she knew that she was most likely imagining it, and yet the sensation felt incredibly real. It was as if she could actually harness the power radiating from each member of her family, but mostly from Annani.

The energy seemed to swell within her, filling spaces between the cells of her body. It was like discovering a new nervous or vascular system that had lain dormant in her body until now.

Imagination. That's all it was.

The head priestess had warned her against letting her mind roam free with flights of fancy. The fact that Ell-rom had a terrible, dangerous power didn't mean that she had one, too. She wasn't an energy vampire who could suck others dry of their life source.

When the second tremor hit, it wasn't notably stronger than the first, but it lasted longer, and suddenly, a fine web of cracks appeared in the ornamental stone mantel above the fireplace. They were so thin that they were barely visible, and no one else seemed to notice. Their attention was on the frightened children as Allegra's block tower toppled.

But Morelle not only saw it, she sensed it, and she knew that it was more than just surface cracks. It was a weakening of the stone, a flaw.

Time seemed to slow as a large section of the heavy mantel broke free, falling directly toward Kalugal's son.

Morelle didn't think—she reacted.

That gathered energy surged through her like a tidal wave as she thrust out her hand, and the falling stone halted mid-air, then shot sideways to crash harmlessly against the floor several feet away from the children.

In the sudden silence that followed, every eye in the room turned toward her. Even the children stopped crying and were staring at her with awe.

The energy still crackled along her nerves like an electric current, ready to be used again if needed, but as the immediate danger passed, uncertainty crept in. What had she done?

How had she done it?

The moment of silence was broken when Jacki uttered an anguished cry and ran to her little boy. Kalugal moved with incredible speed to snatch his son away from the fireplace, and Jacki examined the boy for any injuries. Other parents gathered their children closer, though whether from fear of more falling debris or a protective instinct, Morelle couldn't tell.

She watched the scene unfold for a brief moment and then looked down at her hands, half expecting them to sizzle with an electric current, but they appeared entirely normal.

That power, though, she could still feel it under her skin, and this time she knew it was real, and she wasn't imagining it.

"Well, bravo," Annani said over the din of parents and children rejoicing at a disaster avoided. "It seems we have discovered what else you can do, sister of mine."

"That was telekinesis on steroids," Amanda said after verifying that Evie was unharmed and handing her over to Dalhu. "You are incredibly powerful, Princess."

Brandon's arm wrapped around her shoulders, steadying her as the adrenaline began to fade, and she felt faint. "Are you alright?"

Morelle nodded, wondering if she should ask whether anyone felt tired or drained in any way. If they did, they would ascribe it to the adrenaline spike. No one would suspect her of being a power vampire.

Was that how her nullification worked? She didn't block paranormal talents or deflect them.

She drained them.

Dear Mother of All Life. She really was a vampire.

57

KIAN

Kian looked at the heavy stone fragment lying harmlessly on the living room floor and then shifted his gaze to Morelle's pale face.

"What did you do?" he asked, keeping his voice calm and neutral. "Or rather, how did you do it? We all saw what you did."

Morelle's hands were trembling, and she steadied them by placing them on her knees. "It was instinctive. When I realized what would happen, I felt this surge of power and just aimed it at the falling stone."

"Fascinating," Amanda said. "I wonder if this is an extension of your nullifying ability or something entirely different."

"I've always felt something more inside me, waiting." Morelle lifted her hands and looked at them as if she still couldn't believe what they had done. She then shook her head and looked at her twin with a smile. "I've always wanted to have an incredible power like yours."

Tension shot through Kian's body. Most of the people present knew about Ell-rom's ability, but Kalugal, Jacki, and Brandon didn't, and Kian wanted to keep it that way until they knew more about Ell-rom's death-ray talent and could use it for their benefit.

Kian watched Kalugal's expression, hoping he'd missed the implications of Morelle's words. But the guy was too sharp to miss an obvious clue like that.

"Thank you for saving my son," Kalugal told Morelle. "I'm forever in your debt, Princess Morelle."

"No debt." She shook her head. "Anyone would have done it if they could."

He nodded. "Still, I will always remember that you saved my son." He turned to Ell-rom with his usual smirk. "I wasn't aware you had any special talents. I'm very curious to hear what they are."

Kian saw panic flash across Morelle's face as she realized her mistake. "Ell-rom had a special ability before he went into stasis," she said quickly, "but it's not active now."

Technically, that wasn't a lie because Annani had bound Ell-rom's power, but it wasn't the whole truth either.

Kian caught Ell-rom's questioning look,

reading the silent message: *maybe it's time to reveal everything.*

Perhaps he was right. Once they started testing his ability, secrecy would be difficult to maintain, and after they discovered his limits, Kian planned to inform the council anyway.

Still, it was premature to reveal it now when there was very little he could say about it.

"Ell-rom has a suspected ability that hasn't been fully proven yet," Kian said. "When we've verified it, the council will be fully informed. I don't feel comfortable discussing it before we know more."

From the corner of his eye, he saw Brandon lift an eyebrow at Morelle, who suddenly found the floor fascinating.

Hopefully, she would keep her brother's secret from her mate, but if she didn't, Kian would have to talk with the councilman and ensure that he kept his mouth shut until Kian was ready to reveal it to the council.

Jacki sniffled, clutching Darius to her chest. "Thank you," she said. "Thank you. Oh, dear God, my baby would have died. He's not immortal yet."

Morelle's eyebrows shot up. "He is not?"

"He won't be until his induction ceremony at thirteen," Kalugal said. "That's when boys born to immortals transition." He looked at Brandon. "You've neglected the princess's education on all things immortal, councilman."

As Brandon replied that there hadn't been time, Morelle's hands started trembling again.

"I didn't know," she murmured, looking as pale as an apparition. "Oh, dear Mother above, he could have died. He doesn't have the rapid healing of an immortal yet."

Syssi rose to her feet. "I'll get you something to drink."

Brandon had his arm around Morelle's shoulders. "It's okay. You somehow redirected that piece of stone, and he's perfectly alright."

Kian hissed. "I should sue the company that sold us these mantels. There must have been a flaw in the stone, and it would have happened sooner or later independent of the earthquake."

"We should take the whole thing down," Syssi said. "We might need to take them down in all the houses in this part of the village."

"It's only dangerous to children," Amanda pointed out. "Although having a piece of stone land on your foot is no fun, even if the bruise heals fast." She looked at Kian. "Are you going to get contractors in here?"

He shook his head. "Our community service purebloods can take care of this. I'll just need to give them instructions."

Syssi handed Morelle a mug of coffee. "I don't know if that's what Bridget would have recommended, but when I feel dizzy, coffee helps."

"Thank you." Morelle took a few sips and looked up at Syssi. "It's helping."

"Monday," Amanda said, "we'll start a new battery of tests to examine this new ability of yours."

Morelle nodded, but Kian didn't miss the flash of panic in her eyes. It was gone almost instantly, but he'd seen it.

What was she afraid of?

58

BRANDON

Brandon watched Morelle's composure crumbling by degrees as the family fussed over her. Though she maintained a brave expression, he could see the slight tremors in her hands, the way she swallowed repeatedly as if fighting back tears.

"We should get you home so you can rest," he said, deliberately using the word 'home' rather than 'my house.' When Ell-rom and Jasmine started to rise, he added quickly, "You two should stay and enjoy the rest of the evening."

He needed time alone with Morelle. Though his house was sound proofed well enough that they could have complete privacy in their bedroom, even with others present, he wanted her to have space to process what had happened without an audience.

Something about using her power troubled her deeply, and in turn, it troubled him.

Before they could make their escape, Jacki rushed forward with her son in her arms and wrapped Morelle in a fierce embrace. "Thank you," she whispered again, then turned to her little boy. "Darius, sweetie, can you give Auntie Morelle a kiss?"

The solemn little boy reached his arms for Morelle with complete trust, and Brandon's heart squeezed as she gathered him close. A tear slipped down her cheek as she held him.

"Be well, sweet Darius," she murmured, her voice thick with emotion. "The Mother of All Life has protected you tonight, which means that she expects great things from you. You will grow up and be a fierce warrior." She pressed a kiss to his dark hair before returning him to his mother.

What followed was an overwhelming cascade of hugs and thanks from the family, and with each embrace and each heartfelt expression of gratitude, Morelle's emotional control seemed to be slipping further.

There was panic in her eyes he could only explain as the aftermath of Darius's near death. She looked like she was moments away from complete collapse.

Once everyone was done with their farewells, Brandon opened the door and ushered Morelle out with a hand on the small of her back, and the instant they cleared the front door, he swept her into his arms.

"What are you doing?" she protested. "Put me down."

"It's an Earth tradition," he said instead of following her demands, and kept going toward his house—their house now.

She huffed indignantly but wound her arms around his neck and put her head on his chest. "What Earth tradition are you talking about?"

"When a husband brings his new wife to their home for the first time, it's a tradition for him to carry her over the threshold."

Morelle chuckled. "We are not married. I'm not an Earthling, and this is not the first time I'm entering your house. I was there yesterday and today. I even showered in your bathroom."

The hint of humor in her voice was a relief. If she could still tease and banter, she would be okay. On the other hand, her easy acquiescence to being carried indicated that she was drained and lacked the energy to walk—as he'd suspected.

"Our home, our bathroom," he corrected. "Besides, maybe I just wanted an excuse to hold you?"

It might not have started as a romantic gesture or tradition, but he enjoyed playing the part of the romantic hero, and for once, Morelle was cooperating and playing the damsel's part.

He wanted to ask her about what had happened

earlier and how she'd found that hidden ability inside of her, but first, he needed to get her home and help her process the emotional aftermath of saving Darius's life.

It was up to her to decide whether she was up to sharing after regaining her equilibrium.

As he walked through the quiet village pathways, Morelle's breath grew slower and deeper, and her body went lax in his arms.

She must have been truly drained to fall asleep while being bounced and jolted, no matter how much he tried to minimize her discomfort.

Brandon suspected that what had happened earlier had changed everything.

He'd seen the look Kian had given her and the analytical assessment in Amanda's eyes. Soon, there would be tests, questions, and theories. They would want to understand every aspect of her ability, but something in Morelle's reaction suggested that she already understood more than she was letting on.

She shivered slightly in his arms, though the evening was warm, and when he glanced down at her, her eyes were still closed, but her breathing had changed.

"Cold?" he asked.

She shook her head, curling closer to his chest. The gesture was so trusting, so vulnerable, that it made his heart ache. Whatever she was hiding, she wasn't about to pull away from him.

He would honor that trust.

There would be no demands for explanations tonight and no pressing for answers she wasn't ready to give.

Tonight, his love for her meant simply being the arms that carried her home.

COMING UP NEXT
The Children of the Gods Book 91
DARK PRINCESS
ASCENDING

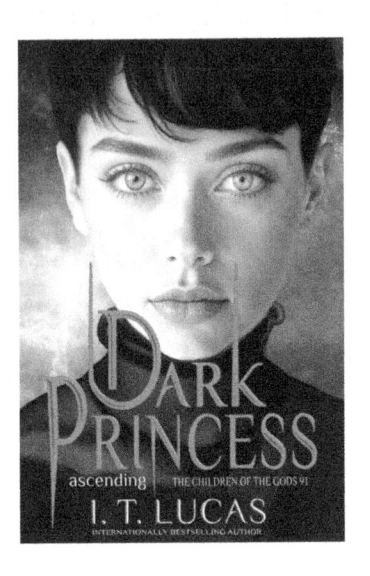

Hidden powers are awakening...

Finally safe with her new family, Morelle is ready to embrace her future, but when an unexpected burst of power reveals abilities beyond her understanding, she must face the truth about her nature and choose between sharing it with those she loves or continue keeping them in the dark.

Some gifts come with a price, and Morelle must decide whether she's willing to pay it.

JOIN THE VIP CLUB
To find out what's included in your free membership, flip to the last page.

NOTE

Dear reader,

I hope my stories have added a little joy to your day. If you have a moment to add some to mine, you can help spread the word about the Children Of The Gods series by telling your friends and penning a review. Your recommendations are the most powerful way to inspire new readers to explore the series.

Thank you,

Isabell

Also by I. T. Lucas

THE CHILDREN OF THE GODS ORIGINS
1: Goddess's Choice
2: Goddess's Hope

THE CHILDREN OF THE GODS
Dark Stranger
1: Dark Stranger The Dream
2: Dark Stranger Revealed
3: Dark Stranger Immortal

Dark Enemy
4: Dark Enemy Taken
5: Dark Enemy Captive
6: Dark Enemy Redeemed

Kri & Michael's Story
6.5: My Dark Amazon

Dark Warrior
7: Dark Warrior Mine
8: Dark Warrior's Promise
9: Dark Warrior's Destiny
10: Dark Warrior's Legacy

Dark Guardian
11: Dark Guardian Found
12: Dark Guardian Craved

13: Dark Guardian's Mate

Dark Angel
14: Dark Angel's Obsession
15: Dark Angel's Seduction
16: Dark Angel's Surrender

Dark Operative
17: Dark Operative: A Shadow of Death
18: Dark Operative: A Glimmer of Hope
19: Dark Operative: The Dawn of Love

Dark Survivor
20: Dark Survivor Awakened
21: Dark Survivor Echoes of Love
22: Dark Survivor Reunited

Dark Widow
23: Dark Widow's Secret
24: Dark Widow's Curse
25: Dark Widow's Blessing

Dark Dream
26: Dark Dream's Temptation
27: Dark Dream's Unraveling
28: Dark Dream's Trap

Dark Prince
29: Dark Prince's Enigma
30: Dark Prince's Dilemma

31: Dark Prince's Agenda

Dark Queen
32: Dark Queen's Quest
33: Dark Queen's Knight
34: Dark Queen's Army

Dark Spy
35: Dark Spy Conscripted
36: Dark Spy's Mission
37: Dark Spy's Resolution

Dark Overlord
38: Dark Overlord New Horizon
39: Dark Overlord's Wife
40: Dark Overlord's Clan

Dark Choices
41: Dark Choices The Quandary
42: Dark Choices Paradigm Shift
43: Dark Choices The Accord

Dark Secrets
44: Dark Secrets Resurgence
45: Dark Secrets Unveiled
46: Dark Secrets Absolved

Dark Haven
47: Dark Haven Illusion
48: Dark Haven Unmasked

49: Dark Haven Found

Dark Power
50: Dark Power Untamed
51: Dark Power Unleashed
52: Dark Power Convergence

Dark Memories
53: Dark Memories Submerged
54: Dark Memories Emerge
55: Dark Memories Restored

Dark Hunter
56: Dark Hunter's Query
57: Dark Hunter's Prey
58: Dark Hunter's Boon

Dark God
59: Dark God's Avatar
60: Dark God's Reviviscence
61: Dark God Destinies Converge

Dark Whispers
62: Dark Whispers From The Past
63: Dark Whispers From Afar
64: Dark Whispers From Beyond

Dark Gambit
65: Dark Gambit The Pawn
66: Dark Gambit The Play

67: Dark Gambit Reliance

Dark Alliance
68: Dark Alliance Kindred Souls
69: Dark Alliance Turbulent Waters
70: Dark Alliance Perfect Storm

Dark Healing
71: Dark Healing Blind Justice
72: Dark Healing Blind Trust
73: Dark healing Blind Curve

Dark Encounters
74: Dark Encounters of the Close Kind
75: Dark Encounters of the Unexpected Kind
76: Dark Encounters of the Fated Kind

Dark Voyage
77: Dark Voyage Matters of the Heart
78: <u>Dark Voyage Matters of the Mind</u>
<u>79: Dark Voyage Matters of the Soul</u>

Dark Horizon
80: Dark Horizon New Dawn
81: Dark Horizon Eclipse of the Heart
82: Dark Horizon The Witching Hour

Dark Witch
83: Dark Witch: Entangled Fates
84: Dark Witch: Twin Destinies

85: Dark Witch: Resurrection

Dark Awakening
86: Dark Awakening: New World
87: Dark Awakening Hidden Currents
88: Dark Awakening Echoes of Destiny

Dark Princess
89: Dark Princess: Shadows
90: Dark Princess Emerging
91: Dark Princess Ascending

PERFECT MATCH

Vampire's Consort
King's Chosen
Captain's Conquest
The Thief Who Loved Me
My Merman Prince
The Dragon King
My Werewolf Romeo
The Channeler's Companion
The Valkyrie & The Witch
Adina and the Magic Lamp

TRANSLATIONS

DIE ERBEN DER GÖTTER
Dark Stranger
1- Dark Stranger Der Traum
2- Dark Stranger Die Offenbarung
3- Dark Stranger Unsterblich

Dark Enemy
4- Dark Enemy Entführt
5- Dark Enemy Gefangen
6- Dark Enemy Erlöst

<u>Dark Warrior</u>
7- Dark Warrior Meine Sehnsucht
8- Dark Warrior – Dein Versprechen
9- Dark Warrior - Unser Schicksal
10- Dark Warrior-Unser Vermächtnis

LOS HIJOS DE LOS DIOSES

EL OSCURO DESCONOCIDO
1: EL OSCURO DESCONOCIDO EL SUEÑO
2: EL OSCURO DESCONOCIDO REVELADO
3: EL OSCURO DESCONOCIDO INMORTAL

EL OSCURO ENEMIGO
4- EL OSCURO ENEMIGO

CAPTURADO
5 - EL OSCURO ENEMIGO CAUTIVO
6- EL OSCURO ENEMIGO REDIMIDO

LES ENFANTS DES DIEUX
DARK STRANGER
1- Dark Stranger Le rêve
2- Dark Stranger La révélation
3- Dark Stranger L'immortelle

The Children of the Gods Series Sets

Books 1-3: Dark Stranger trilogy—Includes a bonus short story: **The Fates Take a Vacation**

Books 4-6: Dark Enemy Trilogy —Includes a bonus short story—**The Fates' Post-Wedding Celebration**

Books 7-10: Dark Warrior Tetralogy
Books 11-13: Dark Guardian Trilogy
Books 14-16: Dark Angel Trilogy
Books 17-19: Dark Operative Trilogy
Books 20-22: Dark Survivor Trilogy
Books 23-25: Dark Widow Trilogy
Books 26-28: Dark Dream Trilogy
Books 29-31: Dark Prince Trilogy
Books 32-34: Dark Queen Trilogy
Books 35-37: Dark Spy Trilogy

Books 38-40: Dark Overlord Trilogy
Books 41-43: Dark Choices Trilogy
Books 44-46: Dark Secrets Trilogy
Books 47-49: Dark Haven Trilogy
Books 50-52: Dark Power Trilogy
Books 53-55: Dark Memories Trilogy
Books 56-58: Dark Hunter Trilogy
Books 59-61: Dark God Trilogy
Books 62-64: Dark Whispers Trilogy
Books 65-67: Dark Gambit Trilogy
Books 68-70: Dark Alliance Trilogy
Books 71-73: Dark Healing Trilogy
Books 74-76: Dark Encounters Trilogy
Books 77-79: Dark Voyage Trilogy
Books 80-81: Dark Horizon Trilogy

MEGA SETS

The Children of the Gods: Books 1-6

INCLUDES CHARACTER LISTS

The Children of the Gods: Books 6.5-10

Perfect Match Bundle 1

CHECK OUT THE SPECIALS ON ITLUCAS.COM
(https://itlucas.com/specials)

FOR EXCLUSIVE PEEKS AT UPCOMING RELEASES &
A FREE I. T. LUCAS COMPANION BOOK

JOIN MY *VIP CLUB* AND GAIN ACCESS TO THE VIP PORTAL AT ITLUCAS.COM

TO JOIN, GO TO:
http://eepurl.com/blMTpD

Find out more details about what's included with your free membership on the book's last page.

TRY THE CHILDREN OF THE GODS SERIES ON
<u>AUDIBLE</u>

2 FREE audiobooks with your new Audible subscription!

FOR EXCLUSIVE PEEKS AT UPCOMING RELEASES &
A FREE I. T. LUCAS COMPANION BOOK

Join my *VIP Club* and gain access to the VIP portal at itlucas.com
To Join, go to:
http://eepurl.com/blMTpD

INCLUDED IN YOUR FREE MEMBERSHIP:

YOUR VIP PORTAL

- Read preview chapters of upcoming releases.
- Listen to Goddess's Choice narration by Charles Lawrence
- Exclusive content offered only to my VIPs.

FREE I.T. LUCAS COMPANION INCLUDES:

- Goddess's Choice Part 1
- Perfect Match: Vampire's Consort (A standalone Novella)
- Interview Q & A
- Character Charts

If you're already a subscriber and you are not getting my emails, your provider is sending them to your junk folder, and you are missing out on important updates. To fix that, add isabell@itlucas.com to your email contacts or your email VIP list.

**Check out the specials at
https://www.itlucas.com/specials**

Made in the USA
Middletown, DE
18 January 2025